Advance Praise for
Under the Dirt Sky

"Callie Trautmiller paints a smart and lyrical portrait of 1920s strife and perseverance. From the Chicago streets of cons and coin-flips to the bleak, drought-ridden Kansas Dust Bowl, *Under the Dirt Sky* illuminates the stories of the brave young people who did whatever it took to survive. Callie Trautmiller continues to do great things for the preservation and accessibility of American history. A great read for any audience!"

—A.L. Mundt,
Author of the Messengers Trilogy

"Set against a historical backdrop, Callie J. Trautmiller weaves a beautiful story still relevant today. Following people who are determined to write their own story in *Under the Dirt Sky*, they hope to find joy despite the challenges along the way."

—Cassidy Mercer,
Author of *Mad Season*

"Callie J. Trautmiller's writing is so enthralling you don't even realize how much you are learning about history. Her characters pull you in and show you the world as it was. Callie takes on the unexplored aspects of an otherwise well-trodden tale of our ancestors in *Under the Dirt Sky* and shows us the whole story. She weaves together the tales of a city boy and a country girl to create a heartbreakingly beautiful tapestry of the roaring 20s through the dusty 30s and beyond."

—Jessica Lee Peterson,
Author of *Thistles & Thorns*

Under the Dirt Sky

Callie J. Trautmiller

Under the Dirt Sky

A Young Adult Historical Novel

Callie J. Trautmiller

Publisher/Executive Editor: Brittiany Koren
Copy-edit: Melinda Peterson
Cover Art Designer: Ed Vincent/ENC Graphics
Interior Layout Designer: Amit Dey
Ebook Interior Layout Designer: Amit Dey

Category: Historical Young Adult
Description: A teenage mobster gets caught up in fast money during the height of Prohibition in Chicago but soon realizes the biggest threat doesn't lie within the city, but in the revolting fields of Kansas where he meets another teen from the Midwest.

Hardback ISBN: 978-1-951375-82-9
Paperback ISBN: 978-1-951375-83-6
Ebook ISBN: 978-1-951375-84-3
LOC Catalogue Data: Applied for. Contact the Library of Congress for info.

First Edition published by Written Dreams Publishing in October 2022.
Ebook Edition published by Written Dreams Publishing in October 2022.

Published in Green Bay, Wisconsin.
Printed in the United States of America.

*This book is dedicated to my family: Freddy, Jada,
Jaelyn & Sterling for their continuous encouragement
and willingness to read early drafts and offer honest feedback.*

*Thank you to all the farmers who are the ultimate providers,
and through the generations, have shaped the landscape
of this country. We all owe them a huge debt of gratitude.*

PART I

CHICAGO, ILLINOIS

Percy James, 1925

Preface

I shuddered off a chill as the Chicago drizzle streamed down the back of my neck and seeped into my bones. This was no place for a kid, but one thing was for sure. I made my own money. Bought my own things.

I wasn't no kid, either. I'm Percy James, the best-selling newsie this city has seen.

It wasn't until the emerald body of a Cadillac emerged from the shadows and slid over the stretch of pavement to where I was standing, that my hands began to tremble. It was a death sentence to associate with the man who owned it.

But what was I to do? Run?

Only a kid would run.

My life was about to sharply turn in a different direction simply because I'd chosen to work in the rain.

CHAPTER 1

Chicago, Illinois
Percy, 1925

I, Percy James, lived in one of the best cities in the United States during the age of growing consumerism—Chicago. All around me, signs were hung by companies interrupting our daily lives with advertisements creating a need for the many products manufactured in their factories. It was as if the world had begun to rotate more quickly, an urgency felt among the millions who flooded to the city in hopes of filling newly built skyscrapers with diligent workers.

Cathedrals in the sky.

During the summer of 1925, all I knew was you either worked on the towers themselves through the back-breaking labor it took to erect such things, or you worked for the empire that occupied them.

Me? I didn't care either way, as long as you bought into my dimples, warm brown eyes and tossed me some change for the rumble I was selling. Ma often told me my eyes were innocent enough to sell any headline out there. I was starting to believe her, and even paid for haircuts to keep my thick patch of chestnut hair clean and tight.

I took a swig of cola, grateful for the sweet liquid that tingled my throat on the way down, a dribble trickling down my suspenders and landing on my brown plaid knickers. The day was early, and if I wanted to bring in some coin, I needed to situate myself to accommodate the commuters, which was the intersection of North Michigan Avenue and East Illinois Street. It also had the best view of the Tribune Tower.

As a kid, I liked to watch the building grow every day, marveling at the balance and coordination of the workers who suspended themselves by wire lines from whichever level they were currently working on. At one point, they weren't harnessed at all, but jumped with ease from board to board as they pulled in a massive stone column.

I shook my head. Fortunately for me, the Tribune Tower held my employer, the *Chicago Tribune.*

"Still the biggest one yet, eh Percy?" Willy's voice interrupted my thoughts as I gazed up to greet my best friend.

His blond hair peeked out from under the same old muddy-colored felt bowler hat he always wore. Like me, he was almost thirteen and worked the streets.

"Don't doubt it," I said, swigging another gulp of soda before offering him the bottle. He took a long drink before handing it back.

"You know my ma won't buy this," he said, holding up the bottle and wiping his mouth with the back of his shirt. "Thinks they're capitalizing off the prohibition."

I chuckled, imagining the look on his Protestant mother's face if she were to see my folks' liquor cabinet. Besides, there ain't no way cola could ever replace a whiskey. Not in my house anyway.

"Well," I said, turning to him with a smile, "lucky for you, I ain't Protestant."

He chuckled. "Hey, you save enough dough for that bike yet?"

Willy worked out of need, bringing home money for the family and it suddenly felt selfish of me to be saving my stack for a new Indian moto bike (or at the very least, a Schwinn), even if my pops refused to buy one in effort of "teaching me the value of hard work."

My cheeks went hot. "Close," I said and smiled, "but need to hit the streets some more if I want to save enough for the one I got my eye on."

Unlike my old man who now covered his work ethic with an over-priced suit bought with new money from the stock market, Willy's pops was typically covered in grease, the result of spending most daylight hours inside an appliance factory while his mother stayed home with the younger kids.

"Awe, breathe in that fresh city air." Willy tilted his chin up and inhaled, his nostrils flaring out like a bull.

I smirked. The city smelled of rotten eggs on a good day. The only thing that flushed that out was either the pungent smell of boiled fish during Lent or the foggy puffs of cigar smoke from the many circles of men we sold our papers to.

He winced. "Sorry," he said, his eyebrows scrunching together. "I forget about your lung ailment."

"What kind of friend are you anyhow," I asked, mocking offense while grabbing the cigarette from his hands. "Anyhow, my lungs aren't that bad." I blew out a ring of smoke adding to the thick haze that hung heavily in the sky, my chest swelling at my newly mastered skill. "This thing here can't be any worse than the city air."

We watched the rings float lazily into the sky before finishing off the cigarette, tipping our hats and parting ways.

Hombres in pinstriped suits and fedoras rushed past in half-hazard directions, briefcases in hand. They resembled ants. *Rich ants.*

I cleared my throat and cupped my hands to my mouth. "HARRY HOUDINI FREES HIMSELF FROM STRAIGHT JACKET WHILE SUSPENDED *UPSIDE DOWN,* 40 FEET ABOVE THE GROUND IN THE BIG APPLE!" I shouted out. "ONLY A PENNY A PAPER!"

Most people went their own way, but a few stopped to listen. Encouraged, I went on. "US ATTORNEY GENERAL STATES IT'S *LEGAL* FOR WOMEN TO WEAR TROUSERS *ANYWHERE!*"

A few disgruntled chumps shook their heads in disagreement, murmuring amongst themselves. Ma had jumped right on the trouser bandwagon, despite the look upon Pops's face as she went about the house as if nothing had changed.

"What's next?" he had asked. "You'll want to borrow my top hat, too?"

"Better put them up higher then," she bantered. "It's to your advantage I'm short."

Ma had always been progressive, representing the one in three women who exercised their new right to vote during the 1920 election.

Presently, a man approached and offered a few coins in exchange for a paper. "Keep the change kid," he said, a cigar dangling from his lips as he tucked the bundle under his arm. He left a trail of smoke behind him. I almost corrected him with my age, but knew better if I wanted a tip.

My next target was a gentleman with polished shoes the color of charcoal and a weak smile upon his face. "YOU!" I pointed my finger at the startled man. "KNOW ANY ARCHITECTS?"

He shook his head hesitantly. I had him.

"$100,000 PRIZE TO THE ARCHITECT WHO DESIGNS THE MOST BEAUTIFUL BUILDING IN THE WORLD!" I boasted.

It was after all, the great owners of the *Chicago Tribune* which were offering such a handsome reward. The man's face reddened as he pulled some change from his pocket and bought a paper, seemingly relieved from the attention of my hollering.

Several sales later, the haze of the heat had begun to float off the asphalt, making me figure it was nearly one o'clock. Ma would be fuming. I quickened my pace to our apartment hotel, a few blocks away.

Mr. Wentworth was already holding the door open when I came running up. "Good day," he said, tipping his hat.

I walked in, grateful for the coolness of the dimly lit entrance. "That it is," I replied.

"Productive day at work, hey?" he chuckled. "I might consider quittin' this bellhop job and makin' my way into selling papers."

I laughed at his usual response, which I'd come to look forward to nearly every day. I straightened up and gave a nonchalant shrug. "Have to get that bike."

I'd be lying if I said I didn't like being treated like a man. I adjusted the herringbone wool newsboy cap I'd splurged my last month's earnings on. I'd stumbled across it through the window of a secondhand store, and though its wear made it resemble more of ashy gray than black, it still held more prestige than my tattered straw hat.

Upstairs, Ma had lunch ready and was waiting at the table with a glass of gin. I sighed, glancing at the watch Pops had given me on my tenth birthday. One-thirty. I was a half-hour late. How many drinks could Ma fit into half an hour?

Judging by her face, *many*.

Looking around our kitchen, you'd never know that up until two years ago, I'd grown up poor. I'd read all the stories and dreamed the dreams. Hell, I sold papers based on 'em.

People striking gold in California or buying up massive amounts of land in new regions of the U.S., some lucky enough to even strike oil, nearly spewing out dollar bills.

Except, none of these things happened for us.

Closest thing was the day Pops came home and told us he'd put money in the stock market. I remember it clear as a blue sky. It took a lot of sweet-talking to get Ma on his side. He could hardly explain how it worked fast enough.

"Where'd you get the money?" she had scrutinized, knowing that on many occasions he didn't earn enough at the *Tribune* to put much food on the table.

"Mr. Montgomery," he shrugged. Though Mr. Montgomery was our trusted local banker, Ma was still skeptical.

"Look," he retorted. "If we don't make anything in the next year or two, we can take the money out and pay back the loan. It'll be fine, you'll see."

And it *was* fine.

Took only three months for Pa's stock to shoot through the roof, money that had been missing in our lives despite all those years of work suddenly flowed like fountain water. It wasn't like the strike of luck that hits oil all at once. It was more of a gradual thing. A building wave in the distance. A new refrigerator here, a washing machine there. Everything endorsed by the notion we'd earned these things as hard-working Americans.

But even the biggest waves break when they hit the shoreline.

Still, Pa insisted on instilling a work ethic in me, so I paid for many of my own things by selling papers.

"Oh Percy," Ma now said, waving her hand at me. "Don't scold me. If I want to have a drink, it's not the government's right to stop me, less a kid. Least I have the luxury of drinking it quietly in my own home and not sneaking off into some dark speakeasy with it hidden in my boot like your father."

She had a point. I dropped a folded paper on the table, knowing it wasn't worth the argument. "You hear about Houdini?"

Ma's hands shook as she carried a crystal vase of pink roses Pops had brought her to the sink, the tip of her cigarette dancing dangerously close to the curled leaves. She filled it with fresh water before placing it back in the middle of the table. "What'd he do now?"

I sat beside her. "Got himself outta' a strait jacket."

"Oh?" She unfolded the paper.

Encouraged, I went on, though less enthusiastic as that morning. I guess repeating yourself a few hundred times will burn your stamina. "Upside down. Suspended in New York City."

She drew in a breath, covering her mouth with her hand as she read. "That man is really something, isn't he?"

I knew that gleam in her eyes. "Sure is, Ma."

I tossed her new patterned pillows to the floor before throwing my legs up on the couch and turning the knob on the radio trying to comfortably position myself against the firmness of the crushed burgundy velvet upholstery.

Ma always had a fix on any man who made the papers. I figured that's why she'd married Pops, even if his column picture never changed and made it seem as if he were about five years younger and a good fifteen pounds lesser than he truly was.

"Your father's working late again," she said, fluffing and tossing the pillows back on the couch. "Up for a big promotion." She smiled, changing the subject. "What do you want for supper?" She scanned the contents of a cupboard and not finding what she was looking for, moved on to the next.

"Not that hungry, Ma." I left out the fact I'd eaten meatloaf ten minutes ago with her beside me. "Don't worry 'bout it."

"You sure?" She slid open the window and flicked her cigarette into the street several stories below. I smirked at the idea of it landing on some unsuspecting chap's hat. Pops didn't like her smoking, but it calmed her nerves. We could all agree she was much more agreeable with it in her system, so we let her believe she had something in common with the starlets on the big screen.

"I don't want you to go hungry." She frowned, years of incessant worry lines pulling together on her face, the result of a time when she wasn't sure where the next meal would come from.

"I know, Ma," I said, offering her a sympathetic smile. Minutes later, I heard the soft purr of her snoring coming from her room. I sighed and knew I only had a small window of time to clean up the empty bottles of booze before Pops came home. Most days he let it all pass, even appeased her ambitions with a night on the town. But Ma was less forgiving of herself. I collected the empty bottle from the kitchen counter and buried it at the bottom of the trash before rinsing out her martini glass.

I gazed in on her from the doorway for a few moments. She was beautiful in her own right with hair the color of the melted chocolate I often eyed through the window of the candy store up the street from my paper corner. Today, she hadn't bothered to take out her rollers, making me guess she'd started drinking early, accounting for the fully empty bottle. I felt a sting in my eyes but blinked it away as I slipped off her heels and laid a blanket across her. She looked almost childlike, and for an instant, I wondered what she had been like as a child on the farm where she grew up. Before getting caught up in the trap of the city life and all its shortcomings.

She was a woman of dichotomies. A skirt voter who wore the latest cutting styles, but gauged her maternal devotion by her dedication to having meals on the table by the time Pops and I got home. It was as if she was suspended on a tightrope between two generations, unable to make up her mind as to which direction to pursue.

Me on the other hand?

I've always known which ledge to make my way to. I was destined to do something. To be somebody people noticed. Somebody important. More than just a newsboy in the street where people threw their trash. More than a son whose father seldom acknowledged him. No, not me. I was going to be something.

Something *great*.

CHAPTER 2

Paper selling was slow and not much was moving on account of the rain. I considered not even going out that day, but was restless with Pops's notorious words ringing in my head. *The papers won't sell themselves.* This was coming from a man who never took a day off.

The pavement glistened with water, and scanning the streets, I couldn't find Willy. More than likely, he was under the covers of his bed. I pushed further south, venturing into an area not as well known to me, my shoes sloshing through puddles and my socks sopping wet.

All around me the city bloated with developments. I was amazed there were enough people to fill all the shotty built flats, but with the World War over, the factories continued to need people for manufacturing and drew them in like flies to a honey trap. Pops was fitting to get me into automobile production once I was old enough. I figured a couple more years and I'd be ready.

The towers cast dark shadows as if sucking in all the sunlight at the top and exhaling the remnants below. I shifted the weight of my bag to pull a cigar I'd taken from Pops's stash from the front pocket, convinced it might warm me up.

I didn't think anything of the car when it pulled up to my corner as I handed newspapers out in the rain. I shuddered off a chill as the Chicago drizzle streamed down the back of my neck and seemed to seep into my bones. This was no place for a kid, but I didn't see myself that way. I made my own money. Bought my own things. I was Percy James, the best-selling newsie this city had seen.

It wasn't until the emerald green body of the Cadillac emerged from the shadows and slid over the slick stretch of wet pavement to where I was standing, that my hands began to tremble. It was a death sentence to associate with the man who owned it.

But what was I to do? Run?

Only a kid would run. And one thing was for sure. I wasn't no kid.

I stared dumbly as the car drew closer, gliding its way toward me like a beacon of light.

Bulletproof glass I guessed, almost an inch thick, or so the stories went. Three-thousand pounds of armor plating with windows that could be raised high enough to fit a muzzle of a machine gun. I wasn't fooled by the glittering green, an illusion from the droplets of rain that fell from the sky.

I began to panic, but couldn't move. The car, it seemed, was coming right toward me. I stumbled a few steps back onto the sidewalk as the window slowly rolled down, exposing a man with a white slouch hat, yellow suit, and bushy mischievous eyebrows.

"You selling papers?" he chuckled, catching sight of the cigar in my mouth.

Don't stare, I told myself. Don't stare.

"Yes sir," I stammered, hastily pulling the cigar out. I could only see the right side of his face.

"Two pennies," I stated, and then realizing my mistake, added, "if you want." My face burned and a drop of rain or sweat rolled down my right temple, tickling my face.

I blinked.

The man regarded me with curious eyes as he pulled a leather wallet from his vest pocket and handed me a folded bill. I clumsily made the exchange.

"Keep the change, chap."

My heart raced as the Caddy began to pull away, taunting me with its red brake lights. I knew better than to trust bright electric signs in the city. All at once, it stopped briefly, its taillights reflecting off the puddles, making them appear as if they were pools of blood.

His head popped out of the passenger window, regarding me from the shadows. "Hey chap, you know who I am?"

In that moment, I had a split-second decision to make. Little did I know it would change my life forever. I nodded my head yes.

"Good," he said, seeming satisfied, "you should. You didn't see me here, savvy?"

"Savvy," I agreed, nodding my head some more. "Didn't see nothing today."

The man smirked and up went his window before the car rolled off into the cocoon of Chicago's dark shadows.

I unfolded the bill. Ten dollars! I'd never seen that much money at once. I glanced up the street, but any trace of the car was gone, save the fragmented appearances of buildings reflected in the ripples of the puddles.

He was my only customer that day.

Al Capone. Scarface.

A legendary mobster who ran the juice joints and had a hundred-million-dollar business of bootlegging, over seven hundred men strong from Canada to Florida I'd read once in the headlines.

And he'd smiled at me and given me a ten-dollar bill.

And he didn't call me a kid.

In that moment, I had to be the most fortunate fella in the entire nation, to be living in the most corrupt city in the U.S. A city of lights and glamour and crooked cops. A city of bootlegging and crime and paid-off politicians.

To think. Of all the thousands of chaps in the city, I got to meet him for the simple fact I'd chosen to sell newspapers on a day when the white collars didn't even step out in the rain for a paper.

But *he* did.

Because he appreciated the underdog. The workers in the world. The men trying to make a living. A better life.

And because above all, he wasn't afraid to get dirty.

CHAPTER 3

"You look ravishing," Ma said, admiring Pops from the reflection of the mirror as she adjusted her cloches hat. "You resemble Rudolph Valentino, even."

I rolled my eyes. The only thing Valentino and my father had in common was the slicked back hair, but he was Ma's favorite screen actor, as well as most of the women around the country.

"Well, you're quite the Sheba yourself," Pops commented, focused on adjusting his tie in the mirror. It was one of the few times they'd been able to go out as he'd been working unusually late most evenings. Didn't bother Ma much so long as he came home with a replacement bouquet for the dining room table and talk of new money. Ma often bragged him up to her gossip circle on the phone about how spoiled she was.

"Here, let me help you with that, dear," Ma said, tugging at his tie.

I had to give her credit. She'd mastered the art of doing almost anything with a lit cigarette in her hand.

"I wonder if we'll bump into anyone important," she pondered, steadying herself with the wall as she slipped into satin heels, the beads of her flapper dress swaying back and forth.

The new dress trends showed off a little too much leg is what Pops thought and told her so often, but tonight he didn't make mention of it. She plucked at the ends of her dark hair, which contrasted dramatically with her crimson felted cloche hat. Pleased with her reflection, she grabbed her clutch.

"Don't wait up for us, Percy," she winked.

Pops tucked his flask of whiskey into the inner pocket of his suitcoat and not long after, they were out the door, leaving nothing but the soft hum of the heater and the echo of eager footsteps growing fainter as they descended the hallway.

I pulled the curtains back and watched the valet pull around with our black Chrysler. Within minutes, Ma's bright red hat appeared from the door, followed by Pops, the waxy sheen from his dark hair visible from fifteen floors up.

I had to be careful for this to work out.

It was nearly six o'clock. Their jazz concert would be out around ten and they'd likely be home by eleven o'clock, half past eleven tops as Ma didn't like to comingle in the "slums" of Chicago, as she called the local speakeasies who catered to the crowds of jazz-goers afterhours.

I walked to the Frigidaire and grabbed a bologna sandwich, waiting to eat it until I was in the confines of the jerky elevator. To my pleasant surprise, Mr. Wentworth was not on service, which saved the step of accounting for my whereabouts.

Chicago was alive with the buzz of Saturday evening.

Briefcases were tucked neatly away, replaced by women dressed to be noticed, dazzling in their reflective sequins and dangling pearls. A haze hung about the city as if the mood of the speakeasies had seeped through the walls and settled into the streets, luring couples who longed to be somebody into the same illegal clubs that often catered to the occasional movie star.

Greta Garbo's face with her bedroom eyes, dark lips, and porcelain skin smiled seductively from a billboard. Unlike Ma's, her cigarette was tall and slender, without a hint of caution as to what fire it could set.

I moved among the shadows, keeping a leery eye out for my folks, a thrill running through my veins and quickening my pulse. Without the daylight, my usual paper posts took on a new caution, secretive and daring. When I reached East Illinois Street, I gave out a whistle to the tune of "Downhearted Blues" and waited, scanning the streets for approach.

"You're a mighty fine whistler." Willy's voice made me jump.

"Got the jitters?" he chuckled.

"Nah," I lied, shaking my head. I rubbed my sweaty palms against my pants. "You sure you know where it is?"

"As sure as my cousin works there," he said, which really didn't give me much relief as I'd never met him. "Spoke with him earlier today."

Willy pulled a cigarette from his coat pocket and slipped it between his lips before lighting it with his striker. "He'll be working tonight."

"Let's get on, then," I urged, trying to make my voice as casual as possible. My heart thumped loudly against the echo of our Oxfords beating the pavement and the occasional siren that screeched of some catastrophe in the distance. It was as it seemed to be—the deadest part of the city.

Low income living quarters stretched along the buzzing hum of flickering streetlights, casting a sickening yellow glow amidst ominous shadows of smokestacks and meatpacking plants, steel factories and automobile warehouses. "You sure we're in the right part?" I whispered.

"I'm sure," Willy's voice wavered, less confident than before. We walked another block in silence.

"This is it," Willy said at last. He sucked in one last drag before flicking his cigarette into the darkness.

There wasn't a single window on the shambled brick building, just a door with peeling paint as if it were shedding a layer of skin. Whitewashed writing was barely visible on the east wall, the remains of a business that'd long gone under, someone's dreams now faded with time.

Willy glanced over at me and reading my face, let out a chuckle. "What'd you expect? A sign or something?"

To be honest, I kind of did. All the stories and allure of grandeur I'd heard whispers about, I expected a sign made of nothing less than diamonds.

Raising his eyebrows, he let out a sigh, as if to say *here goes nothing* and made his way to the door, leaving me to follow. He pushed against the weight of the steel door causing it to scrape against the cracked asphalt, releasing an overwhelming fume of musty cement. I blinked hard to adjust my eyes to the unlit entrance.

A set of stairs descended steeply to another door in the basement.

In the shadows, Willy gave me a nod and I followed him down.

CHAPTER 4

If the dankness of the alley entrance was any indication of what was inside, even that couldn't have prepared me for what was waiting on the other side of the doors.

Muffled noises amplified into saxophones and trumpets accompanying the myriad of colors and booming voices. The many women, most of whom were several years older than me, made me feel underdressed in comparison to their flashy feather boas and cloche hats. Flappers frantically fanned themselves as their skin seemed to illuminate under both the lights and the sheen of their sweat. It seemed every woman had dressed with the intent of outdoing the next as their men sat in suits around whiskey barrels playing poker.

Willy flicked his eyes about the room and then to me, a slow smile mischievously sneaking on his face to match my own. I pulled my shoulders back and stepped inside the speakeasy. We squeezed past circles of people and as we cut through the thickness of smoke, I caught glimpses of dames who drank as commonly as the men. If they thought us to be too young to be there, they mentioned nothing to us. Hell, it was illegal for any of them to be there.

"He's in the back room!" Willy called out from over his shoulder.

I followed his lead, trying to play it cool. Sweat seeped into my undershirt as we inched our way to the back room to where the bar was, people emerging with full glasses of sloshing liquids.

A dark wood of sort, the bar top contrasted greatly with the white-shirted bartenders behind it.

"Dudley's the one on the right," Willy said, nodding to a barrel-chested man with a dark mustache who I guessed to be somewhere in his early twenties. The jazz band rose into a crescendo of quicker rhythm, setting many of the women to dancing, their drinks forgotten on whiskey barrels or in hands as they spilled from their glasses.

Dudley glanced over and nodded, flashing a smile from under the thickness of slicked back dark hair. It wasn't less than thirty minutes later before he finally approached our table, setting his bar apron on the chair.

"Busy night?" I said casually, as if I'd been there before.

"Like any other Saturday." Dudley laughed, his brown eyes sparkling. Nearby, a few gals glanced our way and I quickly realized it wasn't Willy or me they were interested in.

"Heck, nearly *every* night," Dudley went on. "Government had no idea how much the prohibition would hit folks. 'Replace barley in beer for loaves of bread for the troops' or so they said. Hell, they even say pretzels and beer are anti-American and pro-German," he laughed again, shaking his head. "All prohibition has done is made a lot of unlikely bootleggers rich at the draining funds of the police force governed to bust 'em. That is, those who weren't bought off by it all."

I nodded my head in agreement, trying to keep my attention on the conversation. From the crowd I spotted a couple of faces I'd seen in the newspapers, likely politicians or business tycoons of some sort. Though Ma pretended to dislike speakeasies, she'd love this place and all the notoriety of the people who consumed it.

"Don't stare at 'em too much or they get jittery," Dudley said, pulling my focus back to his face. "Never can be too careful 'round those rings of conversation. Business deals go on more in here than they do during the 9-5 weekday. Look at 'em the wrong way and you'll land yourself a one-way ticket to the Chicago River."

I got his point and kept my eyes in our conversation.

Willy shifted. "So, they here?"

Dudley smiled. "Some."

"Is *he* here?" Willy asked pointedly.

Dudley laughed from his belly. "You kidding, kid? Course not. Closest you'll ever get to Mr. Capone's face is by opening the paper. Hell, I haven't ever even seen him."

But *I* had.

Willy's shoulders dropped as he glanced over at me.

"Anyone you can introduce us to? You know, somewhere on the outskirts of his ring?" I asked.

"Look around," Dudley said, gesturing with his arms. "They're all on the outside of his ring. Nearly any drop of rum, whiskey, you name it, puts the boozehound on the outside of his ring. Hell, he owns nearly the whole market."

I let out a deep breath and sensing my disappointment, Dudley's face turned serious as if deciding something.

"Look kid," he said, crossing his arms on the table and leaning in closer. "I can introduce you to someone, but then it's on you."

Willy and I exchanged glances and nodded. "What does he like to drink?" I asked, pulling out my wallet and exposing the crisp ten-dollar bill.

He was an oversized man in every sense of the word, wearing a navy suit and a bright red tie. His cheeks were pink, and his neck bulged from his collar every time he laughed. Women gathered around his table as he sipped his drink from a crystal cut glass. I waited cautiously, noticing his drink was always replaced by the time it was three quarters empty.

I glanced at my watch. Eight-thirty. It was time to make a move. Time was running short.

Willy and I casually cut our way through the crowd. When we got close to the table, the man eyed us with sparkling eyes.

"You boys of age?" he asked, his voice as boisterous as he was. A few of the women giggled as they regarded us. "You don't want to get the bum's rush on outta here!"

"No, sir," I said, shifting uneasily, "not in comparison to this whiskey I hear."

The man studied me a moment before erupting in laughter. "Bring it on over! I'll be the judge of that!"

I slid the glass across the table to which he took a slow sip. "Yes," he said, "it's definitely older and smoother than you."

He took another drink.

"What're you boys doing out anyway?" he asked, light flashing off the diamond ring on his meaty finger.

"Hoping to meet you," Willy jumped in. "We hear you're always lookin' for some good workers."

The man laughed again, his voice bellowing over the hushed murmurs of the crowd around him. "That's the catch, you see. The good workers part!"

"We'll do mostly anything," Willy went on.

I suddenly felt uneasy, dangerously aware of mob headlines I'd read about people being dusted off or shot up by gangsters. Would they ever put that responsibility on a twelve-year-old boy?

"We don't require much pay and we don't have any factory jobs or nothin' else to barter our time against." Willy was a slick one, I had to give him that.

For a moment, the man sipped thoughtfully on his drink. "You good with cars?"

I glanced nervously at Willy. "We can be," he said. Confidence or stupidity, I admired him in that moment.

The man shook his head as if thinking. "One more question."

I braced myself, sucking in a deep breath, waiting for him to ask if we preferred knives or guns. Rope or tape.

"You Irish?"

I had no idea what Willy was, but I was relieved when we both quickly shook our heads no.

"Sure the hell hope not," the big man said. "You're not Sicilian, either?"

"No, sir," I said. I was from Chicago. How the hell did I know anyhow?

"Well then, you passed the first test. I'll tell Dudley where to find me."

And that was how it all started.

CHAPTER 5

The whole thing was thrilling, and I couldn't help but feel different. I held my head higher. I had to admit, I enjoyed being the focus of murmurs and cast glances the other paperboys gave me… It brought a level of respect I'd never known before now.

It was simple, really.

Willy and I met the big suit (as we called him, not knowing his mob name and not daring to ask), at a seemingly abandoned warehouse not far from where the speakeasy was. A dark layer of moss crept up the faded brick walls as if trying to escape what lay beneath the crack in the pavement from which it grew. Of the few windows, most were boarded shut. I shuddered, imagining the kind of things that went on inside.

"Not what I expected," I confessed, grateful to have Willy as a sidekick in the whole deal. There was no way I was going in alone.

"What *did* you expect?" he challenged, his eyes sparkling with mischief. "A mansion in the middle of the ghetto?"

He lowered his voice, as if remembering. "Don't forget he's a button man," he hesitated and looked over. "You know, killer."

"Yes, I know what that means," I whispered back, offended. I drew in a long breath and nodded him forward. "After you."

There was a steel door to the left of a pair of rotting garage doors, large enough for freight. It made me wonder what the place had been used for and why it had been abandoned.

A balding man, bulky in stature surveyed us, his mouth snarling as he stood outside the door, daring anyone to give him trouble.

"You fellas meeting Lefty?" His voice was husky as he studied us.

My mouth began to water.

"Yes sir," I stammered, hoping Lefty was the same man we'd talked to in the club. It was too late to turn back.

He rapped his knuckles on the door, his eyes locked on us.

I shifted uncomfortably.

How do you make small talk with a mobster? Surely, I wouldn't want to land myself on the wrong side of a viewpoint when it came to Chicago politics. I used my smarts and kept my mouth shut, praying Willy would do the same.

After what seemed like hours, someone tapped the door from the other side and the balding man let us in, slamming the door behind us.

"Welcome," Lefty's voice boomed, echoing from somewhere deep within the warehouse. "Come on back."

Willy hesitantly glanced my way. "Where the hell is he?" he whispered.

I shrugged. How the hell would I know?

A numbing quiet settled in my ears, save the nauseating buzz of flickering yellow lights. Dark stains were prominently splattered across the cement floor.

Blood? My stomach twisted.

"Back here!" the voice rang out.

We followed the echo across the empty warehouse and through a narrow hallway leading to a back office where Lefty was leaning backward in a chair, his feet kicked up on the desk.

"You made it." He nodded in approval. "Good for you."

He closed his ledger book, regarding us for a moment.

"You know why I'm giving you a shot?" he leaned forward, his big belly pressing into the desk. "I'll tell you why." He pointed a thick finger at us as he spoke. "You remind me of my boy when he was 'bout your age. Mighty fine worker and smart. You two smart?"

"Yes sir," I said.

"You won't find none smarter than us," Willy cut in. I cast him a disapproving glance.

"Confident," Lefty said, laughing from his gut. "I like that." He leaned in as if letting us in on a secret. "Here's the deal. I need a couple of chaps willing to do some grunt work. Can't be no daisies either."

My stomach tightened and I thought I might be sick. I didn't want to kill people or smuggle liquor. Just wanted some dough and a reputation.

"You know, start off easy with oil changes and such." My shoulders relaxed. "And then, move on to changing tires and the occasional broken mirror. You ever change a tire before?"

"Only once or twice, sir," I lied. If I'd left the talking up to Willy, he'd have Lefty convinced we could change engines and whatever else. Probably have us staked out as hitmen already. "We might need a refresher."

He drew a cigar from a pine case on the desk before clipping it sharply and flicking his lighter to the end of it. "Good," he said, tobacco smoke wafting from his mouth. "You start tomorrow, and we'll go from there. Boss got a car that needs a little work."

I extended my hand out to shake his, as I'd seen my father do with business dealings. I sensed Willy's uneasiness as he did the same.

Lefty nodded in approval, nearly crushing my fingers in the strength of his meaty hand. Willy and I turned to go.

"Oh, and boys?"

We turned to face him.

"You know what happens if you tell anyone?"

I gulped hard and nodded. Even Willy knew better than to open his mouth. Stories of corpses fished out of the Chicago River and images of bodies found in abandoned basements came to surface.

"Good," he said. "Then we won't have any problems working together."

CHAPTER 6

I reported to Lefty the following Monday, hiding my bike in a nearby alley. A chill ran down my back as I thought about what could've been dumped in there or what was currently causing the nauseating stench that seeped from its cracks.

Walking a few steps away, I sucked in a deep breath of the slightly cleaner air.

This was it. No turning back. I was about to become part of the most powerful ring of people in Chicago. Bankers, business owners, politicians.

Me. Percy James.

Already I missed Willy who was reporting to another location on the West side of the city, and I couldn't help but wonder just how many locations Mr. Capone had. What would my training entail? My breath hitched in my throat. I'd asked Pops to show me how to change the oil in the car like he used to before we'd fallen into money, but he assured me we'd never have to change our own oil again. Now I wasn't so sure I remembered anything. Sure, I knew the basics of cars, but would it be enough?

What if it was robbery? I wasn't no dip pickpocketer.

Pops used to tell me stories from World War I when he was so hungry, he'd steal vegetables from the locals' gardens while fighting overseas. Or when he was a kid and would run off and hide in the woods near a golf course, sneaking the balls from the green and placing them in his bucket to later sell.

Plain and simple, sometimes stealing was a necessity.

I pushed through the door at the nod of a bouncer, who though not much taller than me, had a neck thicker than my waist and arms that bulged from under his shirtsleeves.

One thing was for sure: the place was a dive. Lights from the ceiling flickered in a series of zaps, before one of the bulbs went out entirely, casting ominous shadows and shifty shapes onto the concrete. Stepping hesitantly forward, my shoes echoed a reverberating façade of confidence I longed to feel. In the far corner Lefty had his back to me, his bald head gleaming.

For a split second, I thought of turning back.

I scoffed at the idea of it.

Not today. Today, I was becoming somebody important.

Just then, as if sensing the hesitation of fresh prey, Lefty turned and locked eyes with me through the office window. I straightened my shoulders back, sucking in a deep breath of courage as I sauntered to where he met me at the door, his meaty hand holding a telephone receiver up to his ear.

"Yes Boss," he said firmly. "Understood."

He cradled the telephone, his knuckles white and gnarly, ligaments and joints torn and mangled from punching too many faces I guessed.

"Hey kid," he plopped down in his chair and patted his forehead with a handkerchief. "Take a seat."

Heat flushed my face as I fumbled to pull the chair out.

"You ready for your first day?" He regarded me with colorless eyes as he clasped his hands in front of him, the gold chain around his wrist clanking against the desktop.

My throat went dry and all I could do was muster a nod.

"Boss called. There's been a change of plans."

My pulse thumped loudly in my ears as I imagined all the possibilities. Running whiskey across state lines? Throwing bodies into the river?

Murder?

I gulped, trying to swallow down the bile building in my throat as I involuntarily dug my nails into the flesh of my thigh.

"You know much 'bout flowers?" he now asked, intently watching me from behind his desk.

I blinked hard. "Sorry Mr.—" I hesitated, unsure of his last name.

Mr. Lefty?

It sounded ridiculous. I waited for him to reply, shrinking as he silently scrutinized me with his eyes. I'd been there less than half an hour and already I'd failed at paying attention. I cleared my throat. "I'm sorry, I thought you said *flowers.*"

He eyed me carefully before leaning back in his chair and kicking his legs on the desk. Even the bottoms of his shoes were clean, as if this were the first time he'd worn them. I couldn't help but wonder how long it took him to wear out a pair of shoes in his line of work, unlike me who could easily wear a pair down to nothing but a flimsy film of rubber in a few months, a testament to pounding the streets nearly every day before school and on weekends for the past several years.

I laughed nervously along with him, having no idea what was so funny other than the image of mobsters delivering flowers to teachers and mothers. Big Al Capone was a family man who cooked spaghetti dinner for his entire family every Sunday, including his mother and father and siblings who lived with him, but *flowers?*

Lefty stood and pulled his black hat from the table, covering the baldness of his head. He could have been any businessman had I come across him on the street. Crisp pinstriped suit, freshly pressed, a red bowtie that exuded the essence of power and money.

"Follow me, kid. We're off to the flower shop."

What the hell?

We rode in silence as I pondered what we were possibly doing at a flower shop, a mixture of disappointment and relief churning in my gut. The earthy smell of the leather car seats brought back memories of polishing my father's shoes as a young boy when he'd hit the streets in search of his next job. It took him years of overtime to get his current position as one of the lead journalists of the *Chicago Tribune*. Starting as a janitor in his late teens, he put in tireless hours of sleepless nights doing janitorial work until eventually he began to rise in the ranks and find his way into the editorial staff. I was slightly ashamed to admit that I'd never read any of his articles.

When Lefty pulled over and put the car in park, I was surprised to find that the flower shop wasn't a cover up business for another mob spot but was an actual flower shop. *Florence Flowers* was painted in neat cursive lettering on a sign that hung above the front door.

Lefty's voice broke into my thoughts. "Your job is to pay attention, okay, kid?"

I nodded. *Pay attention to what?* As dumb as it felt, I prayed there wouldn't be a shooting in this store where not even a petal seemed out of place.

He reached behind the seat of the car, but instead of pulling out a gun, he pulled out a small notebook.

He couldn't be serious.

I glanced around for Dudley and Willy's laughing faces, but only found the hustle and bustle of nameless people going about their daily routine.

Sweet smells of fragrant flowers filled my senses upon entering the shop. The bells on the door chimed, alarming a frail man who stood behind the counter as he peered up to greet us. Seeing us, his face shifted and for just a moment, he was motionless before shuffling over.

"Welcome, welcome," he said, his eyes twitching from behind round wire-rimmed glasses. "What can I do for you this week?"

"The usual," Lefty replied. "Big. Colorful. Exotic. Nothing but the best."

The man nodded his head eagerly, reminding me of one of the dolls from the dime shop. His eyes flicked to me and then back to Lefty.

"The kid's green," Lefty said. "Teach him what you know. I'll be back in forty-five."

Following Lefty to the door, the old man turned the sign over to *closed* before dropping his shoulders with a sigh as I stood there dumbly. Buckets of ruffled sweetheart roses (I knew this one from Ma) stared at me in hues of pinks and yellows. I didn't feel much like a gangster, but more like a butterfly instead. I shook my head in disbelief, praying none of the newsboys would see me in such a place.

"I'm Mr. Daniels," he said, offering his hand as he approached. "How long you been in?"

I hesitated stupidly. "A while," I said in as much confidence as I could muster. The man's mouth turned up in a small smile as if he knew how naïve I was, despite my best efforts.

Mr. Daniels proceeded to walk me down the aisles of "fresh cuts" as he called them, in his greenhouse, asking me questions. "Do you know what color this is?"

I bided myself to not roll my eyes at him. For all I knew, he was a mobster's worst enemy. Maybe he hid the bodies. In his gardens. It was possible.

"Pink," I said. *Obviously.*

"No," he replied. "If you want to impress the ladies someday, floral tip 101. You woo them over. This is *coral.* I suppose you could even call it salmon or blush," he went on.

I couldn't believe my ears. Was this old man serious?

I began to write it down in my notebook to prove I was listening. I could tear it out later. Good God, I couldn't imagine Willy finding it.

"No," Mr. Daniels said, stopping me. "No need to write it down, that tip is free. Someday, you'll thank me." He winked.

Over the next forty-five minutes, I learned about flowers. Big Al always requested gardenias in his orders, not only for their fragrance, but for the stark contrast of white against whatever color peonies or orchids were when fresh in stock. Everything he did exuded money. While most families could afford the standard carnations, chrysanthemums, or daisies, his bouquets were loud, a firework display of color and fragrance.

When Lefty came to pick me up, he wordlessly handed Mr. Daniels a slip of paper, along with an envelope of what I assumed to be cash. There was an address on the slip of paper, but all I could make out was *Charlie.* Or maybe even *Carlie,* most likely a mistress.

"That's it for today," Lefty said, starting the vehicle.

"Look, kid," he said, seeing my confusion, "some days are easier than others. It's not all bad. Rest up. Wednesday you'll be working late."

Before we parted ways, he flipped me a few bills. "Happy Monday kid."

I shoved the folded greens in my pocket, desperately wanting to count them, but playing it cool instead, giving him a nod before sauntering to the end of the parking lot. I waited until he went inside to count the cash and jump on my bike.

I'd hardly done anything. It would have taken me hours to make that kind of money ($4!) selling papers. Visions of the moto bike raced in my head, and I could see a version of myself driving it in front of my measly pedal bike.

Two days later, I was eating toast, trying to decide whether to purchase an obscure brown or a flashy red moto bike as Pops read the paper and Ma fixed up a plate of eggs.

"Another body was found in the Chicago River," Pops said casually, taking a sip of his coffee. *Red*, I decided. Red would get all the paperboys' attention and would certainly attract the gals. Especially in a new cap and leather shoes. Black leather shoes.

Ma, with her hair still in curlers, came and sat down at the table, her eggs steaming in front of us. "Oh? Anyone famous?"

I rolled my eyes.

"Unfortunately, the body ID'ed was Charlie Franklin." Pops folded the paper over, handing it to Ma.

I choked on a piece of toast, my mouth going dry. How did I know that name?

"Good Lord, Percy," Ma said, slapping my back. "How many times do I have to remind you to chew more slowly and you'll enjoy your food more?"

"Good God," Pops said, shaking his head in disgust.

Suddenly feeling nauseous, I took a sip of water, bracing myself for the gory details.

"Another typo. Spelled the word *dam* wrong. Not entirely Harry's fault, but nonetheless, this is the *Chicago Tribune*, for Pete's sake. Otherwise, well-written."

Pops liked to do that. Always noticing the particularities of the writing more than the article itself. He'd catch a typo anywhere as if it was a fatal threat to the future existence of reading. He was meticulously aware of shortcomings.

"Mob related?" my words came out in a squeak.

"Most likely," Pops said, his eyes skimming the paper. "He was one of the lead campaigners for Robert Koski." He frowned. "Try to clean up the city from thugs and bad politicians and all it does is land you in the muck of the Chicago gutters and in a poorly edited article."

A sickening thought struck me cold.

"When did it happen?" I asked, trying to sound casual as I replayed the past couple of days in my head.

"Says here, they estimate his time of death to be sometime last night." He regarded me from behind the paper. "Percy, would you stop scraping your fork across your plate?"

I felt my shoulders drop and repositioned my silverware.

"His poor family," Ma said, buttering her toast. "He has kids, doesn't he?"

My thoughts drowned out their voices. The floral arrangement was to be delivered by Monday evening, I clearly remember Lefty telling Mr. Daniels.

"Big Al's a polite man," he'd said with a smug smile when he picked me up from the floral shop that day.

But doing the math, I came to a sickening conclusion.

The flowers were a death sentence wrapped in a bow and signed by Big Al, delivered to his next victim while they were alive.

I cleared my dishes, thinking I might be sick.

"*Percy.*" Ma emphasized my name, making me realize it wasn't the first time she'd tried to get my attention.

"Yes?" I rinsed my plate, transfixed on the water running over it in streams.

"How's your breathing been?"

I rolled my eyes. If she'd perfected anything, it was worrying. I was as if it diverted her attention from the real problem at hand, which was her constant need to escape reality through her drinking habit. But now as she gazed out the window, her eyes fixed on the gray sky, the fine lines etched across her forehead and I felt a twinge of guilt.

"Fine, Ma." She glanced over, her eyes narrowed. "Really, Ma. Fine."

She sighed, unconvinced. "You better tell me if the air starts getting to you," she said, her pink (coral?) hair rollers bobbing as she spoke.

My stomach twisted.

"*Percy.*"

"Yes, Ma," I said, appeasing her. Walking to her bedroom, I heard her sigh again.

I laced my shoes and grabbed my hat before rushing out the door. Best to get started early. Today would be a full day of washing mob cars, wiping away any remnants of blood that might've splattered the lacquer.

And if I was a betting man, I'd bet there would be a lot of it.

Wednesday, after all, had come.

CHAPTER 7

At one point in Chicago, there were over 250 robberies a week. That's one per shop, per hour. It took nearly 250,000 policemen to enforce the prohibition and another 200,000 to police the police.

Big Al knew how to run a business, had to give him that. Hell, he'd bought off hundreds of breweries, brewing his own brands and giving the brewers raises so long as they kept their mouths shut and their beer flowing. No one dared to question or look twice at the armored trucks when they rolled about in the city. Texas itself was producing 13,000 gallons of whiskey a day I'd read in the paper. I couldn't even count that high.

There was an equal number of murders.

As requested, I'd ordered flowers to most of their houses and knew their names before their deaths. Their cards had all the same inscription: *Al Capone.*

I can't imagine what it must've been like to be on the receiving end of these death bouquets, knowing you were next, always watching your back. But I wasn't the one killing them; I simply ordered the flowers.

In a city of Poles, Russians, Germans, Swedes, and Czechs, it was the Italians and the Irish who ran the city. If you could get on the inside, you were nearly untouchable, with access to the elusive Colomo's Café where a stage would pop up at the push of a button and gold chandeliers glittered in the large stones of the lavishly-dressed women who danced the turkey trot. Rumor had it, at one point when Scarface had first moved here, his previous employer liked to carry around a bag of diamonds and would run his hand through them when scanning the crowd of celebrities. In a dirty city, this place was a mirage. Ma would love it.

"You're doing fine work, kid," Lefty said one day after summoning me over to his office.

I wiped the grease from my hands with a rag and shoved it into my back pocket before sitting.

He pulled a box from under his desk and pushed it in front of me. I glanced at him, my pulse quickening.

"Go ahead," he said and chuckled. "You afraid it might be a head or something? Go on and open it."

The cover slid off easily. I locked eyes with Lefty.

"You've earned it, kid," he said, clearly satisfied with my reaction of shock.

It would've taken me months to save enough for such an expensive gift. I pulled the fedora from the case, the black felt soft under my fingertips as I admired the pearly silk lining and matching hatband.

I opened my mouth, but Lefty spoke first.

"Hey. You run with us, you gotta look spiffy. Ain't that right?" His eyes glimmered with pride.

"Thank you, sir," I stammered, slipping the hat on my head. I wanted to do jumping jacks right there, but held my glee inside.

I was a man. Not only a man, but a mobster.

Turns out, the mob promotes quite quickly and it wasn't long before I was rising in the ranks. Anything was better than wiping blood off tires or selling newspapers in the early weekend hours to keep my parents in the dark about where my money really came from.

There were a couple of rules when it came to being in the mob.

Rule # 1 in the mob is not talking about the mob (although they seemed to enjoy reading their own headlines in the paper).

Rule #2 is no disrespect.

Hell, even the South Side O'Donnell Gang abided by the Gangster Code of Honor…never be a snitch. They thought they were so important with their polka dot bowties and black hats, but they had nothin' on us. Rat on Big Al and you were bound to get a one-way ride outta the city. They were at least smart enough to know that.

Knowing these rules kept me in the mob. Abiding by these rules kept me alive.

So, when Lefty walked over to me a few months later while I was filling the Caddy tires with air, I was cautiously aware that even a domestic animal could turn on you if you weren't careful. He had a presence about him that made you want to avoid his eyes, while at the same time, I didn't want him to mistake it for disrespect.

"C'mon, kid," Lefty's voice boomed. I tried not to gape at the diamond belt buckle, nor the heat he was packing behind it. "Today's your first promotion."

We rode in silence for a while as Lefty puffed on his cigar, one hand on the wheel, while his arm rested on the window frame. I tried to seem as natural as I could, riding beside one of the city's most wanted gangsters.

"You know what today is?" Lefty blew out a cloud of smoke, its strong smell plugging up my nostrils and making my head dizzy. "It's payday."

We swung through the industrial district, causing people to stop what they were doing and take notice of this large man who exuded success and his side kick who despite his young age, held a certain level of pride in his puffed-out chest and upward turned chin, elbow resting on the rolled down window.

The city seemed, well, a little more dazzling today.

In all my life, I'd never had so much privilege nor had anyone take such great interest in me and in how my life was going as Lefty. It made going home to trivial chores like dishes and vacuuming belittling, and despite the change in my demeanor and my offers to pay for top restaurants, Pops still treated me like a kid.

"Your hat is ravishing," Ma had said the first day she'd seen it. "You must've been saving a while. You could pass as one of those young actors." I waited for Pops to say something, but he just shook his head as if I'd spent my money frivolously.

So, I stopped caring so much about what a column writer thought of me. Hell, I was on my way to out earning him and with half the hours of work.

Lefty pulled into the alley behind a shamble of a building, and though initially caught off guard, I knew better than to read a restaurant for what it was. A tall, thin man in a white apron was pulling a garbage can out to a larger garbage bin, but upon seeing us, quickly shuffled back inside.

"Wait here, kid." Lefty glanced in his rear mirror, surveying the surroundings before getting out and disappearing within the building. My folks would never be caught dead in a place like this. How it could have anything to do with the payroll was beyond me. Most likely, it was someone on the inside working a side hustle and owing money.

Lefty came out with a smile and two paper bags.

"This one's for you," he said, handing me a bag.

The aroma of freshly grilled burgers steamed out of the bag as I peered inside, grateful for the food, but scared shitless to eat inside the car less I spill.

Lefty could be touchy.

Not long back, he showed me this side of him. He seemed to be having a decent day. I was working on replacing the wipers on a car, minding my own business when in walked a stout man, sharply dressed. The yelling that came from that office lasted nearly ten minutes as I braced myself behind the vehicle, my nerves pulsating in my arms. Although the man eventually walked out, Lefty kept his door closed the rest of the day. Countless times, the sharp noise of shattered glasses thrown against the wall (and turns out, he had many in that small office) broke the silence of the shop. He could flip on a dime.

Our next stop was only a few blocks away. Lacking an alley, Lefty pulled up snugly to the curb, blocking the front window of a dimly lit laundromat. I glanced over, expecting him to give me a speech or check a map or whatever, but Lefty slid out the door and waltzed into the place like he owned it—and maybe he did for all I knew. The more I hung around, the more I realized just how much of the city the mob owned. Politicians, newspapers, you name it, they owned it.

I learned very quickly what fear looked like when slapped across a person's unexpected face. The shifting of their glance, the lack of eye contact, the pursing of the lips. It was no different today as the clerk moved erratically about, his head disappearing under the counter as he searched for something, popping up with another brown bag for Lefty.

"Time to count the cabbage," Lefty said, handing the bag to me when he got back in the car.

He couldn't be serious. I didn't feel old enough to handle such sums, but his eyes regarded me steadily and I wanted to prove my worth.

"Should be ten Cs in there," he said, starting the car. "Hundreds," he added, as if to answer the question in my eyes.

I clumsily flipped through the stack of bills with trembling hands. I'd never seen that much money before and couldn't guess at how much money we were collecting that day. I counted a total of three times before confirming.

"All there," I said, trying to steady my voice and trying not to think of the consequences for that poor clerk if it weren't.

"Good." Lefty slowed to a stop at the lights. Turns out gangsters could have impeccable respect for traffic rules. Who knew?

"I don't trust him," he went on. "He's had one shot and that's all he gets. No more mistakes or he'll be seeing Chicago lightning. You see, the strength of the union dues is protection. You break that trust, you don't pay, then no protection. Easy as that."

As I learned over time, Big Al ran "unions" all over the city. You name it, he had a union for it. Waitressing Union, Ice Cream Union to name a few. These rackets paid more money than I could even fathom with a brain my size.

So, you can imagine my sentiment when Lefty pulled me into his office one day and for the first time asked about my parents.

"Your pops," he said, tapping his finger on the desk. "He a newspaper writer?"

I swallowed hard, feeling beads of sweat forming under my shirt. "He's a columnist, sir."

He seemed to think on that a while before answering. "He write anything good?"

I hesitated. "Depends on what you think is good, I reckon."

Lefty regarded me with sparkling eyes and a boisterous laugh. "He print any pictures with his articles?"

I tried to remember and didn't know. I thought back to the first couple of articles Ma had attached to our new refrigerator, but had never paid much attention.

"I'm sure he can," I lied, wanting to impress him.

Lefty retrieved a manilla envelope from a locked drawer in his desk. "You slide this into his briefcase or however you see fit. Don't let him see it's from you. Don't ask questions. Don't let on anything is different. Everything he needs to know is inside. Got it, kid?"

His eyes were serious, and I sensed a hint of sadness—the weight of responsibility he'd laid on my shoulders. Hell, it did weigh heavily.

I nodded, tucking the flimsy envelope inside the front of my shirt as I'd seen some of Big Al's guys do.

"Hey, kid," he said dismally, stopping me before I got to the door. "Do yourself a favor."

I waited for him to tell me to sweep up before leaving or some mundane necessity that fell upon me when we were the only two around.

"Don't get nosy and look at any of 'em. Sometimes, the world we build around our family is better off and stronger if you don't inspect the walls."

CHAPTER 8

Pops came home the next day, and though Ma didn't notice, I immediately knew he'd gotten the envelope I'd tucked into the mail.

He paced the kitchen, absentmindedly opening and shutting cupboards at random, pausing every so often to wipe the sweat from his pasty forehead.

My heart sank under a heavy burden of guilt.

"For goodness sake," Ma said, pouring herself a glass of whiskey, "would you stop rummaging for something to eat? I'm about ready to fix supper."

We picked at our baked chicken in silence, forks clanking against ceramic plates. I rolled my green beans into neat little rows.

"*Percy*," Ma scolded. "What's gotten into you? Good God, would you stop sulking and start eating?"

I shoved a forkful of rice into my mouth to appease her. Satisfied, she went back to pulling shreds of meat from her chicken breast, her attention diverted to whatever else was on her mind.

A sickening nausea had seeped into my stomach and I didn't feel much like eating.

Finally, Pops pushed himself back from the table with a heavy sigh.

"Heading back in," he said dismally, leaving an untouched pile of string beans and a mound of rice on his plate.

Ma's gaze followed him with scrutinizing eyes and pursed lips as he threw on his hat and slammed the door closed behind him.

She silently scraped his leftovers into the trash before slipping into her room, the soft sounds of snoring filtering through the door jamb a few minutes later. This became our routine over the next few evenings as the uneasy feeling that had rooted in my gut grew into invasive tendrils that choked every organ.

What did Lefty do?

That Sunday, for the first time, I read my father's column.

Though I wasn't ordinarily interested in the markets or the Chicago economy, I had a hunch it might be a clue to the envelope. I raced down to the corner where a young newsboy, not much older than me when I started selling, was shouting out to passerbys.

I slipped him a few coins and waited until I was in the privacy of my room to open the paper. Was Pop's column on the third or fourth page?

My cheeks burned. I didn't have to search for it.

Pops, who in his twenty some years at the *Tribune*, had never made the front page, now smiled back at me from the front left corner of the paper.

POLICE DEPARTMENT SCANDAL!

The breath hitched in my throat and my heart nearly stopped.

My eyes flicked to the oversized photo that filled the top half of the paper, the crease of the fold slicing through the pictured men just below the hips.

Two men in suits and bowties were shown exchanging something with Chicago's Chief of Police.

I didn't need to read the subtitle. I knew who they were.

The bowties of the two O'Donnell brothers gave them away, their mugs recognizable by any member of the Catholic Church masses they regularly attended.

Someone was a snitch.

I kneaded the knot that was burning in my shoulder and swallowed hard as thoughts ricocheted in my head. *Lefty.*

"Dear God, dear God," Ma said under her breath, the paper shaking in her trembling hands when she read the article later that evening. "Why did you run this?"

Pops opened his mouth and shut it again.

"Do you know what they could do to you?" Her voice was a whisper as her eyes remained glued to the shaking paper.

This couldn't be happening. This was all my fault. What had I gotten myself into? My family into? Bile burned in my throat. How could Lefty put this on my family? My temples pulsated and I thought I might be sick.

Pops set his fork neatly next to his uneaten eggs. "Had to," he said grimly. "I had no choice if I wanted to keep my job or stay alive. You can't win with the mob. You're always an enemy of one of them."

And that was my first hard lesson.

No one was protected by the mob. Not all the union dues in the world would exclude you from their money-making machine and the grip they held on Chicago. They ran with a reign of fear, coated in the glamour of their nightclubs and the power they held over all of us.

I regretted then, for the first time, being on the streets and selling newspapers on that fateful rainy day so many months ago. I just wanted things to be the way they were.

Over the next several months, things quickly began to avalanche. My family was no longer safe.

I replaced my Indian 151 moto bike with my old pedal bicycle and news cap, envious of the paperboys on the corners who didn't seem to have a care in the world. I was living in a man's world, which meant a man's problems.

But these weren't ordinary men.

The O'Donnell gang was quick for payback, plugging at least four of Big Al's guys in the next month, never getting close enough to the ringleader himself, who was always flanked by two guys on both sides, two to the back, two to the front. He was untouchable. This was bigger than the Beer Wars between the gangs. This was personal.

I kept my head down and did my job, running errands when Lefty gave the order. We made our usual stops: me counting the money while he drove to the next unfortunate chap who happened to own a family business in the city.

"We got one new stop," Lefty said, while making our rounds one day. A glimpse of my old selling grounds caused me to lose count of the money I was sorting. His territory was usually on the East side, so I couldn't hide my surprise when we slid into a parking spot in front of the Tribune Tower.

"Turns out," he said, turning to face me, "your old man is about as compliant a worker as you and has the same smarts to know when he needs protection."

My stomach muscles involuntarily contracted causing me to tighten the grip on the money.

He had blackmailed my father.

Twice.

Run his pictures, then pay union dues for "protection."

Thoughts clustered in my mind as my head pounded and my cheeks burned hot. All the stories of Big Al being a family man meant nothing, seeing his own family as so much more important than anyone else's.

The one grace Lefty gave me was that he didn't make me do it.

He disappeared into the building, his body becoming a shadow through the window, his face obscured. I pounded my fist into the leather seat over and over until my knuckles throbbed. I hated this damn car! Hated *him* and saw him for the cockroach he was.

I imagined Pops sitting rigidly in his office chair, the one Ma had gotten on sale when he'd first been promoted, its arms worn into a soft caramel color in contrast to its varnished dark mahogany edges, a testament to the hours he'd spent piecing together stories, devoting his life to the company. Beside his container of pens sat a framed picture of me as a boy at one of the ball games he'd taken me to, the photo flecked with dust. I clenched my jaw until my teeth ached.

He wasn't gone long.

Always prepared, I'm sure Pops had the money neatly ready as he waited.

I couldn't look Lefty in the eyes. My world was shattering and he held the hammer.

"Look, kid," he turned to face me after shoving the bag under his seat.

My shoulders dropped as something sputtered inside my gut. He wasn't going to have me count just how much he'd stolen from my family.

"It's nothing personal. They got us all. Even my old man pays union dues. It's how the city runs. Who do you think pays for the clean parts of Chicago? The politicians? The business owners who can hardly afford to run their small shops?" He shook his head as if he almost believed what he was saying. "We're doing the city a favor, kid. The quicker you learn that, the quicker you'll succeed."

But as we drove, I couldn't think of many clean places in the city. I wondered if Willy had learned the same lessons as I had. My stomach turned at the realization I hadn't talked to him in a while. I missed my friend.

I had been to the slummiest corners where families ate in the same gutter I sold newspapers in, and I had frequented chandelier-lit restaurants and clubs in which plates of food were left half eaten in fear of missing out on the fox trot.

It all boiled down to this.

There weren't many clean parts of the city; some places just hid the filth behind closed doors. But no matter how much they scrubbed, no amount of cleaning could hide the blood stains on the floors.

CHAPTER 9

"They got my old man, too," Willy said one Sunday while sitting in the park, having a smoke.

"Why?" I nearly choked until I saw the wounded look on his face. His pops delivered bread. What could they get him for? "Why?" I asked again, more evenly.

Willy offered a smug smile. "Bread, Cracker, Yeast & Pie Wagon Driver's Association."

I couldn't help but laugh, and then realizing he wasn't laughing with me, shook my head in disbelief. "You kidding me? What they're doing to this city…"

"No more words about it. We gots to get out, but be careful who you talk to. Everyone is under their so-called protection, and you know you can't trust any of the crooked cops. You'd get yourself plugged quicker than your heartbeat."

As if on cue, somewhere in the distance a firetruck blared its alarm through the streets, the siren exchanging between faint and loud intervals while weaving between office buildings and open streets, then finally disappearing altogether as it pulled farther away from us.

"How?" I couldn't see a way out of this for us, other than a one-way ticket down the Chicago River.

"Don't know, but I'm going to find a way."

"Dudley still around?" My voice was hesitant. I hadn't seen him in months.

"They got him smuggling in rum from the Caribbean somewhere down south."

My shoulders dropped in relief.

"Lot of driving back and forth," he went on, "but it's better than being in the city."

I couldn't agree more.

When I got home later that day, I found the place quiet. Not long ago, my parents used to go out for Sunday strolls around the neighborhood or nearby park. Now, because of me, they were no longer safe. It was a pressing burden to wake up to every morning, a heavy blanket that weighed me down and challenged my willpower to get out of bed.

Ma came home a few hours later, her face blotchy and eyes swollen from crying.

"Where's Pops?" *What if they'd tracked him down?* I frantically searched her face for answers. "Ma! Where's Pops?"

"He's okay," she huffed, dismissing me with her hand. "There was a fire."

My mind raced back to the sounds of the fire alarms earlier that day. Never in my mind did I imagine it was connected to my family. "Where?"

"The office," she sniffled, pulling a handkerchief from her pocket to dab her nose. For a moment, I considered telling her everything, wanting her to blanket me in the warmth of her embrace. I wasn't a kid anymore.

"How?" my voice wavered.

"They don't know. Thank the stars no one was hurt. Your father said the elevator stopped working on Friday. Left everyone at the top of the building to take the stairs. Mighta' been electrical."

A numbness crept up my legs, nesting in my stomach, branching into my arms with a nauseating buzz. I couldn't think. Couldn't breathe.

"It's going to be alright, Ma," I forced myself to say.

She squeezed her eyes shut, tightly pursing her lips. *What was she trying to protect me from?*

"What is it?" I placed a hand on her shoulder, studying her face. "You can tell me."

Ma rested her head on my shoulder, choking out sobs for several minutes.

I patted her back, my shirt growing increasingly damp with her tears.

"There's pictures," she whispered.

I cocked my head, pulling back. *"Pictures?"* Is that what she said?

"Five," she confirmed, her shoulders slumped, eyes fixed on the floor.

"Five pictures?" She wasn't making any sense and my concern was turning into frustration. It wasn't out of the ordinary for her drinking to get to a point of confusion. "Here, sit down, Ma." I pulled a chair out from the table and sat across from her, my eyes not wavering from her face.

"You said Pops was okay," I confirmed.

She nodded her head in agreement and I let out a deep sigh.

"Someone slipped an envelope into our mail. No label, nothing."

My stomach tightened and I thought I might throw up. "And? Was it to run another column?"

"No," she said and dabbed at her bloodshot eyes. "Not this time."

"What *kind* of pictures?" I stammered.

Ma leaned over and reached into her purse, fumbling with an envelope before sliding it to me with trembling hands, her nails hot pink against the sickening yellow paper.

I didn't want to open it.

Don't inspect the walls of your house. Lefty's warning rang loudly in my ears. My eyes flicked to Ma, but she stared vacantly at the wall behind me.

I don't know what I expected to find. Pictures of bloody bodies or more pictures of politicians? My mouth went dry. I swallowed hard, dumping the contents of the package on our dining room table.

I bit my lip, my cheeks flushing as I thumbed through the prints.

"That can't be him," I said evenly.

"It is," Ma said firmly, pushing one of the photos closer. "That's the tie I gave him on our anniversary. Remember?" She shoved it closer as if it would make it clearer. Easier to stomach.

I studied the photos, working the muscle in my jaw until the screeching of Ma's chair against the linoleum snapped me back into reality.

She straightened up and sucked in a deep breath, resolute. "Leave them there. I won't be making supper tonight."

I glanced one more time at my father's face and the bim in his arms who was not my mother. My world fell apart. Right there in front of me in the form of five pieces of photographic paper. Was my old man a tough person to love at times? Yes. His rules and unreachable expectations had put Ma to drinking years ago. He showed his love to us through his hard work and his many "life lessons" he was constantly bestowing upon me. At least, according to my mother. No one could deny the man was a workaholic…the one trait I rested my hat on. Hell, he even worked his ass off to portray a picture of the perfect family, bringing me to ball games and bragging up my newspaper sales to his buddies over poker games.

But now, seeing these pictures made me question everything I thought I knew about him. All the suppers he missed, when Ma would spend hours on a roast and nervously skitter about the kitchen to make things perfect for when he got home. He wasn't at work. He was out galivanting around with some floozy who was probably incapable of cooking a damn thing, let alone knowing how to keep a family together.

A slow burn reached through my chest and it suddenly felt as if the walls were pressing in on me, squeezing every last bit of oxygen from the room. My head began to spin.

I had to get out. I glanced at Ma, who was soundly sleeping, and tucked a blanket around her, covering the tear stains on her pillow. She was too damn good for him.

It wasn't until I reached the drowning chaos of the city outside that I felt my chest loosen. Horns blared out, their shrill bouncing off the brick walls of the surrounding buildings as people rushed by. It was a constant pulse that was as reassuring to me as it was irritating to those who weren't accustomed to the rhythm of city life. I'd always have the city.

I pulled a pack of smokes from my front pocket, slipped a cigarette between my lips and sauntered down the sidewalk, letting the sea of people swallow me whole.

CHAPTER 10

The mobsters, at least the really divisive ones, were electric in every sense of the word. Lefty was Chicago bright lights and flashy billboards. So attractive, it was easy to forget that in high volts, electrical storms were capable of draining every power source it encountered while expanding into something more volatile.

But, it could also be controlled and used to serve your own purposes if you knew what type of storm you were dealing with.

Well, I'd learned a thing or two, and a plan began to formulate in my mind over the next couple of weeks. There was a lot of room for thinking in a apartment without spoken words.

I couldn't look Pops in the eye.

Part of me wanted to grip my fingers around his neck and give him some chin music now that I saw him for what he was. *Who* he was and whether he was that much better than the gangsters I'd come to know. Scarface after all, lived with his entire family. Hell, even his mother lived with him. The guy had a religion of cooking them all homemade spaghetti every Sunday and set up soup kitchens throughout the city. He might have a hot head, but he was loyal where it counted and he loved his wife.

As crushing as it was, I had to come to terms that Pops, as it turned out, was a ringer. An asshole who didn't rate much.

The worst part about it was my mother's reaction to it all. She refused to confront him. At least not directly, nor in front of me. Every day, she got up, put on her makeup and pretended as if nothing had ever happened. The night of the photos, in silent protest, Ma didn't make supper. I braced myself for the screaming, the drinking. Any shred of emotion left on the bones of their marriage.

But instead, we roamed around in numbing silence, ghosts incapable of feeling or speaking.

Finally, I'd had enough.

"Why Ma? How can you let him get away with this?" I fumed one day while Pops was at work or *wherever* else he was.

Ma took a sip of whatever it was she was drinking that day. "Look, Percy. I'm not new to this rodeo. It's not the first time, you know," she said.

Not the first time? Her words stung. Or maybe it was my realization at the true cause of her drinking "habit."

She let out a soft chuckle the way she did when she'd had too much to drink and I knew she'd been drinking the really heavy stuff. I'd learned there was a difference in her demeanor when she drank "light" or drank "dark" and I braced myself for an argument. "Your father likes to think he's something special, you know," she slurred, "like one of the actors on the screen. A real catch." She took another sip, struggling to keep the contents in her glass.

As upset as I was with him, her words sucker punched me and I pushed off an instinctive urge to defend him. "Ma, why don't you do something?"

She flailed her arm out, her drink sloshing over the edge of the glass and spilling onto the floor. "Like *what,* Percy? What do you want me to do? Leave him?" She laughed.

I didn't know exactly what she should do, but she should do something! *Anything.* This was unforgivable. I still couldn't wrap my head around my father's actions, one of the hardest working men I knew, doing this to my mother.

"Where would I live, Percy? I don't have a career. I have no money of my own. Where would I go?" She slumped down in the chair. "What lawyer would defend me if I could even come up with the money?"

I sighed. She was right. Damn it. I knew she was right.

My mother, who tried so hard to appear independent, had always been quick to appease my father in every way, showering him with compliments and flattering him with her submissive manner. Women's rights stretched only so far politically, but socially, it was another battle altogether.

My cheeks grew hot, and I found myself hating the man who had brought this about my family. I clenched my jaw and slammed the door shut behind me. I needed to walk and think through what was spinning around in my head.

I needed to get out. Out of the mob and out of this family. Out of this city with all of its flashing lights and seductive illusions of grandeur that were nothing but empty promises and outright lies.

I needed out of this so-called family.

Was it even possible?

Lefty and I ran our usual stops. I had learned to keep a stoic face, even if I couldn't stomach the sight of him. He'd stolen more from my family than money. I cringed.

I didn't know who to be more disappointed in. Knowing what Pops had done was devastating. I asked myself if it was better Ma knew, but I wasn't so sure. Not like Lefty had done us a favor or anything. I'd be damned to think he did my mother a favor. I was the stupid kid for trusting him in the first place. For assuming there was some kind of gangster family code of ethics or something.

We ran our routes in silence, me wearing my best poker face, giving an occasional nod of agreement to whatever he happened to be rambling on about.

Timing.

Perfect timing is crucial to every system, every assembly line. And, it was crucial to any shot I had at leaving.

The tension hung in the air like a thick fog, choking out visibility beyond what was right in front of me. I couldn't see past the volatility of my emotions enough to reach any kind of clarity of reasoning.

We ran our usual routes that week and the next, but when I was done and fared Lefty good-bye, instead of turning toward home on my bike, I pedaled in the opposite direction. I pedaled furiously, my legs burning, my ears alerted by the spinning tires of every approaching car, every screech of brakes that sent tingles down my spine. I biked nearly twenty blocks away and already darkness was threatening to swallow me up.

When I arrived, I parked my bike carefully in the bushes by the street. The brick house was nothing less than I'd imagined. Fat and tall with windows that peered at me from within the comfort of their cream-colored shutters, the soft glow of light spilling from their glass, casting distorted shapes across the neatly mowed lawn.

The street was quiet, nothing like my own that was alive with the heartbeat of the city. It was a dream house in a quiet neighborhood, bought with the blood and grime of the worst in the city, neatly trimmed in flowering lilac bushes that scented the breeze as it wafted across my face.

I tiptoed to the front door, the croaking of frogs hardly louder than the thud of my pulse in my neck. *This was the way out*, I reminded myself. I owed this to my family.

To Ma.

Sucking in a deep breath, I tapped my knuckles against the thick slab of wood, and after the soft thuds of shuffling from within, I was greeted with a familiar smile. Wordlessly, I pulled a slip of paper from my pocket and handed it over.

The man opened it, and scanning the name, frowned before giving a slight nod and clicking the door shut behind him.

I was in bed by nine-thirty, after I had easily slipped past Ma who was already asleep from what I suspected to be the empty liquor glass on the counter.

Different scenarios played in my mind like a movie reel over the next couple of days. Had I done the right thing? Surely it was justified. What was done, was done and I knew it was too late, even if I had second thoughts. I spent hours upon hours willing myself to sleep at night while lying in bed, horrified at the outcomes of my decision.

And then, it happened.

I was squatting down, checking the pressure on the tires of the Caddy. The door busted open, the silence violated by a posse of stomping feet and deep voices, intent on finding someone. My heart beat wildly as if it wanted to get out of the confines of my body.

I shrunk myself down, sliding behind the car. *Had they seen me?* Ma's face flashed in my mind, her lips turned up into a loving smile as she pitched a ball to me in the alley as a kid, back when she smelled of clean cotton and sweet lilies, not the aftertaste of strong liquor.

Don't breathe, Percy. Don't breathe.

Heavy footsteps echoed, reverberating against cold, bare walls and smooth cement. How many were there? Three? Four? Five? At least three.

I pressed myself against the floor, the smell of oil calming as I peered out from under the car. I imagined snarled faces and burly chests belonging to the feet of the men stomping their way closer to me. Two, four, six, eight. Eight feet. Four men.

They knew.

I clasped a hand tightly over my mouth and balanced myself with the other, my arm now trembling under the weight of my body and the chill in my hand from the unwelcoming floor. The shadow of a body stretched out from beneath the car. I let out a light sigh, realizing it belonged to me.

I slowed my breathing against the mumbling of voices in the commotion that had broken the whistling of the furnace. My legs were burning as if at any minute the weight of my body would bust my kneecaps. I didn't dare move.

Just a glimpse.

No, too risky. The consequence would be deadly.

Big Al was an elusive man and always guarded by a circumference of men twice his size.

A door slammed shut. Slowly, ever slowly, I stretched out my tingling legs until I was sitting on the cold floor. I took a chance and craned my neck to the window of the office where an oversized man filled the window with his back. Awkwardly, I sucked in a breath and held it as still as I could while sliding myself under the shelter of the car, the underside inches from my face as I stared into the darkness.

"I don't care if you pay me with your first-born child! You're nothin' but a swindler with shells. A skid rogue who can't be trusted and it's time for you to sing!" Big Al had gone off track, his voice booming through the walls of the office, setting the door to rattling in its frame. "You think you can get away with giving *me* the squeeze? That's *my* dough you've been skimming!"

My muscles tensed, burning like fire. Beads of sweat bubbled on my forehead before trickling down the sides of my face and onto my neck.

"I don't know what you're talking 'bout boss," Lefty pleaded.

"Close your head! This ring is built on trust! You've broken it. Well, I'm 'bout to give you some bad news. The only place you can be trusted is in a wooden kimono six feet under!"

A shot thundered through the building. I clutched the rim of the tire to steady myself. Lefty, the man who had invited me into the mob, had been rubbed out.

The office door squealed as it opened, and footsteps grew louder and closer. Each step sending electrical impulses through my veins until all of a sudden, the men stopped and all was silent save the few crickets that had wedged their way into the warehouse and never left. My heart thudded wildly; my pulse raced faster.

"Hey kid?" a voice called out.

Big Al.

My hands trembled. *Oh my god, oh my god, oh my god.*

"Yeah?" I tried to play it casual, but my voice came out squeaky and shaky.

"Take the day off. You just got promoted."

Moments later, the shop door slammed shut and was followed by the faint sound of tires against gravel.

It seemed as if the air had been sucked out of the room.

I stayed under the car in the piercing silence that followed for what seemed like an eternity. The reality of it was about half an hour.

When I finally had the nerve to push my body out, I ran for the shop door and didn't stop until I was on my bike. The buildings were blurred by my need to feel safe and yet, when I reached home, it wasn't until I closed my bedroom door tightly behind me and collapsed onto the bed, that the reality of my situation sank in and the silent sobs began.

One of Chicago's Biggest Mobsters Found Dead in the Chicago River read across the headlines of nearly every paper a few days later. It was an extravagant funeral filled with fellow mobsters; Big Al in his classic yellow suit, surrounded by his bodyguards. And for maybe the first time ever, Lefty's warehouse didn't smell of grease and fuel, but the overwhelming sweet fragrance of fuchsia gardenias and crimson roses tucked neatly amongst leatherleaf.

It was as beautiful and misplaced as a Garden of Eden in a concrete park.

I brought an arrangement home to my mother not long before biking to the old florist's house to place that deadly order. She deserved better than the withered roses my father had neglected to replace since the envelope had arrived. She had refused to toss them out, hanging on to something that was nearly dead.

I believed she deserved some beauty in her life again and I could afford it. So without a second thought, I had pulled the brittle stems from the vase, the musty smell of dust and neglect wafting around me as I walked them to the window and threw them into the street, admiring the skill of the old florist as I centered the fresh arrangement on the table in a spray of color and fragrance.

Lefty had grit.

Had to give him that. Didn't run when the flowers were delivered. Went to his office the next day and waited in his chair, his face red with anticipation of what was to come. Skimming off the top is bad business and Big Al wouldn't stand for it. He had enough class to send flowers to all the mobsters he dusted off. That's what Lefty had told me.

But for once, Big Al had it wrong.

Right location, wrong target. Because not much credit went to a kid who was in charge of counting and organizing the money. I was after all, just a kid.

Not many mobsters noticed I had been riding a new moto bike and secretly putting envelopes of money in my mother's purse.

As the saying goes, revenge is a dish best served cold, but that day, I was ready to prepare it either way.

CHAPTER 11

A few years had passed since Lefty's murder, but I still recalled it as any other pivotal memory that stands out in a young fella's mind. They say transition into adulthood happens ever so slightly and a little at a time, like erosion or something. But for me, in that season, I became a man. A man ready to take on the world, vowing never to chase fast money again.

I could now change a tire in ten minutes flat. Hell, I could crack any safe on a soup job in ten minutes flat, provided I have the main ingredient to the soup: nitroglycerine.

But still, I couldn't shake my last conversation with Willy and those haunting words that were my last tie to Chicago. I was sixteen and had seen more crime than the coppers.

"He always had your back, you know," he had said.

We were smoking on the park bench, watching the Chicago River on a day when I needed to escape the suffocation of the apartment. The currents were strong and steady, despite the hindrance of underwater boulders, evidence only seen in the rough ripples they cast.

"Who? Lefty?" I asked, turning to face him. His name hadn't been mentioned in years. Guess everyone was too afraid to talk about the chumps who didn't follow the rules.

Willy's face held the experience and wisdom of several more years than he'd lived. I guess the mob had the ability to age people, too. I ran a hand through my hair, consciously aware my face probably held the same concern. I shook my head in disagreement. "He didn't care 'bout me. Just his rounds."

"Not true," he said pointedly. "You know, when I was working with Dudley, I overheard him talking to Stubs." Stubs reported directly to Big Al himself. Rumor had it, he'd followed him here from New York in the early years. "Lefty was trying to convince him to leave your family alone. Even offered to take some of the dough outta his own share."

Willy sucked in a drag from his cigarette. An aching burn climbed up my back and into my shoulders. He blew a couple smoke rings into the air, seemingly larger than the skyscraper beyond it.

Lefty had my back? A sickening feeling filled my stomach, threatening to force the contents of it to spew out of my mouth.

"*You okay, Percy?* I know you two were tight." Willy's words hung in the air, reaching my ears from some distant place.

He didn't know. No one did.

In the end, I'd like to say it was my moral conscience as a law-abiding citizen that pushed me out. That I had a change of heart. But it wasn't, and I never claimed to be a prime role model citizen. It made it easier that no one ever questioned the suspicious amount of money I suddenly brought in. Hell, not even the crime ring shootings had soured my taste of the city.

No, it was the combustion of everything else, all the little fires that no matter how much water I tried to drown them with, I just couldn't put them out. I wanted to scream anytime my parents ate together, pretending to be something we weren't. No amount of cash could fix it. God knows I tried.

I could stomach a lot of things, but that one wasn't one of 'em. Not anymore. Ma wouldn't even grant me the grace to confront him in fear of him leaving.

And the guilt.

God, the guilt. It stalked me by day and tortured me by night. I killed him. I'd killed Lefty in a fit of revenge. *I couldn't have known,* I told myself. How could I have ever known?

I'd learned a tough lesson. Revenge runs deep. Deeper than the layers of the mob. I was responsible for taking the life of someone who trusted me. Liked me. Had my back.

It haunted me for a thousand miles and several months removed from the situation.

My lungs were the easy alibi. The smoking habit I could kick, but Chicago was a slow death sentence. Her gray skies had wedged its way into my body and become a part of me, slowly choking, making it hard for me to breathe.

Convincing the folks my lungs were in need of fresher skies was an easy task. I think we were all just willing to do whatever it took to break the tension that had mortared our family unit together. We were living in a sandcastle house and the tide was coming in.

The mob? Well, let's just say that so long as I was compliant and didn't rat out anyone, my folks would stay alive. Willy promised to keep his tabs on them. Keep them safe.

So here I was, a world away from Chicago and thousands of dollars lesser, gazing out over a prairie of nothing. Nothing for as far as the eyes could see. Gone were the honking horns and flashing lights. Gone were the tall skyscrapers and men in suits, hustling by so quickly they hardly glanced my way. All of these things had been replaced by blue skies and the soft whisper of wind as it bent the grasses through which it traveled, rolling up to greet me in a glowing wave of copper.

I took in a deep breath, filling my lungs with the promise of new beginnings and a little luck, exhaling out the frustration I harbored for my parents and their charade of a relationship as the wind wrapped me in a quiet embrace before lifting the weight from my shoulders and carrying it to the sky.

I stretched my hands out over the grass, their blades gently tickling my calloused palms. These were working hands. I might've left the city, but I had brought some of it back with me, its grime etched in the grooves of my fingers.

All I needed from the city was contained within my hands.

And with work ethic and a usable skill, you could go nearly anywhere and things would work out.

Or so Pops always said…

PART II

WICHITA, KANSAS

Carrie Lexington, 1929

PREFACE

Ilooked to the sky and said a silent prayer, as I'd seen Pa do almost every day since spring. The hem of my cotton dress hung on to its ruffle sadly, threatening to let go with any breath of wind, as if no longer caring to hold onto the frill that once dignified the garment. Nonetheless, the skies were a bleak gray, not with the promise of rain, but with sand that could choke the life right out of you at any minute, with any breath of wind.

I searched the vast expanse of land that had once been an endless emerald green against blue skies. It was land that would sustain us, even as the stock market was crashing. The land, when treated right, was reliable or so I was told. More reliable than placing borrowed money you never touched into places in the market you couldn't see.

I thought back to when we had first moved here several years earlier. "Says here, Carrie," Pa started, squinting his eyes against the sun and looking at me, "that Oklahoma grows better corn than both Kansas and Minnesota…better cotton than Mississippi and better fruit than Arkansas or Missouri."

He never smiled much, but his lips curved up slightly now. No one mentioned how many times he'd told us that story already. Still not a good enough reason to leave Minnesota, but no one asked me.

"Let's hope they're wrong about Kansas," Pa said.

"Well," Ma said, biting the side of her cheek. It had been a long drive and she'd had as much as she could take. "It certainly sounds like a dream now, doesn't it?" She winked at me. "The real estate folk promised artesian wells and wide streets lined with elms and maples far as the eye can see." Ma scanned across the field, her eyebrows raised in scrutiny, but the closest things to trees were patches of buffalo grass that popped up sporadically across the horizon.

I knew better than to ask. Besides, I already knew the reason for our move. After Pappy and Granny passed, we had lost our only real connection to Minnesota. Irish immigrants, they'd come to the U.S. during the potato famine to start a new life as farmers. Growing potatoes here wasn't the problem. Finding land to own was. Here we were, a generation later, still renting our farmland.

"It sure is hot," Ma said, frowning. "Not quite like Minnesota."

"Well, reckon we'll get used to it," Pa said, his voice wavering.

I searched the fields at the expanse of land. "Where are the trees?"

Ma flicked her eyes to Pa, who was stuffing the brochure back into the pocket of his pin-striped overalls. "Give it a chance," she said. "We've only just crossed the border."

Nothing was interesting about the vast plains that lay before us. Nothing vertical anywhere in sight. Horizontal barbed wire fencing, horizontal land. A horizon that cut a slice between the dull sky and the colorless land, save some grass patches here and there. Ma reached over and slid her hand in mine, giving me a reassuring squeeze.

Not a house in sight. *Not a single one.*

Pa busied himself with the roping which held all of our family's belongings to the back of our beat-up truck, tugging on the twine to make sure it was secure despite the miles of road we'd covered over the past few days. A couch, a few mattresses, a couple of chairs, and whatever else we could fit in the bed of the Chevy.

He didn't say much now; then again, never really had. I didn't need him to convince me of anything.

I'd already decided I didn't like the place.

We never did find those trees they promised.

Nor did the other thousands of people who had arrived by excursion trains with all the professional-looking men in suits who promised fancy houses with picket fences and land ownership as far as the eye could see. We made a life for ourselves nonetheless, tilling the soil of the land at the urging of our government, because wheat had won the war according to the president. The Germans had cut off our access to it, leaving it up to us farmers to produce it. We were, after all, the backbone of our nation as Pa said.

In the early to mid-twenties, produce it we did. Heck, everyone did round here.

As soon as Pa was able, he went out and bought himself a tractor, its rubber tires and steel frame replacing our worn-down horses, their backs bowed from years of pulling plows and other necessities around the farm. They weren't useful for much after their work had been drawn out of them, the best years of their youth spent working to yield the crops. Pa was adamant we'd save on the five acres of alfalfa, oats, and hay it took to feed them, replacing those crops with cash crops to cover the cost of kerosene and fuel for the tractor.

Now, we could plow two, three times the amount of land we could cover before, discing dirt clumps into a powder fine enough to resemble the softest beaches on the west coast. Or so I imagined.

I was happy to not have to fix meals for all the men it had taken to run those old plows and thrashing machines and separators, along with those who ran the racks and hauled the grain away. The best part of my days were spent helping in the kitchen or stacking wheat stalk bundles to dry in the windrows. The process was exhausting, requiring a small community of neighbors to come together to work the fields from sunup to sundown.

Running sandwiches to all these men, I was grateful to leave the steamy, overcrowded kitchen in exchange for the ninety degrees of dry heat outside, finding it more bearable than the slick condensation that rolled up from pots of boiling green beans, soups, and gravies as the women prepared supper, the smell of fried chicken wafting from the house.

Little did I know how much I'd miss those days, as exhausting as the work was, the multitude of savory food aromas and the fulfillment of a successful hard day's work taken for granted.

It was said that from 1925 and for the next few years, enough land had been plowed up in the southern states to equal the entire state of New Hampshire. We were too busy to slow down enough to notice, breaking our backs to keep up with the large amounts of wheat our fields were producing.

What could possibly go wrong?

CHAPTER 12

Carrie, 1929

Today was the day.

Though it was early, I knew I wouldn't be falling back asleep so figured I might as well pull myself out from under the covers. The smell of crackling bacon wafted its way down the hall to my bedroom, bringing my senses fully awake. I slipped on a loose-fitting baby blue frock and adjusted the collar before pulling my dark hair into side clip and tiptoeing out, trying to find the sturdiest parts of the creaky floorboards.

"Dat you, Cawie?" Benny's voice called out from the corner of the room we shared.

"Good morning," I said to him and smiled as he reached his arms up to me, his blonde flips matted together from most likely his previous meal. I picked him up from his crib and set him on my hip. At three years old, he was a bit old for a crib, but I liked to think of it as a cage to ensure he didn't get into unsupervised trouble. "Are you hungry? Ma's making some bacon."

"Ba-con!" His eyes lit up. "*Down*," he demanded, squirming his way out of my arms and onto the floor, running ahead of me with damp patches from the sagging cloth of his diaper.

"You're up mighty early for a Saturday," Ma said, setting a plate of crispy bacon on the table. "Pa's already in the fields, so we'll have to save a plate."

Ma's specialty of silver dollar cakes and homemade maple syrup, which had traveled with us from Minnesota, was my favorite. I smeared a pat of butter on the hotcakes, watching the gold stream trickle down into a puddle on my plate. Benny was already munching on bacon, syrup smeared across his face as he shoved more in his mouth.

"Looks to be another fine day for plowing." Ma smiled.

I'd never seen her happier. Heck, everybody was happy. Folks might say money don't bring happiness, but I was smart enough to know that the lack of it never helped.

"That's swell, Ma." I was tired of everyone always talking about the crops. Seemed to be the only thing people talked about here. That, and the weather. "Today's the day," I said, changing the subject.

Ma's eyebrows furrowed in contemplation before realization crossed her face. "It is! What time is your father bringing you?"

"Not until ten," I sighed. "I reckon I'll take a walk and fill my time 'til then."

"Smart idea, Carrie. Would you mind doing those dishes first while I clean up Benny?" Ma asked.

"Sure, Ma," I said.

Ten minutes later, I was walking in 'fields of gold' as Pa would say. Endless acres of golden winter wheat lay stretched before me in all directions, ripples of light shimmering across it in breeze-blown waves, cut in half by the old gravel road that wound its way to our house from the street to town.

The sputter of Pa's new gas-powered combine churned away. Where he'd put all that grain, God only knew. The grain elevators were near full and already, there were heaps of surplus piled up on the main road in town. We'd never had so much newness in our lives. Not back in Minnesota anyway. Pa even got the family a new Model A pickup and a new gas-powered tractor. And Ma got new fabric for clothes for us.

A handful of crop seasons into Kansas and we were pert near plum rich. We might've been only a handful of states away from Minnesota, but it felt like another world and we didn't mind.

CHAPTER 13

Pa and I rode in silence a while, enjoying the sunny warmth that poured through the windshield. I stretched my arm out the buggy window, cupping the air as he drove, my skin rippling with the pressure of the air. The sky was a clear blue, the air clouded only by the belches of dust kicked up from the gravel behind us.

"Have you thought of any names?" Pa's voice interrupted my thoughts.

"Goldie," I said and smiled up at him.

He considered. "Goldie seems fitting."

I knew he'd like it…a good reason for ruling out competing names such as Daisy or Trixie. In my opinion, there were far too many dogs named Trixie in the world already.

"You know the responsibilities that come with a dog?" He raised his thick gray eyebrows, bunching up the tan lines on his forehead as he threw me a glance.

"You do realize I'm sixteen, Pa." It was more of a statement than a question. "Anyhow, I've read plenty on Labradors. They're a social breed and great with kids. I reckon she'll be part of the family before you know it. You won't even know she's around."

"Uh huh," he said, unconvinced. "Well, you just keep her from chewing up anything and get her potty-trained and things'll go mighty smooth."

A weathered white farmhouse appeared at the end of the dirt driveway, and like most farmhouses in the area, it seemed to be swallowed up by a sea of crop fields. Immediately, a German shepherd bellowed out and charged the buggy, announcing our arrival. The place was chaotic but inviting, with its wraparound porch and blue wicker rocking chairs, chickens squawking about as they pecked at the ground while the dog continued to bark.

"Banjo! Settle down!" a voice hollered.

"Mr. Meyer," Pa reminded me. "Gotta be well into his eighties, I reckon."

The old man made his way over in stiff strides, though his tanned face made him appear much younger than he was. Banjo, unwilling to leave, had at least stopped barking, his tongue hanging from the side of his mouth as he panted.

"God blessed us with another dandy crop season," Mr. Meyer commented, tucking his thumbs into the top of his suspenders. They seemed to be the only thing keeping his worn jeans up.

"Sure did," Pa said, getting out of the truck to shake his hand. I followed his lead.

"You only been here a few years now, hey?" The man spat brown tobacco juice into the gravel, his lower lip bulging from his teeth.

"Yes," Pa nodded. "Came down from Minnesota."

"That right? Minnesota, hey? I hear it gets real cold up there in them parts."

"Sure does," Pa said, his voice swelling with pride. Minnesotans wore their weather badge with honor and Pa was no different. "Some stretches fall well below zero."

Mr. Meyer shook his head. "My family's been here for two generations. Cattle ranchers. Came here not long after the buffalo were slaughtered."

The sun was scorching hot, bringing a cloudless heat that came with early afternoon in the plains. I shifted my stance and glanced around the yard for any sign of the puppies. Farmers could talk for hours, and they seemed to be in no hurry of wrapping up any time soon.

"The *beef bonanza* papers called it," Mr. Meyer went on. "Cattle everywhere. Good cattle, too. So many they'd set the dishes to rattling like bones in a casket anytime they were herded up."

Pa's gaze settled on the man's face as he spoke.

"We ate steak almost every meal and I'll tell you somethin'. My ma sure could cook a mean T-bone." The old man licked his lips as if he could taste the grizzle of the meat.

"Your family still own cattle?" Pa asked.

The man laughed. "'Course not, son. The winds rolled in one season and killed 'em all. The storms turned to drought and killed damn near everything." He wiped the glean from his forehead before stuffing his hanky into his front pocket. "Now we just got a few measly horses and some chickens. *Noisy squabblers.*"

For a moment, there was a lull in the conversation.

I looked at Pa. *About those puppies. You know, the reason we're here…*

"After that, they said God had left these parts." Mr. Meyer spit again. "But, they also say rain follows the plow," he shrugged, pulling on his suspenders. "So now hear I am, growing wheat."

He shifted his gaze to me. "So, I hear you're interested in those puppies."

"Yes sir," I said, my heart fluttering. We'd been begging for a pup for years and with Pa in the fields so often, he'd finally decided it might be a good thing to have a watch dog.

A wide smile spread across Mr. Meyer's face, exposing coffee-stained teeth. "Well then, why don't y'all follow me back to the barn and you can have a pick of the litter."

I wanted to skip behind him, but paced myself in mind of my age and manners of "being a lady," as Ma often reminded me. It couldn't stop my heart from racing in anticipation.

If we'd told Benny a puppy was coming home with us, he surely didn't show his excitement or understanding of the situation 'til I carried her fuzzy body through the door. I held her close enough to feel the thumping of her heart as she nuzzled her wet nose into the crook of my arm.

"PUPPY!" Benny screamed, his chubby bare feet thumping toward us on the wood floor. "PUPPYPUPPYPUPPY!"

"Shh, Benny. You don't want to scare her now, do you?"

He showed no concern for what I had to say as he pulled my arms down to get face-to-face with the lab, the smell of syrup lingering in his hair.

"This is Goldie," I said, stroking her back. She was the silkiest thing I'd ever touched, her pale fur shining in the light.

"Goadie?" he mimicked, burying his face in her fur.

The lab trembled as he roughly patted her head.

"Me hold Goadie!" he cried, reaching for the pup. Benny could hardly contain himself.

"Okay," I sighed, pushing aside my selfish plans of bringing her out back to snuggle. "How 'bout you sit right down on the couch, okay?"

The faded floral cushions bulged out beneath his weight as he plopped down beside me.

"Now be real careful with her, okay?" Goldie began to whine, her legs dangling helplessly as I placed her on Benny's lap. "She's just a baby."

"I wuv you, Goadie," he whispered into her fur. "You a good puppy, Goadie."

Turned out, Goldie was a *good puppy*, which also meant she was good at chewing up everything! Keeping her away from Pa's leather boots was like trying to keep Pa from his fields. He'd traded some things for the boots years back at a hide-tanning place up in Minnesota. Goldie, it seemed, had expensive taste in all things leather and no matter how hard I tried, she would patter across the floor, get hold of those laces and pull the boot right behind her as she clumsily ran through the kitchen.

And she was quick.

Quick to get into trouble, quick to chew on the legs of the supper table and quick to give anyone with food those warm brown puppy eyes, effectively convincing them she hadn't eaten in days and desperately needed a table scrap. I even caught Pa at supper one night reaching down with a bit of something. When he realized I'd noticed, he gave me a wink. It was the first time he'd ever winked at me.

Things were good and life felt complete.

I couldn't imagine how things could get any better.

CHAPTER 14

"It's about time we got some tenants 'round here," Pa said one night while I was grooming Goldie outside on the doorstep. She was wriggling around in my arms, anxious to run off and explore. "I just can't keep up, even with the new machinery. Another pair of hands could get me out of the fields by supper at least."

Goldie squirmed, and when I was sure no one was watching, I handed her a shred of chicken, which she immediately swallowed before regarding me with sad chocolate eyes, her tail thumping against the floorboards. *Don't give her eye contact,* I told myself.

"It would be nice to have you 'round more," Ma said, sitting beside me on the step. "Won't be long and Carrie here will be moving out and starting a family of her own." She smiled, bumping her knee against mine.

I choked back a gut laugh. Benny was enough work to scare that thought right from my head and Ma wore the exhaustion lines just under her eyes.

"Heck, a good wheat crop equals about ten years of raising stock," Pa went on. "With money like that, we can surely afford some help. Can't have a factory without more'n one employee." He wiped the sweat from his forehead with the back of his sleeve.

"You got anyone in mind?" Ma asked, watching Benny, who had now moved to the sandbox and was currently talking to himself while digging sand into a big pile.

"In fact, I do," Pa said. "Algott Meyer's grandson moved down here from the north for some health reasons. Says he's a real worker…not afraid to get his hands dirty. Even knows how to handle the mechanics of the farm machinery. God knows I could use another set a hands to help with harvesting."

"When would he start?" Ma asked, turning her eyes back to Pa.

I released my grip on Goldie and she clumsily leaped into the yard before waddling her way toward Benny. Her gangly legs had outgrown her body almost overnight, making it a struggle for her to keep her balance as she zigzagged her way over to where Benny was sitting.

Within minutes, she was furiously digging, a spray of dirt pelting Benny in the face as the upper half of her body disappeared into the hole, leaving only her bottom and wagging tail exposed. Ma chuckled.

Encouraged to have a partner in crime, Benny squealed in delight as he clapped his hands and tossed handfuls of sand up into the air.

"Benny," Ma yelled. "No throwing sand!"

He dismissed her with another fistful aimed in our direction, buffered by a good twenty yards of grass, his toothy grin a testament to his disobedience.

"That boy's scalp will be caked with it and he'll need another washing," Ma said and sighed.

Pa, who had briefly disappeared inside the house, returned with the click of the screen door behind him. He gazed out across the fields, his eyes sparkling in wonderment. I had to admit, I'd never seen the wheat as tall as this season—shoulder high in places.

"Boy's name is Percy," he replied. "He can start Monday."

Percy? It had been a while since there were any new boys in town.

As if reading my mind, Pa added, "He's a year older than you, Carrie. Don't be afraid to introduce yourself."

I rolled my eyes.

"I'm back to the combine," Pa said. "There's money standing tall in those fields."

Farmer Meyer dropped Percy off 'round seven a.m. the following Monday.

I peered out the window, craning my neck to get a better look at the figure who was stepping out of the passenger side of the truck.

"What're you looking at?" Ma asked as she came over and stood beside me, pulling back the lace curtains and following my gaze.

"Oh, I *see*." She smiled. "Seems like a fine young man now, doesn't he?" I could see the wheels turning in her head. "Didn't Pa say he was your age?"

Good God, she wouldn't stop until I was walking down the aisle.

"Seventeen. A year older," I said evenly, praying she wouldn't notice my anticipation.

She raised an eyebrow, her eyes fixed on the boy. "Well then, he should be a great help to your father."

Throughout the day, I stole a few glances at Percy. I'd forgotten where he'd moved from and Ma couldn't remember. Minnesota? Wisconsin? Michigan? Illinois? There were plenty of states north.

His style screamed city, not a single tear or worn spot in his dark denim jeans, his plain gray work shirt devoid of grease but nearly white against his tanned arms, and the rust-colored hair which was sharply parted to one side.

He was unlike any of the other boys 'round town. I could sense it. The way he held a quiet but respectful confidence as he intently listened to Pa and toured the farm, pointing to certain parts of equipment while Pa, seemingly pleased, nodded with pride. Percy held his shoulders back and took deliberate steps, giving him the appearance of being much taller than I suspected he truly was. But Pa, comfortable in his six-foot five lean frame, made anyone appear short when standing beside him.

He must be smart, too, if he knew how to fix machinery.

"Why don't you go on out and let them know lunch is ready?" Ma winked as I tried to get into reading a book later that day.

"Busy," I lied, flipping a page I hadn't read. My heart raced at the thought of approaching Percy, who I'd only viewed from a distance.

"That so? Well, I coulda swore it's taken you at least half an hour to read that page. Come on now. Go introduce yourself."

Nothing escaped Ma. When her back was turned from me, I pinched my cheeks for quick color before glancing at my reflection in the mirror and heading out to the shed. My heart was a time bomb, ticking louder with every step closer to this mysterious boy.

I found him, or his legs rather, sticking out from under the tractor, the soles of his boots frosted with dust. What do you say to someone's feet?

Hi, lunch is ready? Nice slacks? Where're you from anyhow? I cringed, standing dumbly beside the tractor.

"Carrie?" Pa's voice saved me as he walked in from the fields. "Lunch ready?"

I nodded, my eyes fixed on Percy's legs until he slid out from under the tractor and sat up, his brown eyes meeting mine in a flash of curiosity, his lips turning ever so slightly into a smile.

Pa regarded me for a moment. "Well, are you going to introduce yourself, Carrie, or do I have to do it for you?"

My cheeks burned and I wanted to hit Pa upside the head.

Percy sprang to his feet, his face twisted in a smirk as he wiped his greasy hands on his jeans, breaking them in to farm life.

I extended my hand. "I'm Caroline, but everyone calls me Carrie."

"I'm Percy and everyone calls me, well, Percy," he said and grinned when our hands touched. It was as if electricity passed through me. His skin was calloused, but gentle when he took my hand in his. I'd met some boys who seemed to think they could impress ladies by the extent of squeezing the blood right out of them. Not Percy.

"Well, I reckon I'll call you Percy then," I said.

Dimples played upon his face as he regarded me, the slightest hint of mischief in the sparkle of his eyes. I saw a confidence in him unlike the boys around town who always seemed unsure. Unsure of the skies, unsure of the crops, unsure of how to approach girls.

"So, where're you from?" My words came out fumbled and awkward, making me suddenly aware of how fast I spoke.

"Chicago. Moved down a few days ago. I'm staying with my grandpops just outside of town."

Chicago.

So far from the dirty skies of Kansas. I suddenly felt a bit sorry for him for having to leave such a place. What kind of health problems could force you out of a glamorous place like that?

"Well now," Pa said, interrupting my thoughts. "Let's go fetch us some lunch."

Grateful for the interruption, I followed them to the house to where Ma was waiting with plated sandwiches and an outstretched hand.

"Pleasure to meet you, Percy. I hear you came all the way from Chicago." She spoke softly as to not wake Benny from his afternoon nap. "How're you liking Kansas?"

"Hell," the word hardly slipped from his lips when he caught himself at the look upon our faces. Pa didn't allow cursing in the house. Least not around the ladies. "Sorry ma'am, I meant to say heck. I'm more than happy to dust out of Chicago."

Ma's eyebrows raised and she glanced to Pa, who lathered his hands in the sink, a ritual before every meal.

Percy's face flushed. "Chicago ain't all that bad, it's just quick-paced," he said, shaking his head. "Fellas trying to make a living with too many highbinders in office making all the rules and exploiting who they can."

I looked to Ma and grinned. I could see she was also impressed with how he carried himself, but possibly reserved about his maturity for his age. A thrill raced through my body.

"You got that point right," Pa said, making his way to the table and beckoning us all to sit. "Ain't far from the truth round these parts as well."

Ma said grace and poured milk into our glasses. "Tell us about your family then," she asked, realizing Pa was more interested in his food than in the background of his new worker.

Percy shrugged and I noticed for a fleeting moment, a sadness brushed across his face, quickly replaced by a winning smile. "Not much to tell. Ma is progressive and likes to dress to the nines. She'll do all she can to keep up with the flappers in the juice joints, but she's got a heart of gold. Always taking care of everyone."

"Is that so?" Ma asked. I could tell she was taken aback. Things were slower to catch on round our parts and I could tell she was intrigued, but too polite to prod. "And your pa?"

Percy hesitated, his jaw muscle flexing. "Pops is a hard worker. Works for the Chicago paper as a columnist."

Ma smiled, waiting for him to go on and seeing he wasn't going to elaborate, seemed grateful for Pa's sudden awareness of the tense topic.

"So that's where you get it from then," Pa commented, waving his fork as he spoke. "He teach you how to change a tire and do all the mechanicals?"

"Yes sir," Percy said, rather quickly. "Mostly taught me to work for what I wanted from a young age." He glanced at me and I swear I saw his eyes sparkle, making my heart nearly leap right from my chest. "Worked a paper route from twelve years old to the age my sales started declining on behalf of losing my little boy charm."

I nearly choked. Ma shot me a look.

"I hear the crime ring is getting bigger every day there," Pa said, shaking his head in disapproval. "You ever run into any of that on the streets?"

Percy's eyebrow raised slightly, and I could feel my cheeks burn at such a ridiculous and insulting question. Poor fella would probably never come back. Not after this interrogation. But if Percy was insulted, he didn't let on.

"Films and papers glamourize everything, sir. I would know. I made a living off from selling the buzz."

This seemed to satisfy Pa, who finished his last bite and brushed the crumbs from his hands. But I had a burning question.

I cleared my throat, working up the nerve to ask it. "So what'd you do with all the money you earned all those years?" I couldn't imagine having a job other than farming, at such a young age.

"Carrie," Ma warned, her voice scolding.

He looked me square in the face, his eyes flashing a hint of mischief as they held my gaze. A toothy grin crossed his face. "I did what any smart teenage fella would do: I bought a moto bike."

I learned a little more about Percy over the next few days. Turns out, his family lost most everything after the stock market crash. According to Pa, his folks couldn't carry the financial burden of Percy's health and his grandfather was willing to take him in while his folks stayed back in Chicago on account of his father's work. I regarded Percy in a new light then, a little sorry that his mishaps landed him here.

"We're fortunate, us farmers," Pa said as he sliced into his piece of chicken one day at lunch. "They figure there's over three million people out of work, sleeping in public toilets and shantytowns along railroad tracks, eating outta garbage cans."

Ma shook her head, her face dismal. "How in God's world, do 27,000 businesses fail?"

Pa shrugged. "Newspaper says three billion dollars in deposits were lost. I reckon that's what happens when people borrow money they don't have to invest it into something they can't see." He took a sip of milk. "That's why it's good to invest in the known. Like land. Bible even says, 'you reap what you sow.'"

We filled our stomachs with baked chicken and green beans canned from last summer's produce of Ma's garden.

"Not much rain lately," Ma spoke quietly, almost to herself.

Pa chewed thoughtfully.

"True. Mississippi River's down. Hard to believe it flooded just three years back. Sure, the crops are a little wilted, but droughts happen." He raised his fork, gesturing with his hands as he spoke. "It's nature's cycle. It can't last forever."

All I knew is it had been one of the hottest summers yet, reaching temps near 118 degrees. So dry that most days, it landed me with a scratchy throat and sore eyes, the walls of our home, a shield against the constant assault of heat.

"I'll pray on it," Ma replied, cutting chunks of meat for Benny, who continued to stack his green beans into a tower.

I wanted to remind Ma she'd been praying on it nearly every night for the past three months, but decided against it. Seemed like every time Pa read the paper, wheat prices were dropping. *Plow more field and plant more crops* was always his answer.

My mind drifted to Percy, and something stirred within my stomach at the thought of seeing him again and I couldn't help but smile.

"So, how's he working out then?" I asked and diverted eye contact as I took a drink of water.

Pa regarded me with inquisitive eyes. "Who?"

Ma snickered.

"Percy," I added, my voice a little too high.

"Oh." Ma wiped Benny's face with a napkin. "You mean the tan boy whose been helping Pa out on the farm? I didn't realize you'd even noticed him."

"*Carrie,*" Pa said, his eyes flicking from Ma to me. "You met him. The other day, remember?"

Ma chuckled, clearly satisfied with herself while I focused on the piece of chicken in front of me.

Pa shook his head, dismissing his confusion. "Smart kid. Knows his mechanicals."

I bet he does. I stifled a laugh.

"That's all?" Ma asked, raising her eyebrows at Pa's vagueness.

He shrugged, oblivious to our prying.

"Hard worker," he added.

Ma nodded her head, encouraging him to go on.

"There's not much he can't do. Asked him to change the tire on the trailer and he got right to it without needing any help. Witty, too. Good kid."

A man of few words and high standards, Pa was black and white. Reliable and confident in the land and the skies and the promise of God's harvest. His opinions were nearly fact.

My heart swelled.

Percy was a good guy.

A hard worker and a good guy, which translated to a person worth getting to know better.

For the first time ever, my summer held more than just the promise of wheat.

CHAPTER 15

I made it a point to be more helpful on the farm after that night. Ma scrutinized me nearly every morning when I put together sandwiches of wheat bread, cheese slices and bologna (extra bologna for Percy's). Obviously, it would be rude of me to eat in front of Percy, so naturally I'd fix him one, too.

"Don't forget your father," Ma would scold, narrowing her eyes.

What did she want with me? Most days, she'd happily wed me to the first bidder and then when a legitimate boy my age was a prospect, she questioned everything I did.

When I found Percy that afternoon, he was working on the combine harvester and greeted me with a spark in his eyes and a slow smile, shooting shocks right up my arms. He treated me unlike anyone ever had before. Like an equal. As if he believed I could do just about anything he could, even though I was a girl.

"Why don't you give me a hand," he said.

I was taken aback, so I stood there dumbly, holding a basket of bologna sandwiches like some kind of idiot.

Sensing my hesitation, he laughed. "Don't tell me you've never worked on the combine. You've been on a farm your whole life."

I bit the inside of my cheek. "It's just that…no one's ever shown me."

"Well," he smirked, one eyebrow raised, "there's a first time for everything."

My cheeks burned.

He pulled a tin of oil from amongst the many containers Pa kept on the high shelf, the back of his shirt stretching against his shoulder blades as he reached up. "So, what do you know about the combine?"

I swallowed, unable to distract myself from his forearms.

"The basics." I shrugged a shoulder.

He set the tin on the floor and pulled a towel from another shelf, spreading it across the floor and beckoning me to sit beside him.

"I know it reaps, threshes, gathers the wheat, and winnows the grain from the chaffs all at once. Saves a lot of work and frees up a lot of time and men," I explained.

He nodded, clearly impressed. "Women, too."

I gave him a questioning look.

"You said it frees up a lot of men." He shrugged. "Women, too."

"Yes," I said, warmth flooding my face. "Women, too."

Whether it was growing up in Chicago or his family's upbringing, he had a different way of looking at things, which made me anticipate my conversations with him even more. He listened to me. He asked me questions. About the land, the history of the area, *anything*. He'd watch me while I spoke, twisting his mouth as if he might be biting the inside of his cheek, considering my opinions or debating some internal question I knew nothing about.

Already, he was becoming the best friend I'd ever had.

"So, where'd you learn how to do all this anyhow?" I asked. I had never imagined anyone in Chicago *changing oil*. It was like one of those unglamorous tasks of life you never saw in movies so couldn't even picture it happened.

His face shifted, the muscle in his cheek bulging as he clenched his jaw. "My pops," he said pointedly.

He turned his back to me, grabbing another rag from a pile of old cloths. Something tickled the back of my brain. An itch I couldn't reach.

Was he lying? It didn't seem likely that a newspaper columnist would know about the mechanics of machinery.

"I'm impressed," I said, lifting my chin.

His shoulders relaxed and he turned to face me with a warm smile. "Well, as long as you're impressed," he teased, "it makes all those hours under the car worth it." His eyes met mine and lingered there, catching me off guard.

"Want to learn how?" he challenged, a spark in his eye.

"To do what?"

"Change oil. Change a flat tire. You know, life skills." He shrugged again as if it was an ordinary task for a girl to learn how to do things other than sew and cook. "Or are you too high-hat?"

"Of course I want to learn." I grinned.

"It's a date then," he teased.

Heat rushed through my body.

"Or, we could call it *training* if it makes you feel more comfortable." His eyes flashed to mine, a calculated smile playing up the dimples on his face. "Whatever works for you, long as you're up for a challenge."

A slow smile played on my lips. "Am I ever."

CHAPTER 16

The sun streaked through the bedroom window, suspending specks of dust in the air like a beam of light cutting through a dense fog. I pulled back my curtain expecting to see Pa in the field, the chugging of the tractor an indication of sleeping in, but the fields were empty.

"Morning, Carrie."

Pa was sitting at the table when I walked into the kitchen and upon seeing me, folded his newspaper in half. "How 'bout you come with me to town?"

My heart surged. "Can I bring Goldie?"

Squinting his eyes, he considered. "I suppose that'd be okay."

Town didn't hold the usual hustle and bustle of farmhands gathering supplies or mothers making grocery runs, other than a few scattered vehicles parked along each side of the road. Pa pulled in by the town bank and set his straw hat on the dash before turning to me, beads of sweat already bubbling up from the skin on his forehead.

"I reckon this won't take long." He smiled, giving Goldie a pat on the head. His eyes were apologetic and sincere. "Why don't you go on and show that little pup off?"

Moments later, Pa disappeared into the bank while I tried coaxing Goldie into allowing me to slip the rope through the ring on her collar.

"Sweetie, we need to tie this rope round for a leash, you see." She defiantly shook her head back and forth, making it tough to wrangle her furry head through the loop.

"It's the law 'round here," I reinforced, cringing that my voice had taken on that annoyingly high pitch people often used with kids. "If you want to walk 'round town, you've got to let me put this on you."

In the end, it took sheer strength to lasso the thing around her neck as I braced her in the crook of my arm. Several times she wriggled herself away from me, backing her bottom up and then proudly regarding me with a toothy grin and hanging tongue. Nonetheless, soon we were stepping out of the truck and on our way toward the heart of town, the rope strung loosely through her collar.

Goldie had a tendency to slow me down as usual. She stopped to investigate a suspicious looking bush, stampeded through the landscaped grasses in front of the bank, their brittle stems crunching and busting as she trailed through their pale plumes. At one point, she lowered her head to the pavement and came up smacking on some pink chewing gum. She tugged me over to anyone who happened to be walking the sidewalk, expecting to get a pat on the head, assuming everyone loved dogs and if not, she would be the exception.

And as it turned out, most people *adored* puppies.

"What a sweet puppy," they'd say as Goldie would nuzzle into their eager hands. "What's his name?"

"Goldie," I'd reply patiently. "*Her* name is Goldie."

"*Goldie,*" they said in that same high voice, as if talking to a baby. "What a *good dog* you are."

Goldie played the part, giving them wide eyes while wagging her tail proudly as if to say, "Why yes, yes I am. And aren't I pretty, too?"

Already my arms were reddening from the sun, its constant assault relentless as it shined upon everything beneath it. I swallowed hard, attempting to moisten my parched throat. Goldie was panting now, her tongue dangling from the corner of her mouth. I scanned the street for shade, but the few trees were skeletal, their leaves curled and withered.

The grocery store was just 'round the corner but Lord knows they didn't give out anything. Specially water during the dry season. But Goldie, being a natural sales dog, had a way of using those chocolate eyes to entrance those around her into giving in to her advantage. It was sure worth a try.

"Well," a voice called from behind me. "If it ain't Miss Caroline, *but people call me Carrie* Lexington."

I spun around to face Percy.

Goldie's ears perked up as she tugged me closer to where he was standing, closing the space between us. My heart beat wildly, as if at any moment it might explode into a million pieces.

"Percy." I nodded.

He squatted down, stroking Goldie's fur while she licked his boots in appreciation.

"Looks like you found a friend," I said and laughed, relaxing my shoulders. I owed Goldie more than she would ever know.

He stood up, and I slid my gaze from his lips and the way they curved into that mischievous smile of his—as if he was about to disclose a secret.

"Grandpops is getting some things at the store."

Our eyes locked long enough to flood my face with heat.

"And why aren't you helping him?" I asked pointedly.

His cheeks flushed. Maybe he wasn't as confident with girls as he let on. "Well, he's no daisy. Besides, he doesn't need *that* many things."

Just then, a man approached, his forehead gleaming with sweat, the underarms of his white sleeves damp with perspiration as he carried his navy suit jacket over a shoulder.

Percy's body stiffened.

The man gave us a sympathetic nod as he trotted past, his shoulders slumped. Percy visibly relaxed, exhaling loudly.

"Suitcase farmer," Percy scoffed. He shook his head in disgust. "We'll see how long these hotshots from Hollywood last out here without rain. Think they're so much better than everyone, buying up all the land with no intentions of settling here. Well, I'll guarantee that most of them will be packing up with the drought and dusting right outta here."

I hadn't seen that side of him. He'd always been so cool and collected.

I opened my mouth to correct him. This wasn't a drought, just a dry spell. But thought better of it. "Well," I said, "tell me how you really feel." I attempted to lighten his mood. "I don't know, I kind of liked his bowtie."

In actuality, I felt sorry for the man. He looked so…*defeated.*

Percy's eyebrows scrunched together in disgust, and for a minute, I thought he'd argue with me. I couldn't be upset with him. He'd said aloud what nearly every farmer in the area felt.

When he realized I was messing with him, the creases in his forehead smoothed. "Caroline Lexington," he teased, his eyes leveled on mine. "I reckon we'll get along well."

I replayed our entire conversation in my head on the way home as Pa listened to the radio broadcast going on about the droughts in the Midwest and along the Ohio and Mississippi river valleys.

"Not a drought," he mumbled to himself.

Muffled voices drifted from the kitchen later that night. It must have been nearly midnight and I reckon Pa had just come in from the field, awakening me with the latching of the door. I slowed my breathing, the ticking of the dining room clock matching my heartbeat. In a house with wooden floors and mostly bare walls, overhearing conversations, especially in the middle of the night, wasn't a difficult task.

"All this wheat and prices are dropping," Pa said, his voice low. "Can you believe it? They're *dropping.* We'd be further ahead financially if we spent the year sleeping."

I felt every muscle in my body tense. He never showed anything but confidence.

"What can we do?" Ma asked softly.

Tick, tick, tick.

The scrape of a chair being pulled across the floorboards pierced the silence and I imagined Pa sitting at the table, head in his hands.

"Don't know," he said. "Sure, next year will be better, but in the meantime…"

"What did the bank say?" Ma whispered.

Pa sighed. "This is the last time. They're stretched as much as the rest of us, maybe more."

Ma's footsteps paced the hallway in a rhythm of light thuds, unlike the creaking of the uneven floorboards when pressed upon by the mass of Pa's body. The patter approached my room before descending back toward the kitchen.

"Local church is holding a prayer service this Friday," Ma offered. "Praying for rain."

I rolled my eyes.

Prayer services. The answer to everything around here. It wasn't the first prayer service and there wasn't much to show for their past efforts. Besides, Percy had invited me to do some exploring and I had no intention of interrupting those plans for sitting in a church.

"No," Pa said, agreeing with me.

Thank goodness someone had some sense around here. "We're not going if we can't put in an offering. Besides, I'll be in the fields and I'm not looking for any handouts."

Always Pa's prayer…plowing and sowing more seed in the fields.

Ma sighed.

"The bumper crop'll help," Pa insisted. "You'll see."

CHAPTER 17

*F**riday!*

My stomach did flips all day and I was grateful Percy wasn't needed on the farm as I pranced around the house, frantically trying to piece together an outfit. After a few changes, I settled on a baby blue sundress; casual but flirty.

"If it were any other boy…" Ma's voice trailed off as she put away dishes later that evening. How could she want me married off so quickly, but not want me to go on dates?

Dates.

Was this a date? The thought sent a thrill down my spine.

"I know, Ma," I said, keeping my voice even as I wiped my shoes down with a cloth. *Ugh.* This dust! It coated everything in sight, sneaking through the sideboards of the house, settling on the floors and rising up to reach even the highest places.

She sighed, watching me wipe my shoes. "Hopefully this grime will go away once it rains."

Once it rains. When it rains. Everyone's answer to everything.

"Remember to let him open the door for you," Ma suggested.

Benny rammed a toy truck into the wall as he spit out chugging noises breaking up the quietness.

"Oh, and tell him thank you. He must really like you to pay for a movie." Her voice was distant. Envious. When was the last time she and Pa went out? I couldn't remember.

"Ma." I slipped an Oxford on my foot, pulling the lace tight. A recent hand-me-down from one of her friends from church, I'd polished them to the point of appearing store-bought new, the black gleaming in the light.

"I don't even know if this *is* a date."

A date!

I peeked out the window then glanced at the clock. After what seemed like several minutes, a distant cloud of dust emerged up the road. My heart fluttered. I gave one last glimpse in the mirror, pinching my cheeks for color.

"Remember!" Ma called after me. "Have fun!"

I raced out the door, closing it behind me before Ma could even think about following me.

Percy jumped down from the truck.

I swallowed hard.

He was almost unrecognizable—donning a fancy black hat, like the ones the bankers in town wore, with a gold watch that glinted in the pink hues of the setting sun. My heart danced at the thought of him dressing up for *me. Me!* Yes, this was surely a date. Thank goodness I put on the sundress and Oxfords.

He met me at the passenger door, his eyes not leaving mine and I could feel the pull of electricity between us.

A smile played across his lips. "Well aren't you the cat's pajamas, Caroline Lexington." His arm brushed mine as he reached across to open the door, sending an electric surge through my veins. I couldn't help but giggle. His city talk somehow took me away from this place and made me feel like I belonged on the big screen.

He was within inches of me, his typical smell of oil and kerosene replaced by the fragrance of spice and cedar aftershave. "You aren't secretly some kind of suitcase farmer, are you?" I teased.

"Hmph."

Without warning, he slipped one hand in mine, his grip strong and reassuring as he hoisted me up into the truck, his other hand lingering on the swell of my back.

"Is the hat too much?" he asked, pulling his hand away. Uncertainty swept his face, so different from the confidence he showed on the farm. There was a vulnerability to him that was endearing.

My heart swelled. "Not at all," I said, offering him a smile, wondering what he could ever see in me.

"Good," he replied, tipping his hat with a smirk. "I like to throw on the glad rags every now and then."

The interior of the truck was clean, but when I thought about the meticulous way he lined up and organized the oil cans, cloth, and anything else he needed when working on equipment, I wasn't surprised. Scanning everything, a tattered photo wedged between the dash and the window caught my eye. I leaned in closer to study the picture.

"My folks," Percy said, following my gaze as he climbed into the truck. "It's an old photo."

I sensed something in his voice. *Apprehension? Sadness? Regret?*

His father's face was stoic, his chin held high and shoulders pulled back. A wide smile spread across his mother's face and a trendy (but slightly scandalous) dress silhouetted her curvy form, strands of hair peeking out from under the cluster of flowers that detailed her cloche hat. She was beautiful, like someone from the magazines they sold at the stores in town. I wondered what they were like. What traits he had gotten from them.

But Percy's image was the one who caught my attention. He must've been about twelve? Thirteen? A toothy grin was plastered across his face, his eyes twinkling from beneath his newsboy hat as he clutched the bars of some sort of pedal bike.

I waited for him to say more and when he didn't, I decided to change subjects.

"So, what's it like in Chicago?"

I thought of a trip our family had taken to St. Paul when we lived in Minnesota. It was like another world. *Minnesota.* My heart ached thinking of it. The intensity of the burning colors of changing leaves on maples and oaks in the fall. The first snowflakes of winter. *Change.* Here, everything remained the same.

Same colors, same weather, same people.

"Roaring twenties," he grinned, pulling me back to the present. "Automobiles crowding the street, jamming up the city. Lights flashing everywhere. Honking, yelling."

I tried to imagine what life would be like not having to depend on the weather in order to eat or pay the bills.

"What about the theater and the clubs and the music?" I asked.

Surely, he was downplaying how wonderful the city was.

He shrugged. "Juice joints everywhere, disguised as dives. Ma liked to dress up and go to the theater; Pops and I would go to ball games. Even got to watch the Cubs play against the Yankees," he marveled, his voice reminiscent as he shook his head. "To watch Babe Ruth play ball was something…" His eyes fixated on the gravel road before us.

We'd listened to a few games on the radio, but had never imagined what it would be like to actually *go* to a game. That luxury was reserved for the elite. I thought of Pa and how much he'd probably love to go, but never got ahead enough to get outta the fields. My heart dropped.

"Anyhow," Percy sighed, "those days are gone. When the market crashed, I knew something was wrong when Pops came home early." He hesitated. "He never left the office early. Ma fixed supper in her best dress and made his favorite meal: broiled steak with parsley butter and baked potatoes."

He cleared his throat, and I noticed his eyes had gone glossy as he scanned the road ahead. I regretted bringing the subject up.

"Next morning, he left unusually early in his best work suit. It was weeks before I knew he'd lost his job and was standing in food lines, dressed in his work clothes. We'd lost everything. Everything, but this watch he gave me."

His face shifted slightly; *guarded.* The way it had been the day we came across the suitcase farmer.

"I'm sorry," I said, not knowing what else to say. The crash had been all over the papers and radio, but we were so far removed, it hadn't affected us much. Not when the crops were so plentiful.

"Don't be," he said, his eyes meeting mine. "Less you're one of the highbinders who took all the money from the banks we trusted." He laughed, but a hint of regret laced his words.

"Anyway, here I am. Ma and Pops lost the place we called home and are renting a flat in a less glamourous part of the city. It was hardest on my mother, who had gotten used to a certain way of living. Now, both my folks work in factories. I miss them, but I'm sure glad I'm not there to see it. I'll never forget the despair that swept over the city…like a heavy blanket."

I thought about the day of the crash. We were swimming in wheat. I remember Pa feeling guilty. Times were good for us and the only real connection we had to the event was through the newspaper, the haunted faces of those looking for work, worry lines carved into their gaunt faces. To hear about it now, firsthand, stirred a sadness within me.

We drove in silence the rest of the way to the theater, the gravel crunching rhythmically beneath the tires.

"Look," I said hesitantly, turning to face Percy after he'd parked the truck in front of the movie house. "We don't have to go to the movie. We could take a walk instead."

His eyes became so intense I thought I might spontaneously combust under his stare.

"Carrie, I'd pay three times as much to bring you here. I ain't no flat tire date," he said, his face serious. "Besides, if it makes you feel better, our good chicken laid a few extra eggs this week." He flashed me a grin.

It had become a regular thing now for people to barter with fellow businesses and the cinema was no different. One egg could get you a first-rate movie.

"Well, in that case," I teased, "I feel much better."

He chuckled, but then his face grew serious again. "I'm really sorry I didn't bring you flowers."

"Flowers?" I couldn't hide the confusion on my face. "Where in the world would you find flowers 'round here?" I laughed lightheartedly and he joined me, relief crossing his face.

"Well, I tried looking for some. If I could've, I would've brought you something beautiful and extravagant. Chrysanthemums or orchids maybe."

Seeing the surprised look on my face, he mocked offense. "What? Did you make me for some kind of chump?" He shook his head. "Carrie, you underestimate me."

I blushed. I had no idea what chrysanthemums even looked like. "Percy," I said, "you could pick me daisies and I'd be happy."

His lips turned up in a smile as he gazed thoughtfully into my eyes. "I'll keep that in mind."

My stomach dropped when we crossed over to the theater. A few girls from school were there, watching us with narrowed eyes as we stood in line. Bethany Williams, the banker's daughter, was among them in her new Hollywood Oxford pumps, the ribbons tied into delicate red bows. She was lanky, a good couple of inches taller than me, with golden hair tied effortlessly back, exposing the thick straps of her black and white checkered dress.

"Hi Percy," she said, her voice perky and confident. She exuded luxury, the aroma of lilacs wafting from her hair.

My cheeks burned.

"Bethany." He tipped his hat.

They knew each other?

I stood there dumbly while the other girls whispered amongst themselves, thinking they were so much better than us farmers, even though they lived in the same dirt as us.

"How do you know Bethany?" I asked, trying to keep my voice casual as we moved forward in line.

"Carrie Lexington." His eyes gleamed as he studied my face. "Are you jealous?"

Heat rose to my cheeks. I opened my mouth but couldn't think of anything witty to say, so closed it again.

Satisfaction crossed his face.

"I met her when I first moved here," he said pointedly, his eyes quickly shifting away from mine.

An uneasy feeling snuck into my stomach and settled there.

Much later, Percy reached over in the dark and slid his hand into mine, strong and protective, sending a thrill up my spine, making me feel as if I might jump out of my skin at any minute. I tried to focus on the movie, but couldn't concentrate. I fixated my eyes on the screen even if I had no idea what the movie was about.

Outside the theater, shadows stretched across the street in distorted shapes; tall grasses jutting sharply from the dead lawn, their blades slicing through the pavement as a quiet, empty sky watched us from above. We walked a bit, our shoes clicking rhythmically against the cement, their echo keeping perfect time with our pace.

Percy's expression changed all of a sudden. His eyes narrowed as he glanced over his shoulder.

"What is it?" I whispered.

He shook his head but said nothing as he protectively grabbed my hand while his pace quickened.

And then I heard it.

Click, Click.

The echo of our footsteps bounced off the brick wall of the town store. But it was followed by something else.

Another set of footsteps. Much heavier.

Percy flicked his eyes toward me.

Click, click, *thud, thud.*

The pace quickened with our own. Someone was approaching. *This is ridiculous*, I thought.

Percy didn't seem to agree with me, turning every so often to glance behind us, his hand becoming moist with sweat.

This is so ridiculous, I thought again. Though his jitters made my own nerves stand on edge. A shiver ran down my spine.

And then, all at once, Percy spun around, protectively shielding me with his outstretched arm. My heart jolted.

His eyes were wide, his lips tight.

Within seconds, his grip loosened as another couple who were out for an evening stroll came into view.

I laughed nervously. "Jittery?" I asked, trying to lighten the mood.

"Carrie," he turned to face me. "You can't ever be too trusting. There's derricks and clouts even here, looking to brace somebody. Well, it ain't going to be us."

It was the first time he'd spoken to me like that. I exhaled.

"Look," he said, his shoulders relaxing, "I just want you safe. That's all that matters."

I imagined his caution came from living most his life in a city and supposed moving to a place with unlocked doors would be a place that would take some getting used to.

The danger gone, we continued our walk.

"I had a swell time tonight," he said later when walking me to the door. He was looking at me in a way boys didn't look at me, as if I were someone else. Someone who could afford the latest styles and go to the busiest clubs. Someone boys would sacrifice their day job responsibilities and ball games to be seen with. And for a minute, I was a girl out of Chicago.

"Me, too," I said wistfully.

The moon hung low and bright as stars speckled the sky. The soft light of a lantern spilled from the windows and onto the yard. Ma must've been waiting up for me.

Thoughts swirled around my head and my heart raced. *Was he going to kiss me?*

He gave my hand a squeeze before bringing it to his lips. His mouth was within inches of my own, his breath sweet and warm.

Our eyes locked and for a moment, the world was still, save the buzzing of my own anticipation. He seemed to feel it, too, this magnetic pull between us. His lips brushed mine, soft and full while the world around me melted away.

After a few beats, he pulled away.

"See you tomorrow, Miss Caroline," he said with a wink.

I could hardly speak.

As he sauntered to his truck, I thanked my lucky stars for my father's insistence on bringing a tenant to the farm.

CHAPTER 18

That fall, the bumper crops were too successful. Grain elevators were overfilled and mounds of surplus piled high along the gravel roads going into town, their kernels only enticing to the mice that scuttled through them.

"Prices are dropping."

Percy's voice held a hint of worry, much unlike him. We were taking a break, sitting on the fence rail under the shade of the shed's roof, the rough splinters snagging at the cotton of my dress. Our knees were almost touching, creating an electric barrier between our bodies and now this little stated fact pulled my attention away from the pounding in my heart and thoughts of a first kiss.

My stomach tightened "They're dropping?"

He nodded his head. "Too much supply."

Never in a million years would I have imagined this would be a problem. Pa hadn't said as much, his answer to any issue always being *more wheat*. "What's going to happen?"

He sighed, the lines in his forehead creasing. "Most of the wheat will rot away. Beyond that, don't know. I imagine I won't be needed much round here unless somehow this wheat starts selling again."

My pulse quickened, a mix of panic and dismay drowning my senses. *Would he move back to Chicago?*

"I can tell it kills your pops to let me go so he finds small tasks to fill my day. I can't justify getting paid for it like some kind of wrong number. Without him tied up in the fields, they're things he can easily do." He paused. "There's not much oil changing needed without tractors running. Hell, the few cows we have at our place aren't doing so well, either so grandpops could use my help." His voice wavered.

Heaviness pressed upon my shoulders. "The wilting crops are hurting everything." I sighed, trying to think of what Pa might say, not knowing much about cattle or stock and not really ever paying attention.

"They need food," he said, shaking his head. "As Grandpops says, *never forsake the cow, the sow, or the hen.* You never know when you'll need them."

"What are you fixin' to do?" Herds of cattle were already dying in the driest states, but I was sure he already knew that.

He shrugged. "Try and sell them. Sell them off before things get worse and we're fully behind the eight ball."

Get worse?

Things weren't going to get worse. Pa, who had so much experience in farming, believed things would get better. We just needed to wait for the rain to come.

"There must be *something* we can do."

He bit his bottom lip in thought and flicked his eyes to mine. "I'm working on it."

That was the last official day Percy worked at our place. It wasn't the surplus of grain that pushed him out, but the opposite. There was nothing to take care of. It was as if the fields were throwing a tantrum, refusing to grow anything at all while the skies refused to give in to the earth's demands for rain.

Cracks splintered the ground, splitting the earth and peeling its skin into curled edges as the sun plotted its next assault, glaring at us by day, lurking deceptively in the shadows of nightly retreat, only to regain strength in the morning.

Death filled the lands and breathed upon the few wilted plants that defied the odds of breaking through the dry dirt. Pa didn't say much. He wore his thoughts upon his face as he watched the skies.

He came in early on one of these days and hung his hat on the hook by the door. "No use," he said, his voice exasperated. "Nothin' to tend to. The crops are nearly destroyed."

It was as if someone had let all the air out of the room. Ma shook her head. "I'm sorry. Anything I can do?"

"Nothing, less you can bring rain."

His face registered defeat, the lines that had formed above his brows, now crevices of trapped dust. Dust that had settled onto everything around us: plates, cups, drapes, clothes. Ma had begun tying a scarf protectively over her blonde hair, her exposed braid ashy from the skies.

Benny screamed just then, unaware of the gravity of the conversation as he jumped up and down. My nerves, already frazzled, jittered in annoyance.

"Gwasshoppas!" he yelled, pointing out the window. He began to jump up and down. "Gwasshoppas!"

Ma followed his gaze, her eyes growing wide as she clasped her hand to her mouth and gasped. "Good lord! John!"

She abruptly jumped up, knocking her chair to the floor in a thud as she scrambled to where Benny was standing, her eyes fixed in horror at the window. Her face dropped.

"What is it?" I asked, making my way over. What was all the fuss in grasshoppers?

An ominous cloud blanketed the crops, hovering over them in a thick haze. But not a cloud after a cool rain or lifted frost like in Minnesota. No, something wasn't right.

I moved closer to the window, wiping the dust with the back of my sleeve before peering through the circle I had made.

I strained my eyes. The fields appeared as if they were moving. I squeezed my eyes shut for a moment, knowing I was seeing things. But when I opened them again, nothing had changed. I jerked my head to Pa, but his face was frozen in shock.

I couldn't move. Couldn't believe my eyes.

It was as if the ground was sliding closer toward us.

"My God," Pa stammered, more to himself than anyone. We stared in horror as the cloud grew larger in size, drawing closer. "I've never seen anything like it."

Grasshoppers began to tap the glass window, causing me to draw away. That's when I noticed the yard…

A chaos of insects jumped in a frenzy throughout the yard as if trying to escape the cloud that would soon consume them.

But as the cloud grew closer, I suddenly realized the yard of grasshoppers were not trying to escape but were the front line and had reached our house. My heart stopped. The haze wasn't a cloud of dust after all, but a thick of grasshoppers.

Millions of them.

They covered the entire patch of our dirt yard, jumping sporadically, hitting the side of the house in a series of light pings like Minnesota hail.

Panic filled my body. *Would they get inside?*

"Where'd they come from?" Ma stammered, her face registering shock.

Pa shook his head, his eyes glued to the fields. "They're doing what every other living thing is. Looking for food."

Despite the heat, a chill ran down my spine. Bible stories of plagues I'd dismissed as childhood lessons were suddenly true.

Within minutes, they covered nearly everything outside, shading the sun as they ate across the space of the plains, blanketing our yard in squirming shades of green; their natural predators long since gone due to lack of food.

The invaders stayed the entire day, occupying every inch of space they could as we helplessly watched from inside, my heart jolted by their bodies flicking the glass windows and squirming their way every so often through the bundled clothing we had shoved into the nooks and crannies of the house. My nerves were frayed and my patience thin. I wanted to be anywhere but in that house.

We later discovered they'd eaten the wood fence posts and shed beams to nearly nothing, not stopping until everything edible was depleted, their swarm rolling on to their next destination East.

Over the next days, several stray hoppers remained in the yard, confidently reminding us of the final insult to our crops. I envisioned the feel of my foot squishing the life out of one of them, but no matter how hard I tried I couldn't catch them.

Later, Pa and some neighbors would burn the fields before spreading arson, molasses, and bran to be sure to keep them from returning.

There we were, farmers of America who couldn't farm and couldn't keep anything alive but the pests who fed upon our hopes.

Soon, there was nothing for the farm animals to eat. Their painful pleas filled the sky as they cried out for food. The horses and cows on the neighboring farms chewed desperately at the dirt, gnawing their teeth right down to the gums in an effort of finding any growth.

But there was nothing to find in the cracks of the earth. Nothing at all.

The plants died first. The farm animals next.

How long before it was our turn?

CHAPTER 19

The jackrabbits were the next to come in. The vibration of thousands of thumping feet against hollowed dirt reverberating across the land like the growing moans of a volcano about to erupt.

But this time, we were prepared.

Percy stopped by one morning, grinning despite the heat and despair of the fields.

"Your pa around?" he asked when I answered the door.

"Sure is," I replied, disappointed he wasn't coming 'round for me. "Not much for him to do right now besides *pray for rain*." I rolled my eyes.

Percy shook his head, reaching inside his pocket to reveal a rolled-up piece of paper.

"What's that?" I asked, peering at him over the paper.

"A flyer for a rabbit roundup," he said, matter-of-factly.

"A what?" I scanned the flier.

WAR ON RABBITS!

Citizens are invited to a big rabbit hunt at the Lexington Farm
next Sunday afternoon at 4 o'clock.
Men, women, and children may take part in this drive.
Dogs prohibited. Meat will be split among families.

"What do you think?" he asked.

My cheeks burned as he watched me, seemingly eager for my approval.

"Hmph," I said. The thought of eating meat again made my mouth water. "What? Do we lasso them like old cowboys?" I chuckled at the image of Percy in a cowboy hat, his biceps bulging as he intently scrambled after not a bull, but a measly rabbit.

"Clubs," he confirmed, shaking me from my daydream.

I frowned. The image was ruined.

"Anyhow, I'm ready to do whatever it takes to taste meat again. These jackrabbits are destroying anything that hasn't already been destroyed by the weather and hoppers." He glanced at me. "And they're HUGE."

The following Saturday, at least fifty people came out to our place. So many, that most of them had to park along the side of the road and walk in as if going to a town parade. Children ran about, zigzagging between knees of adults who were discussing the best way to go about rounding up the rabbits, some holding clubs, others leaning against them.

I craned my neck, scanning the crowd as they filtered in.

"Who you looking for, Miss Carrie?" Percy's smooth voice from behind me set my heart fluttering.

"No one in particular." I blushed, then went out on a limb. "Looking for cowboys, that's all."

He smirked, exposing his dimples. "Find any?"

"No," I teased. "Not yet."

"Percy!" Mr. Meyer hollered, beckoning him to the growing crowd of men.

"Well," he said, turning to face me, a sparkle in his eyes, "I might not be a qualified cowboy, but they know how I rate."

I stifled a giggle as he sauntered away. He began talking with another man, his eyes periodically glancing toward me with a cocky nod of his head, as if he were the one responsible for this whole escapade about to happen. And I guess in a way, he was. He'd brought the idea to Pa after all. Not that I would tell him so.

The men spread out in every direction until they made a circle about a mile or so in circumference. Twenty some minutes later, the murmurs of the women and the laughing of children were interrupted by a shrill shrieking that hurt my ears and overpowered any other noise. My feet began to vibrate with the thudding of the ground as hundreds of rabbits fled to the makeshift pen a few of the farmers had built a several days prior.

I covered my ears against the screaming as I hurried into the house to where Benny watched through the window in fascination. Men appeared from the field, enclosing the circle, clubs raised over their heads.

People lingered throughout the day, posing for photos and for the first time in ages, had smiles upon their faces at the prospect of meat to can. I locked myself in my room, haunted that night by the high-pitched shrieking of rabbits. A sound I was sure I would never forget.

The next day was quiet. The gentle breeze was a blessing to our blistered skin and sweat-slicked foreheads as we helped Pa dig holes for new fence posts.

That night, the taunting aroma of sweet jackrabbit stew wafted through the kitchen, savory enough I could taste it in the air.

Food! One word with so much promise of fulfillment. *We finally had food.*

And not just food, but meat.

CHAPTER 20

Ididn't see Percy for several days. He had told me that sometimes he needed to "dip out" to help around his grandpa's farm.

Something ticked in the back of my mind. I couldn't put my thumb on it, but something was off. Pa was around, but spent his time absentmindedly staring at the fields, coffee swishing about untouched in his cup, unaware of any of us. Ma would frown sympathetically at me, and as if knowing something was wrong, Goldie would lay upon my feet, her ribs protruding from her soft fur, her heartbeat softly tapping against my skin. My heart swelled when looking at her and I wished there was more I could do.

When Percy finally stopped by, I met him in the driveway, kicking myself for being so damn eager to see him.

For a minute, he sat in the truck as if debating something, a distant look fleeting momentarily over his face before getting out.

My heart jumped in spite of itself.

"Carrie Lexington." He tipped his straw hat to me as he approached, his voice smooth as butter.

"You miss me?" I asked coyly, catching his gaze.

Something flickered in his eyes. "Maybe." He shrugged, taunting me. "You want to take a drive?"

"I suppose I could do you that favor."

"Thank you for your generosity, kitten," he countered.

"Where you going?" Ma asked when I stepped inside. She was plunging some cloths in cold water to soak, the liquid already clouding into a murky gray.

"Just a drive," I snapped, a little too quickly.

She scowled at my weak attempt of downplaying my desires as she dried her hands with a dish towel. "Be back by supper."

A few minutes later, I was climbing into his farm truck.

Percy drove toward town as I bounced along next to him.

"I just have to make a quick stop," he mentioned when reaching town, pulling into the back alley of the general store.

"What?" I asked. "Are you embarrassed to be seen with me?"

His face dropped, wounded. "Of course not," he said, his eyes serious as they met mine. "How could you even think that?"

A twinge of guilt pinged in my stomach for even bringing it up.

He let out a sigh. "Carrie, you—" His voice trailed off, as if he was about to open the door to some secret, but after thinking more on it, slammed it shut again. "Look, I'll be back in a couple of minutes."

I swept a few strands of loose hair behind my ear, despite the breeze's best efforts of tossing them about my face. His parents stared at me from the tattered photo as it flitted about and finally came loose from the dashboard, then floated to the carpet.

Percy's handwriting was scrawled across the back of the photo. It was an address here in town. I secured the picture between the plastic and the dashboard. And then, for no other reason than my own curiosity, I unlatched the compartment of the truck's glove box with a click. I glanced to the general store before peeking inside.

There wasn't much in there. At first glance, there was a dirty rag, spotted with what appeared to be grease, and his mask, compliments of the Red Cross who had handed them out to nearly everyone in town. The dust had gotten worse by the day, crusting our noses and the insides of our eyes, let alone our lungs. I dreaded the day I had to be seen wearing one of them.

When I went to close the lid, something caught my eye. The corner of a piece of paper revealed a few receipts from local stores that had been tucked under the rag, along with a small notebook.

Stop, I told myself. This wasn't right. Guilt burned the edges of my conscience before being watered down by my curiosity. I flipped open the thin cover.

It was a ledger of sort. Dates and times, dating back to a month and a half ago. The itch returned.

I thumbed through the pages until they went blank. Turning back to the last entry, I scanned the page, glancing up again to be sure he was still inside.

Today's date. *Seven O' Clock. Meet B.*

B? Thoughts whirled in my head in an endless riptide of suspicion. *Bethany?*

I glanced at my watch. Half past five.

Percy emerged from the building. I quickly tucked the notebook under the rag, clicking the door shut and rested my hands in my lap before he reached the truck with a smile.

"Told you I wouldn't be long," he said, roaring the engine to life.

"I was thinking," I said casually, taking a shot. "How about you stay for supper tonight?"

An undiscerning look crossed over his face. "What time?"

"Usually Ma puts it on 'bout six-thirty or so." I studied his face. Noticed the way his lips tightened at the corners and I thought I might get sick.

"I wish I could," he said, his eyes unwavering from the road. "I really do. It's just that I have something I need to do back at the farm."

His voiced hitched. He was lying.

"Well," I said, trying my best to keep my voice sincere, "that's too bad."

We drove the rest of the way back in silence, his thoughts lost in some other place. Mine resting on Bethany and the fact that he'd left the general store without purchasing a single thing.

CHAPTER 21

"**S**TORM!"

Pa's voice was a gut punch that shook me awake the next morning. It wasn't so much his words as the sharpness in them as he yelled into the house from the front door. How long had Goldie been barking?

I jerked the covers back. With the windows now covered in boards due to the recent happenings, it was hard to tell the time these days, as if nature had confined us into a box for its own safe keeping. Or punishment.

"Carrie! Go help Pa!" Ma yelled.

Ma didn't so much as glance my way as she shuffled around the kitchen, tucking rolled sheets against the frames of the windows and any other crevice that could invite sand into the house. Goldie paced the kitchen.

I pulled the mask from the hook by the door, fitting it to my face. Outside, the wind was fierce and hungry, making me lean into its force just to stay standing. Without any vegetation to hold the yard in place, already the dirt was spinning in circles in the sky, spitting sand at anything that came in its path. Narrowing my eyes, I scanned the yard.

"Pa!" I cupped my hands over my mouth, but my voice was useless against the roaring of the wind, making it barely audible even to my own ears.

I hunched over, making my way to the shed in slow, heavy strides, my legs feeling like they weighed hundreds of pounds each. It was a Red Sea closing in. Panic gripped my throat.

Dust storms were becoming more and more frequent here, coming out of nowhere, but passing through quickly. They reminded me of windy Minnesota snowstorms, with the added effect of sand that pelted the paint off the buildings and rubbed a person's skin raw, drowning the fences in towering mounds of collected sand.

The shed door was hoisted open. Inside, Pa's silhouette moved frantically about with preparations.

"Pa!" I stumbled into the shed, gasping for oxygen through the confines of the mask.

"Carrie! Grab the other end of the sheet!"

I took half the bundle from his hands and awkwardly, we managed to spread the sheet across the tractor, securing the corners with field rock from the pile Pa kept beside the shed. The combine was much too large to protect against the spray of sand that streamed through the boards of the walls.

Within hours, the wind subsided to a careless breeze, oblivious to the devastation it had caused.

Percy's truck pulled in later that afternoon and a sense of peace passed through my soul. He was safe. Part of me hated how necessary he'd become and how vulnerable that made me. Pa had always taught us to be self-reliant, but already, much of my happiness was reliant upon Percy's existence in my life.

Instinctively, I ran into his embrace. His arms were strong and sturdy as they held me tightly, a harbor to the storm. His breath was warm upon my neck and nothing else mattered in that moment.

After several minutes, he finally pulled away.

"Thank God you're okay," he said, his brows furrowed in lines of concern. It was rare his guard was let down.

"You worried about me or something?" I cocked my head, assessing his reaction.

"Of course I was worried about you. Carrie, I don't know what I would do if…"

"If what?" I doubted he cared about me as much as I did him. I needed to hear him say it. Open up for once.

"You know what I mean," he said, dismissing his previous thought. "Anyhow, I have to dip out, but wanted to make sure you were safe."

An alarm went off in my head.

"I understand. I'm sure your grandpops has a lot of work for you to do."

His face shifted, his eyes diverting away from mine. "Yes," he said. "He does."

"See you tomorrow?" I asked.

He thought for a moment. "That'll work, Miss Carrie."

I stepped down and away from the vehicle.

He turned his truck around in the bit of the driveway we had shoveled out and disappeared down the road. Things would be okay.

Percy was safe and still cared at least enough to check on us.

But still, I couldn't help but wonder why his truck had gone in the opposite direction of his farm.

CHAPTER 22

"I dare you to touch the car," I teased the next day, pushing aside any thoughts of suspicion as to his whereabouts the night prior, let alone *who* he was *whereabout* with.

Percy narrowed his eyes at me, a grin plastered across his face. He couldn't, nor wouldn't *ever* turn down a dare.

"You like me that much, huh?" His eyes flashed mischievously.

My heart skipped.

"Well, if I die, please let my grandpops know, and don't forget to tell him you were the sharper who conned me."

He hesitantly took a step closer to Pa's parked car, turning to face me as he approached. Already, his hair was standing on end from the static charge. He winced slightly, but sent me a half-cocked grin.

"Go on city boy." I nodded, feeling slightly guilty at egging him on, but it was probably the most entertaining thing we'd done that day regardless. Besides, there wasn't much harm in a little fun with all the gloom and doom.

The car now within inches of his body, he tentatively reached his arm out to shield himself. With the other, he stretched inch by inch closer and closer.

Suddenly, an invisible force thrust his body backward, flinging him helplessly into the dirt. It was as if he'd been shoved by an invisible giant.

I laughed uncontrollably as he lay stunned in the dirt at my feet.

"I'd offer you a hand," I said, my words slipping out between my laughing fits. "But I'm not sure how many volts you have running through you right now!"

He pulled himself up, patting the dirt from his jeans. "I see how you are," he chuckled.

His expression grew serious as his eyes met mine. "Best keep Benny away from anything that could be charged from the storm."

Percy knew how to kill a moment, just as quickly as he knew how to create one. It was that elusive door that kept all of his feelings and thoughts shut out from me, closing without warning anytime we were growing closer. As if he couldn't handle the idea of maybe caring too much or caring for only one person.

"C'mon, let's go," I urged, annoyance creeping into my voice. It was nearly five in the evening and Ma had finally cleared me for going outside. The heat was too much of a risk midday to leave the house.

"Masks on," he instructed, taking his wet handkerchief from me.

We wrapped them around our necks and pulled them up over our mouths, breathing in the damp moisture amidst the dryness of the land. Ma had made me also swab my nostrils with Vaseline to trap the dust.

We started across the field and walked until we could no longer see the house.

"Where should we start?" I asked. I tried to keep my balance but wearing a sundress found it difficult walking through the uneven sand.

"Let's cross over the creek. Used to be ranchland on the other side."

"Pa mentioned that," I said.

We were quiet as we trotted through the dunes, as if the sound of our voices might be enough to agitate the stillness and stir up lurking monsters from the ground. All around us, the sand rolled in and out with waves of colorless grays and browns, giving the appearance of a strange planet incapable of life. The sky was a brilliant blue, cutting into the landscape with the precision of a sharpened blade as it carved the horizon to its liking, painting over barbed wire fences and erasing other manmade boundaries it saw unfit.

"Can't imagine what it must've been like," Percy said, breaking the silence.

"What's that?" I shook loose my thoughts and pulled my attention to him.

"Losing all that cattle." He shook his head.

A hollowness filled my heart. "How're the chickens?" Last we'd talked about it, they were down to just a few from the twenty-some they had.

Percy sighed. "Okay, considering. We keep them in the shed, but nothing can keep the sand from blowin' through. On top of that, they're starving. The stress is too much. They stopped producing eggs a long time ago."

He frowned. "Grandpops is talking about the possibility of butchering them if they don't start producing soon."

"How many you got?"

"Two left."

When I'd been to the farm last, there were far too many to count. It was a sad reality.

He grinned, casting me a sly smile. "Henry and Ford."

"Really?" I choked back a laugh.

He shrugged. "Had to pay tribute to the man. He is, after all, one of the best machinists who ever lived. He's half responsible for your pa's equipment, you know."

I raised an eyebrow. "Must be some sophisticated chickens."

"Well," Percy said, stepping over some barbed wire, "They are quite swanky. When they kick the bucket, I'll bring you over some meat."

I cocked my head. "Are you implying I need more sophistication?"

"No," he said rather quickly. "Of course not, I—"

"Good Lord, Percy, I'm teasing." I tilted my chin up. "I know my sophistication level. Although I have to admit, I'm a little disappointed you wouldn't hold a proper burial." I swatted at his arm. "What kind of person are you?"

He regarded me thoughtfully, a gleam in his eye. "A hungry one."

The bantering quickly died when Percy abruptly stopped chuckling; his lips pursing tightly.

"What is it?"

I craned my neck to follow his gaze but didn't see anything different from the rest of the sand mounds. His face told me otherwise.

"The creek," he said, dropping his shoulders. "It's gone."

I couldn't remember the last time we'd had rain and never would've believed it would be so long until we'd see it again. No one could. Not even Pa, whose knowledge of the land dated back to our ancestors in Ireland who were potato farmers before the blight. He had cultivated knowledge and knew about seasons, throwing around the whole *reap what you sow* verse.

But yet, they'd been sowing. *And sowing. And sowing.*

Maybe too much.

It was as if God had stored up all the reaping and threw it in our fields all at once, relieved to move on to some other place in the world.

"You think anything will ever grow here again?"

"Don't know," Percy said, his voice distant. "Grandpops thinks next week's service will help, but I have my doubts."

I sneered. *Prayer services.* The answer to everything.

"Doubt isn't even the word for it. Ma's making us all go, too. The posters said to bring a hat and umbrellas," I said.

I waited for him to laugh, but he shook his head dismally. "We'll see."

Just then, something caught my eye in the valley between the dunes.

"There!" I said, throwing my arm up to point.

"Good eyes!" His voice matched my own enthusiasm. Thank goodness all the doom and gloom talk was over. "Wagon wheel? Race?"

He cast me a mischievous smile, and without giving me time to respond, was pushing ahead, leaving me no choice but to chase after him through the uneven sand in my dress.

It felt good to run. To be free and wild on the open plain just like running through endless rows of wheat during better days.

Even despite the thoughts in the back of my mind, in that little corner where people tucked away their innermost longings, where a pocket of guilt was. A few weeks ago, it was neatly boxed and wrapped tightly shut, small enough to overlook. But recently, it had been violently ripped open, spilling its contents messily in my conscience until I couldn't ignore the burning question: *How can you be so happy when so many people are suffering?*

My own family included.

It wasn't just the guilt of happiness that weighed down my conscience. It was the guilt of not believing in much besides the feelings I harbored for Percy. It seemed to be all I could count on.

More than the rain. More than Pa's hopes for our future, always dependent on the crops and the weather. And as much as I hated to admit it, more than the thought that simple pleading prayers would be enough to turn this wasteland around.

The guilt grew heavier with each blue sky and every unanswered prayer. Guilt, because unlike the farmers, I no longer believed rain would come.

And what kind of farmer was I to think that?

CHAPTER 23

Ipeeked inside the oven door and the warm aroma of baking bread wafted out, instantly transporting me to the old days of harvesting when the kitchen was crowded not only with cooks, but with food *to* cook.

Chicken, beef, ham.

Memories of all the luxuries made my mouth water. What I'd give to taste meat again. Still, despite all the trouble grain had caused my family, I loved fresh baked loaves of bread and I loved to cook.

The cooling rack was in the top shelf of the cupboard and I had to stand on my tiptoes to reach it. Ma kept a step stool around here somewhere but only she knew where. It was too dangerous a temptation for Benny. That little boy could and would destroy anything in his path, and wasn't afraid to do so.

Sifting through the cupboards, I spotted some of the jarred jam from Minnesota we'd brought. I missed that place. A place with the coldest of winters, but *never* the fear of being drowned by your own land.

"Goadie!" Benny's voice nearly tipped me off balance.

"Benny!" I snapped, steadying myself with the open cupboard door.

There it was. My favorite blueberry jam. Sliding it from the far back area of the cupboard, I debated whether to grab strawberry, too. What if Percy didn't like blueberry?

"Goadie!" The padding of quick feet followed by the scraping of the chair's legs against the floor signaled havoc behind me.

I snatched both the strawberry and blueberry jams for good measure.

"Benny!" I said sternly, setting the glass jars in the basket. "*Stop* chasing her! You're going to wreck this place more than those damn storms."

Benny, who never listened to anything, paused, a blank look on his face. "You said a bad word!"

"No, I didn't. *Wreck* is not a bad word."

He opened his mouth, but I cut him off before he could protest. "Now settle down and stop that running and screaming, or I'll tell Pa when he gets home."

He ran to the other room, and I breathed a sigh of relief. Finally, I could pull myself together and clean up the mess before Percy got here.

I glanced in the oven again, pleased to find the round loaf of bread had turned the shade of golden honey. I slid the loaf out and set it on the cooling rack, careful not to burn my arms as the steam floated to the ceiling.

There was a tap on the screen door. "Anyone home?"

Percy.

A rush of heat filled my body. Would my body ever adjust to his voice?

"Just a moment!"

I gave my cheeks a quick pinch of color in case the heat of the oven wasn't enough. Goldie began barking from the back bedroom. *Damn Benny and his taunting.*

"Benny! Percy's here!"

I drew in a deep breath and opened the screen door with a smile. Immediately, his eyes met mine and my heartrate quickened, the breath catching in my throat.

"These are for you," he said, his face flushing with color as he pulled a bouquet of flowers from behind his back.

Daisies! He brought me daisies!

"Well, that's unexpected," I said, taking the flowers.

"You're welcome and hello to you, too." He laughed, letting himself in. "Smells fine in here. Not like Grandpop's house. Today's *laundry day*."

His hands were red and raw from what I suspected to be from the lye. Instinctively, I reached out and gently took his hand in mine, his skin rough with blisters.

"I noticed," I said and frowned.

"That bad?" He raised an eyebrow.

Oh, he was so handsome. "I mean, it just looks painful."

His hand squeezed mine and he leaned in ever so slightly, causing a twinge of electricity to run up my legs and into my stomach.

Benny's stomping grew louder as he approached.

"Percy!" Benny shrieked as if on cue, barreling into him with Goldie right behind, barking.

I dropped Percy's hand, exhaling in annoyance at the stolen moment.

If Percy was annoyed, he gave no hint, but hoisted the boy up from under his arms. "Hey there, little man!"

He threw him high up in the air, causing Benny to screech in delight, his arms and legs flailing loosely about him.

Percy caught him as easily as he tossed him up, the strains of his muscles lean and taut under the tanned skin of his forearms.

I couldn't help but smile. Benny *adored* him.

"Don't worry, Goldie," Percy said, bending down to stroke her fur. "I didn't forget about you. You're the big cheese 'round here, ain't you?"

Goldie wagged her tail in delight, nudging his side with her furry head.

I pulled a mason jar from the cupboard, filled it with water, and placed the daisies in it. Percy was full of tricks. Who else could find any living thing in this area or afford anything from the floral shop?

My heart did little flips. He cared enough to put forth the effort. *For me.*

I tucked the bread loaf neatly in the red checkered cloth of the wicker basket, alongside the jams and a spoon.

"How are you, girl? You being good?" Goldie's tongue hung out the side of her mouth, her tail thumping against the floorboards as she took in Percy's affection.

"Alright y'all. Let's go," I said.

Outside, the slightest hint of a breeze blew through the air as Percy held the door open for our little parade. We chose a spot near the shed to spread out the blanket.

"You're going to fatten that pup right up now, aren't you?" Percy said, narrowing his eyes at Benny who was already sneaking Goldie pinches of bread.

Benny grinned, stealing off with a chunk of bread, Goldie keeping pace with his feet.

"Hard to imagine these same skies carried storms that took out nearly half the wheat crops." Percy shook his head, a slight frown on his face as he sprawled out on the blanket, his lanky legs stretched nearly to the end of it.

I nodded in agreement, with nothing to add. It was on everyone's minds. It might as well be said out loud. All their effort and sweat for what? To be destroyed? The drought couldn't last forever, could it?

"Next year will be better," I offered, handing him the basket as I hoisted myself up to sit beside him.

He broke off a chunk of bread. "Reckon you're right. Farmers think so anyway," he said, smearing blueberry jam across it. (He liked blueberry jam!)

His eyes locked with mine. "But what if they're all wrong?"

The question startled me.

"What do you mean? It *has* to be better next year." I was taken aback by my defensive tone. We'd lived here longer than Percy and we'd seen flourishing crops. Sure, it had been a while, but we knew it was possible. What could he possibly know about farming that Pa didn't?

"I just mean, there's history in the sand here," he said. He laid back and casually threw his arms behind his head, unbothered by my hasty response. "Ask any of the cattlemen. The land here is fragile."

He leaned up on his elbow and popped another piece of bread in his mouth. "I mean, the buzz is that farmers plowed up as much grassland as the state of New Hampshire."

My cheeks grew hot. I had every right to blame my father and the other farmers, but how could *he* when they'd given him a job?

"Yes, but thirteen bushels an acre in the good seasons. How do you argue with that?" I asked.

He thought for a moment.

"I won't. But it's gambling. And with gambling, you're not always going to end up the butter and egg man."

Looking at the sincerity on his face, I couldn't stay mad. Seeing my raised eyebrows and stifled giggle, he rolled his eyes. "C'mon Carrie. Butter and egg man? The bankroller?" Seeing I was still confused, he clarified simply. "The fella who rolls into the casino with a big wad to spend."

It was a constant thing. Him throwing out some city term and having to explain it to me. It was all foreign, but part of his intrigue as well. Chicago, or any large city for that matter, seemed like a world away. At least to me it did.

He grew quiet, his gaze somewhere off in the distance as if his mind was deep in a concealed past. More and more often lately, he seemed to be doing that.

But he had a point. I'd never considered farming as a gamble. Pa had always reassured us there was predictability and dependability in the land and in the seasons. Gambling lived in the stock market and in the cities. Not on farms in rural places.

Wanting to learn more about his past, I shifted gears. "Tell me about your life in Chicago." I tossed a piece of bread at him playfully.

He frowned slightly as he usually did when I brought up the topic. "Look Carrie, I've told you all there is to know. I know you think it's the cat's meow, but there's a side you don't see in films. There's a lot a people right now behind the eight ball, down and out and either bustin' it in factories or spending the rest of their dough in some clip joint or dive." He shook his head. He seemed so much older than he was and I wondered what he could possibly know about such things.

"Okay. Not about Chicago then, but about *you*."

Something shifted on his face. "Carrie, I…"

Not many things made Percy speechless. I could ask him about politics or farming or what he knew of distant places overseas, but when it came to personal questions about his past, he withdrew. Shut me out.

"Percy," I said softly, reaching over and grabbing his hand in mine. "It's okay. We don't have to talk about the market crash. You were one of the top newspaper boys to make enough money for that moto-bike. I'd be a fool not to know that. Tell me more about it." The thought of him as a young newsie wearing a paperboy hat and knickers warmed my heart.

He shook his head in disagreement. "You don't understand. I'm not the good person you make me out to be."

I frowned. He was one of the best people I'd ever come across. How could he say otherwise? Why was he always so hard on himself?

"It's just… There's some things I haven't told you about me."

"Oh?" I attempted at picking up his mood. "Elusive. Are you some kind of undercover agent or spy? Is this how you got all the girls in Chicago?"

"It's not like that. Not at all." He shifted his eyes away from me, his face wounded unlike the usual cockiness he embraced. "It wasn't always duck soup. I did some things I regret."

Like what? I wanted to demand. Like lied to your parents? Stole something? Did poorly in school? I couldn't imagine sweet Percy of utmost morals doing anything regretful.

"You can talk to me, Percy," I reassured him softly. "Please…"

He considered me for a moment until a shrieking cut through the silence.

Benny!

"Wabbit!" Benny broke between us in pursuit of a rabbit that jumped out from the field.

Seemingly grateful for the interruption, Percy jumped up. "Time to get those getaway sticks moving!" he said, pulling me up to standing. "Wait up, Benny!"

I exhaled heavily, frustrated. He could be so…evasive.

I packed up the picnic basket and shook the blanket in quick snaps, spraying crumbs of crust across the brittle, yellowed grass of what was once a yard.

Jackrabbits.

They scurried about the land, squatting here and there in a sort of chaotic frenzy.

"Carrie!" Percy yelled, catching my gaze. "Help us catch supper before they lam off!"

He was pouncing at a skinny gray rabbit, whose bones protruded from under its skin like the cracks in the dry land around us.

"Well, as absolutely charming as you are, jumping 'round in the sand, I think I'll pass."

So much for a romantic picnic or a first kiss. A warmth spread throughout my body and I hated how he could bring out the extremes of my emotions, but couldn't help but give in.

"Oh, alright," I said. "I suppose."

For the next hour, we chased rabbits until Percy, Benny, and I collapsed in exhaustion. The temperature seemed to be dropping and I shuddered a bit from the chill.

Caught up in the moment, without warning, Percy reached over and pecked me on the cheek. It happened so quickly, I almost questioned whether it had actually happened. But it did.

A real kiss.

"What was that for?" I teased.

"That," he said confidently, "was for heroically chasing all those hoppers and saving my back."

I giggled.

"I could go chase some more, you know," I said, raising my eyebrows.

He leaned close enough for me to smell the woodsy scent of sawdust coming from his shirt. His breath caressed my ear, my cheek, as he was now within inches of my lips.

And then, he *kissed* me.

Really kissed me. His lips pushed gently against mine and I was grateful my pa wasn't there to see it.

When he finally pulled away, I smiled coyly. "I think I like Illinois boys."

"I thought you might."

My pulse quickened as he slid in close enough for our legs to touch. That same electric feeling took hold of me. A magnetic pull.

As I gently placed my hand on his arm, something caught my eye over Percy's shoulder. Off in the distance, dark gray thunderheads flashed meanly as they rolled in across the plains, lighting up the fields against a darkening sky. The land was vibrating beneath me, accompanied by a low rumble from off somewhere in the field.

Shadows quickly grew in size, stretching across the prairie in twisted and uneven waves, making the lifeless grass bend at odd angles until breaking in quick snaps.

Percy whipped around to see what had stolen my attention, his face registering sheer panic. A wall of sand rolled hungrily toward us, consuming everything in its path. We needed to get out and *fast*. It covered the entire width of the horizon and had to be nearly 10,000 feet tall. These were not ordinary thunderheads or dust storms.

"Holy Hell!" He jumped up, jerking me with him. "Benny!" he screamed. "Get inside!"

Panic surged, and I couldn't quite catch my breath or pinpoint what was happening. Thudding pounded in my ears and heart, my arms trembling with it. But it wasn't my heartbeat. The clothing line was bouncing with the earth, the thudding growing louder like an approaching cargo train. What scared me most was the fear on Percy's face.

My heart nearly stopped.

Panic seized my body.

Jackrabbits!

Only a few at first, hopping wildly from the field. I stammered back, unable to take my eyes off the wall of sand that was growing in size as it neared the yard. My legs rooted into the dirt and I couldn't move. The ground tremored with the heavy thumping of rabbits. More than I'd ever seen in my life. Hundreds, no, thousands.

They were everywhere, scurrying round like a machine kicked up a den. But it had been months since any chugging of an actual farming machine. Percy grabbed my hand with an urgency I'd never seen and was pulling me toward the house as my own feet failed.

"Get to the house!" Percy yelled, pulling me forward. "Where's Benny?"

I hardly registered his voice. I couldn't speak. Couldn't breathe.

"Carrie!" he yelled. "Where's Benny?"

Benny! The thought jerked me back to my senses. Where *was* Benny? A new fear seized me, cutting off my senses.

The pounding of jumping feet against the dry ground was a drum roll echoing through the lifeless field. The sky grew darker and darker until I could hardly see a thing.

"Benny! Goldie!" Percy yelled.

If any time was a time for Goldie to listen when called, this had to be it. I couldn't help myself and turned again to stare at the fields behind us.

"It's coming!" I shrieked, instinctively covering my head with my arms.

Percy's voice was faint as he called Benny's name over the shrieks of the birds.

Birds.

They were everywhere around the dirt yard, frantically flying about.

"Get to the house! Now!" Percy yelled, the sand wall towering over the land.

I could hardly see the house through the darkness. Tears streamed down my face. I couldn't lose Benny. Not my brother.

"To the house, Carrie! Get wet towels!" Percy's voice was distant.

It would drown us. That brown sand. Drown us all. The houses, the cars, the people. The whole damn county.

The sky had turned, carrying with it a tsunami of sand and dirt that would destroy it all. Even the birds and grasshoppers.

Tears stung my eyes and my legs threatened to buckle from under me at the realization that the land was not at all predictable. Not even in its bluest of skies.

Percy was right. The farmers were all wrong, and now the time had come.

The land had revolted and was coming for us.

CHAPTER 24

Iscrambled clumsily to the house, shielding my eyes from particles of sand as I leaned into the wind.

Dirt blocked the sun, filling the air with dust as it screamed out in sharp shrills that pierced my ears and shook every part of me to the core.

The wood splinters dug into my shoulders as I fumbled with the door handle until it finally gave in against the pressure, tossing me carelessly to the floor. Sand sprayed the house.

Stand up! Damn it, Carrie, stand up!

Bracing myself on all fours, I crawled behind the door and leaned all my weight into it until it latched securely into the frame. The roaring was reduced to a sharp, but inconsistent whistle as the wind spit sand through the bottom door crack.

My shoulders dropped. I tried to gain my senses.

Benny. Percy. Goldie.

Urgency twisted my stomach as I frantically jerked open kitchen drawers to fetch towels. The boarded windows and dark skies made it impossible to see. I blindly reached out my hands to the hard surface of the counter, gliding my fingers along the dust until they bumped into the kerosene lantern, knocking it over in a hardly audible ping. Finding the handle, I set the lantern on the table.

Ma? Pa? Where were they? Were they safe?

I lit the lamp with shaking hands, hastily setting it on the countertop. I couldn't just sit there. I had to do *something*!

Running some rags to the sink, I dampened them until water trickled down my arms as I charged toward the front door and turned the handle. Violently, the pressure of the wind shoved it against the wall with a loud crack, throwing me to the floor.

"Percy! Benny!" I screamed at the top of my lungs, clutching the wet towels to steady my nerves. *"Percy!"*

We were all going to be buried. I could feel it. I pushed the thought from my head and focused on the yard. If anybody had a plan, it would be Percy.

Then a dark figure grew larger, a moving blob of shadow, fighting its way through the winds and darkness. I squinted against sand particles insistent on hitting me in the face.

"Carrie!" My name was barely audible.

Percy.

The blob steadily grew closer until I could make out Percy's form as he pulled himself to the house along the barbed wire fence, Benny limp in his arms.

"Benny!" I shrieked as tears stung my eyes.

I clutched Percy's shirt when they neared, pulling them inside before quickly closing the door. Confusion swept over me. Percy's shirt was off and wrapped around Benny's head.

Percy was coughing uncontrollably, bent over the kitchen table. Benny wiggled the shirt off his head, his hair covered with sand.

"Benny!" I cried, grasping the flimsy boy. Sand coated his entire body in a sickly orange dust. Water dripped to his face, forming pools of mud. I realized it was coming from my eyes.

Percy reached toward me, grabbing a towel and pulling it to Ben's mouth, even as he continued to cough himself, spitting out clods of dirt into the yellowed towel.

"Benny!" I demanded. "Open your mouth!"

I forced my finger between his lips, running it along the inside of his cheeks despite his protests as he shook his head from side to side.

I pulled out little sand, I guessed, due to Percy's quick thinking with his shirt.

I grabbed a cloth and pressed it to his nose. "Blow!"

"No," Benny whined.

"Blow the sand out, now!" It hurt me to be so firm. I'd almost lost him. He could've been dead right then, but I knew it was the only way to reach him.

He did as he was told, coating the towel with orange and brown residue. Percy was now at our side, his arm wrapped protectively around me as he led us to the couch where we huddled together, Benny's legs stretched over Percy, me cradling his head and stroking his hair.

How long could this last? This storm wasn't like the others. *Were Ma and Pa safe? Where were they?*

A sudden thought pierced my conscience.

"Where's Goldie?" I asked quietly, turning to Percy.

He shook his head, his eyes heavy. "Couldn't find her. I tried. It was just so dark, and the sand and wind…"

Benny's eyes flinched and he began to sob. *"Goadie! Goadie!"*

I hastily readjusted Benny and jumped to the door, but Percy followed me and was now pulling me back, preventing me from opening it. "Carrie, I'm sorry. We can't open it."

"No!" I yelled, jerking away from him. Tears streamed down my face. I knew he was right. The sand would swallow us right up.

Sobs caught in my throat. My lungs burned. Goldie's furry little body played in my head, from the day we brought her home to just this morning when she melted me with those brown sparkly eyes, full of hope at stealing a piece of bread. She counted on me. And I let her down. I let her die.

"What kind of caregiver am I?" I sobbed. *The worst,* I decided. The very worst.

"A great one." Percy pulled me into his chest and held me tightly. His shirt grew wet with my tears, but I didn't care. I didn't care what anyone thought. My Goldie was gone.

Life would never be the same.

CHAPTER 25

It was too dark to tell what time of day it was. All we could do was helplessly wait and pray as desperation tore at the wall I had placed between God and me.

"I'm scared," Benny whimpered, his eyes flitting in the lantern's glow as his head lay in my lap. It killed me to see him so still.

"Do you want me to tell you a story?" I asked, stroking his hair, grateful he couldn't see the tears streaking my face.

He nodded.

"Okay. Let me think." I wasn't the best storyteller. Heck, I didn't even like telling stories. Rarely read anything. No time for it really. I racked my brain for some kinda history lesson from school.

"How about I tell you about the people who used to roam this land?"

His eyes widened, two egg whites in the dark as he slipped his thumb into his mouth, a habit Ma had tried to break him from.

"*The Comanche* they were called. They came from Wyoming, I think it was. And came in so strong, over twenty thousand, on horseback, that it was as if they rose from the Plains' grasses."

I had his full attention now.

"The Comanche used hand signals, their own secret language. You know how loud the wind gets when it goes whipping around the plains?"

Benny shook his head.

"Well, that's why they used hand signals. To communicate over the noise of the wind. They put markings up their arms." I traced my fingers up Benny's arms, noticing for the first time, just how frail they had become. He shifted slightly.

"Anyhow, they bred horses and were the best riders you've ever seen. You know those cowboys you hear 'bout on the radio shows? Well, the Comanche were better, stronger, tougher. They rode bareback and even while carrying their weapons. Sometimes, while fighting, they'd even slip sideways on their horses to avoid being shot."

Benny whispered, his voice raspy and weak. I leaned closer to his face. "What's that?"

"What color horses?" he repeated, his voice wavering. A thought gnawed on my heart and I pushed it away, focusing on the story.

"All different colors, but I s'pose they were mostly dark to avoid drawing attention to the God-awful lightning out here cross these plains."

Benny shook his head in agreement, thumb still in mouth, waiting for me to go on.

"So, the Comanche traded horses with the gold-seekers bound for California. But the Republic of Texas got mad and organized the Texas Rangers."

"The Wanjers?" Benny asked.

I nodded my head, unsure of whether he actually understood anything I was saying.

"These Rangers thought they could match the Comanche, but they were no match. You see, the Comanche had been hunting bison by horse for years. They used the bison for nearly everything. Some say it took twenty bison skins to make one teepee." I'd heard of them being portable and intricately decorated, and it still amazed me.

Benny's eyes started to twitch as he struggled to stay awake. I gently shook him, desperation racing through my body. When his eyes popped open, I exhaled a sigh of relief and went on.

"Well, eventually, despite the treaty," I continued, my voice soothing him back to sleep, "the White men broke their promises and invaded. They killed the bison by the millions."

I left out the part that over seven million bison tongues had been shipped out of Dodge City alone and over twenty-five million bison were killed in only two years, a thought that sickened me.

Benny's eyes were closed now, his chest rising gently up and down with the hum of his breathing.

White men had slaughtered all the Comanches' horses. *Over one thousand*, I'd learned. The people didn't stand a chance. Starving, they were forced out on foot, ending up in various camps throughout Indian Territory. Took barely ten years to eliminate the bison, the horses *and* the Indians. Wiped out nearly everything, until there was nothing left but the crying of the grasses in the wind.

I leaned into Percy and must've dozed.

At some point, the sky grew light, streaking just enough through a crack that I knew it was the next day.

During the night, Percy's breathing grew labored and he wheezed each time he sucked in air, so I replaced dried out clothes with damp ones on his nose and mouth. His chest and back were covered in red blotches from the blasts of sand. I gently rubbed a salve on them, my eyes stinging with tears. He didn't look like the Percy I knew. I kept waiting for him to open his eyelids and pull me into an embrace or throw me some slick Chicago line in his cocky style, but instead, he struggled for air.

I grew uneasy. Even though his face held a peace about him while he slept, Percy wasn't one to let his guard down and the thought of it twisted my stomach. Several times, I shook him awake, relief pouring through me at the sight of his open eyes.

When he and Benny finally awoke, we hesitantly made our way to the door. We were unprepared for what lay before us. I could hardly speak. None of us could.

The roaring of the skies had died sometime in early morning, replacing the clamor with a stillness that was just as unsettling in its quiet.

Percy's face registered awe as his mouth dropped open. He shook his head slowly while searching the landscape.

Dunes of sand in varying shades of oranges and browns swept over all of Pa's fields, making it hard to tell where the fields stopped and the roads began. Death blanketed the fields like ash, a rolling famine devouring any life left in that place as it licked the land with a thirsty tongue. Dead birds and rabbits lay scattered about the fields, victims of the storm.

"Sand!" Benny pushed past us, rejuvenated from sleep.

"Careful," I warned. I reached down, expecting to stroke Goldie's fuzzy head and my heart broke in half at the realization she was gone.

I choked back tears. My poor Goldie was buried somewhere out there. She'd stayed by Benny, protecting him from the storm with what little energy she had left, shaking with fear but loyal to the end. When would we find her? *Would* we find her? My thoughts raced as memories flooded my mind and heart. It was foreign to watch Benny in the sand without her. I choked back sobs.

As if reading my thoughts, Percy reached over and grabbed my hand, giving it a squeeze.

We sat on a mound of sand, which only the day prior had been the porch. Words escaped us. I couldn't bring myself to talking.

I wasn't sure how long we'd been sitting there before the spitting of a tractor stole our attention. We ran out to greet whoever was still alive, awestruck by the damage and beauty of the dropped sand, which spread over the landscape of nearly everything…the only evidence of man being there was the ugly wood poles for the phones, a dismal reminder of what once was.

"Grandpop," he said. Percy's shoulders dropped in relief at the sight of the man.

Ma! Pa! I restrained Benny from running to the giant tractor's wheels as it spit up clouds of dust behind it.

Pa jumped down from the tractor and ran to us, pulling us both into a strong embrace.

"Goldie," I cried, despite Percy's presence. "Storm got her, Pa. She's gone."

He patted my back and in the reassurance of Pa's arms, I sobbed, childlike and uncaring of who might've seen me. He was a harbor of strength.

Percy was coughing again, and Pa gave Mr. Meyer a worried glance.

"We have to get you to a doctor," the old man said, his eyebrows knitting together as he helped Percy up to the tractor.

Percy looked at his grandpops and gave a half-cocked smile. "And here I thought Chicago was dangerous." He clutched his side and winced. "Better drop Ma a dime or we'll never hear the end of it."

Ma held Benny close as she rocked him, kissing his sandy head, a million worries settling into the fine lines in the corners of her eyes.

And for the first time, I remembered why Percy had come to this God-forsaken place to begin with. Nausea filled my gut, and I began to get light-headed at the realization.

Asthma. Percy had asthma.

As deadly as the storms could be, dust pneumonia or worse, silicosis of the lungs, was even deadlier. Several locals who had died of pneumonia surfaced in my mind. All ages, young and old. Healthy and sick. *Babies.* God, babies even.

I suddenly didn't care about his past life. I wanted him safe. *Needed* him to be safe. All I cared about was his future, whatever it may be.

And then, when the tractor shrunk into a pinpoint on the horizon, I wept.

CHAPTER 26

Pa had brought home a few dead rabbits to cook up.

Once cleaned out and skinned, Ma boiled one of the rabbits, filling the house with rich smells of real food again. Not just food, but *meat*.

How long had it been since we'd even smelled meat? Not since the rabbit round up months back. She set some of the liquid aside for future soup stock and added ground wheat to the rest for the jackrabbit porridge, minus the carrots or any kind of vegetable for that matter.

Moisture involuntarily seeped from the insides of my mouth as I savored the aroma in the kitchen, its steam billowing up from the stove and coating the insides of the windows in a slick of sweat as Pa and I silently slipped out to begin the overbearing task of shoveling the yard.

"Goldie!" I shouted into the stillness of the prairie, straining my ears, not wanting to believe she was gone. The hopeful part of me imagined her hopping playfully through the sand as she made her way toward me, her tongue hanging out the side of her mouth as she gave me a toothy grin as if to say, *Here I am and aren't I cute?*

But she didn't come.

Pa began to shovel out the back shed door. At this rate, it would take hours to get near the ground with a shovel. My heart was a lump of lead in my chest.

"Where'd you say Benny was found?" Pa asked over his shoulder. He threw another pile of sand to the side of the shed, dust clouds forming lazily above it.

"Somewhere near the shed," my voice wavered. I rubbed my sleeve over my eye, the grit of the sand scratching my face.

"Well," Pa said, scooping out another shovelful of sand. "Why don't you help me? We'll get the job done faster."

He leaned against the shovel and wiped the sweat from his forehead with a handkerchief, the dirt on his face settling in the worry lines of his forehead, making him appear much older than he was.

It was a grueling job, shoveling that sliding sand. It was hot, dusty work, despite Pa instructing me to pull my handkerchief over my mouth. The cloth of my shirt clung to my skin in patches of sweat and everything seemed to scratch. I imagined Ma sweeping out the house again, an endless task against the persistent dust. It settled on everything. Clothes in closets, cups in cupboards, the bedding, everything…

"You think Percy's going to be okay?" I asked, trying to fight the tears.

Pa's body stiffened, just for a moment, but enough for me to sense his uncertainty.

"He's a strong kid," he said, scooping another shovelful of sand.

In the past few days, we learned a couple more babies and elderly people had died from dust pneumonia. But Percy was different. He was strong. Healthy. Larger than life. With all of the mischief and reckless things he'd done, there's no way he could die like this. Pneumonia? Not my Percy.

Reluctantly, we took a break and went in for supper when Ma called out to us. Every muscle in my body burned, but I owed it to Goldie to find her.

The table was wiped down as best as could be, streaks of chalklike gray still visible against the dark surface. I reached up into the cupboard and grabbed a glass, leaving a ring of darker wood where it once stood. Ma handed me a cloth.

"Best to wipe it out, Carrie," she reminded me. Despite stocking all the dishes upside down in the cupboards, dust still managed to crawl inside somehow. Dust was choking out the air around us.

Ma had fried leftover oatmeal from the morning to eat with the soup. I missed meat. I missed potatoes. Sometimes before bed, I was so hungry, I imagined a feast of what I would eat if times were good. The way they used to be. Last night it was chicken breasts and fresh corn on the cob with Ma's cornbread. My stomach grumbled as I bit into the crusty patty, which only earlier that day was wet, soggy oatmeal.

We ate in silence.

Even Benny, who was usually making a fuss over something, dismally ate his food and kept to himself.

"Cellar's almost down to nothing," Ma mentioned more to herself than anyone. Pa swallowed his oatmeal, a glassy look in his eyes. Out of habit, I broke off a bit of Ma's bread from the loaf and lowered it to my feet before remembering.

I sniffled, pulling my full piece of bread back up to the table, untouched.

Ma cast a worried glance in Pa's direction, but he was in another world, staring at his plate. My family felt foreign to me, like some other family had been switched with mine. They'd never acted like this before.

When we were finished eating, Ma excused us from the table and allowed me to go back outside.

"Let's take a break, Carrie," Pa said, resting his hand on my shoulder.

"But the shed…"

"The shed can wait. I want to show you something."

I followed him 'round back of the building to where the ground sloped up in a gentle curve of sand that muted the separation between land and structure. Pa trudged ahead of me, stopping every so often to regain his footing. When he reached the top, for a moment he was still as he gazed out in the distance.

The sand was slippery, constantly shifting beneath my knees as I crawled. Eventually my knee hit the solidarity of the roof, making it easier to brace myself as I inched my way to where Pa was standing. He reached down and clasped his strong hand around mine, my arm aching as he pulled my limp weight up to the top of the roofline.

When I gained my footing, I didn't see anything out of the ordinary. Just the void of nothingness. Any remnant of life had been smothered by the relentless sand that now sat upon it, suffocating any opportunity the crops had of growing. An entire season of profit wilted in the unforgiving heat.

I exhaled, the dryness of my throat aching for water. I braced myself for Pa's disappointment. Surely, the fields were completely doomed. Another year of crops wasted away.

"Beautiful, ain't it?" Pa said, his voice reminiscent and quiet.

My eyes darted to his face. His eyes scanned the horizon that was broken only by the box of a house we called home, sticking out ugly against the colorless sand.

"I wonder if heaven looks something like this," I said.

"The golden glow of wheat under the reflection of the sun is breathtaking," he said, his lips turned up into a slight smile. "It's as if the sun was kissing the fields, leaving her glow right on them." He shook his head.

Had he truly gone crazy?

"Even still," he continued, "this truly is God's country and there's no amount of manpower or will that can change that."

My heart burned at his words. I had nothing to add. The problem was, there wasn't any wheat. Nowhere in sight. Still, I knew how much the land meant to him and couldn't bring myself to throw the heavy reality of it all onto his shoulders. Not in that moment of peace.

"Still gold," he said softly, more to himself than to me. He regarded me and smiled. "Someday, Carrie, everything you see will be yours."

He shifted his gaze back out at the fields and my heart was as hollow and void of promise as was the land. How could he not see I didn't want it? Any of it? Even so, I couldn't break his heart. Not the way nature did time and time again. He wasn't broken yet and I wouldn't be the one to do so.

Instead, I reached over and took his hand in mine, giving it a squeeze. "Still gold," I agreed.

CHAPTER 27

I rubbed my eyes, trying to get the sleep out. Sun leaked through the cracks of the window boards in my bedroom, spilling onto my quilt in thin lines of light. My heart sank, anchored to the bottom of my stomach.

Ma was in the kitchen, scrubbing the countertops methodically, an unending necessity that never seemed to pay off in this godforsaken land.

Seeing me, Pa drew in a deep breath. His face was unshaven, aging him by several years. I'd left him digging late last night and wondered if he'd even gone to bed.

"I heard from Algott Meyer," he said, pursing his lips together.

Something was wrong. My gut cinched and I felt like I couldn't breathe.

Benny rolled a toy truck along the countertop, leaving a winding track in the dust that stopped abruptly where he shoved the truck into Ma's hip, pressing against the faded fabric pattern of daisies she wore.

My heart plummeted into my stomach. "Percy?"

I hoped Pa couldn't hear the wavering of my voice. Ma solemnly wrung out the dishcloth, a stream of brown water running into the sink.

Pa opened his mouth and closed it again, lines of concern carved above his tired eyes.

"*Percy?*" I repeated. My voice didn't sound like my own, but a frantic mother's who had lost her child.

"Carrie, he's been sleeping since he got home. They're not sure…" Pa's shoulders dropped.

"What do you mean?" I prodded. "Who's *not* sure? Not sure of *what*? He was fine after the storm! You saw him! This is a sick joke. SICK!"

"Carrie," Ma started in, her voice hesitant. "Percy took a lot of sand into his lungs." She pulled up a chair and sat beside me at the table, her face suggesting a fate more serious than she was willing to let me in on. "He's at home resting. It's in God's hands."

My pulse beat wildly in my neck. *God's hands?* Like the land and crops were in *God's hands*? What kind of God would do this? Not Percy. No God would do this to Percy! He wasn't the type of person who died young. Not him! My cheeks burned.

Not willing to repeat my thoughts aloud, I asked sharply, "Can we see him?"

"Not yet. Algott said tomorrow, considering…" Pa's voice trailed off.

"CONSIDERING *WHAT*?" I snapped, unable to take this vague bullshit anymore. "Considering he doesn't *die* tonight?"

Rage scorched my cheeks, rumbling through my veins. Didn't they know what he meant to me? What I stood to lose if I lost him? He was everything. He was my very existence.

"Carrie," Ma tentatively said, and reached over. She placed her hand on mine, her face wounded with concern.

I jerked away. I didn't want to be coddled. I couldn't even believe this was happening. Percy was coughing sure, but he was still breathing enough to cough and talk and crack small jokes to pass the time during the storm. He couldn't be dying. He couldn't be. It was a gut punch at a kid's birthday party. It didn't make sense. He was larger than life itself.

I had to get away.

I stormed out of the house, slamming the door behind me.

Already, the sun was beating down in its cruel and sadistic nature. It was a desert of a place, once holding the promise of green crops, golden wheat and a future. I sought out the little bit of shade under the roofline over our front entrance and hugged my knees to my chest, letting the tears stream down my face.

It couldn't end here, it just couldn't. Not like this.

From behind me, the door screeched open, followed by Pa's heavy footsteps as he plopped down beside me.

"Another hot one," he said, his face drawn. "Algott stopped by this morning on his tractor and helped me shovel out the Ford. Heck, the train even derailed from the storm. Electricity surge shut everything down."

Pa's small talk drove needles into my skin. All the air in the world couldn't fill my lungs fast enough. Lightheadedness filled my head.

"Is he going to make it?" I asked as I searched Pa's face.

His eyes met mine. "Carrie, it's—"

"Don't give me any crap about God, Pa. I want to know if Percy's going to make it."

He heaved out a heavy sigh, looked away and then gave me the most honest answer he had. "I don't know."

I squeezed my eyes shut, determined not to cry in front of Pa.

"Look, Carrie, I'm as worried as you are. I don't like relying on things we can't know or see. But that's what we need to do. Faith lives in the blurry places between black and white."

Tears slid from the corners of my eyes and puddled on my knees. The heat was suffocating, and all the dust and emotion made it difficult to breathe through my nose. I swallowed hard in an effort of wetting my throat.

"When can we see him?" I asked.

"This evening. Ma's fixing to make Mr. Meyer something for supper."

She must be some kind of modern-day miracle to find any kind of food to make in surplus. I bit my lip and nodded.

We sat there for several minutes and studied the horizon, the razor cuts of a thousand worries etched across Pa's face. My body was a hollow vessel, all my insides void of feeling. I suddenly felt claustrophobic in this world. In this life.

Benny's footsteps approached and I heard the screen door slam behind him.

"Cawie?" He plopped down next to me and placed his hand on my leg. Were they large enough for a boy his age? Worry flooded my brain. Was he growing at all with the little bit of food we had?

"Don't worry 'bout Percy," he said, his voice small but resolute. "He's a Comanche. Strong and smart."

He stood up and raced out to the backyard, leaving me in awe of his resolution. Heck, I didn't even think he'd remember the story from that fateful night when my world collapsed.

I spent the afternoon lost in memories of Percy. Some were mere moments, glimpses of his smile when making a wise crack, others morphing into adventures that made me laugh. Time ticked by in heavy strokes of the clock's hands as if taking glee in my agony.

Ma handed me a basket later that evening to give to Mr. Meyer. "Carrie," she said, in all her audacity, "it wouldn't hurt for you to pray over him."

We drove in silence.

The landscape had transformed the familiar into unrecognizable places. Dunes melted into smooth ravines of sand that stretched across the plains and into the dirt roads, making it hard to tell where the fields ended and the roads began. Pa drove cautiously, turning our ten minute route into a twenty-three minute one.

About a mile before Mr. Meyer's place, he glanced over and rose his eyebrows as if to say, "Here goes it."

My stomach twisted into tight knots.

What if I broke down and cried? What if he could hear me? What if he couldn't? What would I say? What was I thinking?

"Just talk to him about positives," Pa said, as if reading my doubts. "Daily things. He can hear you, Carrie," he said, his voice unwavering. "He maybe can't respond, but he CAN hear you, so make your words count."

As we neared their drive, a black pickup pulled out of the driveway, turning in the opposite direction from which we had come. It was shiny enough to reflect the clouds as they rolled across the inky surface in a way that was almost romantic, if not symbolic. The silhouette of a man in a fedora framed the driver's side of the truck and upon seeing us, he gave a slight nod before going about his way.

"Model A Ford," Pa scoffed, shaking his head in disgust.

He'd never really trusted anyone wearing a suit. Be it lawyers, insurance agents, or government officials, they were all lumped into the same category: untrustworthy and pretentious. The sole exception being the local bankers when they approved our loans and seemed genuinely interested in seeing us succeed.

I scanned my brain for things to say to Percy, but nothing seemed worthy. It wasn't fair. It wasn't fair that he'd risked his own life to save my brother's. It wasn't fair he had to leave Chicago on account of his health to begin with. For what? Only to die here instead, and shatter my heart in the process?

Pa rapped his knuckles against the door. I still had nothing in my mind. Inside, there was a clamoring of footsteps.

"Algott?" Pa called out, peeking inside when he didn't reply.

Thudding reverberated against the creaky boards upstairs. I tentatively followed Pa inside, setting the basket on the table before taking the stairs, bile rising up into my throat with every lumbering step toward the unknown.

I'd never been inside Mr. Meyer's house. I was surprised to find it quite tidy and comfortable. A homemade crazy quilt casually rested over the arm of the couch, a proud display of various strips of pattern, colors, and fabric still vibrant despite the obvious aging of the rest of the furniture.

From what I could tell, the tables had been routinely dusted, assuming Mr. Meyer hadn't done so recently in expectation of visitors. A worn ring stained the coffee table in a halo of lighter wood, and upon further inspection, I noticed a much more faded one beside it, a reminder of the late Mrs. Meyer whom I'd never met.

Along the staircase, the walls were bare, save two pictures. The first of Mr. Meyer, along with his late wife and presumably their two children, a boy and a girl who appeared to be somewhere in their teens. I peered closer at the girl searching for the similarities between Percy and his mother. It seemed tedious, given the situation, but I was both curious and desperate to avoid the inevitable as Pa disappeared around the corner.

She wore a rather simple dress, devoid of any pattern. I imagined it to be a light blue or gray. Her face was solemn, and she had clearly inherited Mr. Meyer's thick eyebrows and her mother's straight nose. Another photograph at the top of the stairs revealed the same girl, now somewhere in her twenties and with her husband. Her eyebrows weren't quite as thick, likely she'd found herself a pair of tweezers amongst teenage friends. But still, something nagged at me and I couldn't put my finger on it.

"Carrie!" Pa interrupted my thoughts.

I threw one more glance at the picture and with flittering in my stomach, made my way to the bedroom.

A splinter of light seeped through Percy's doorway, followed by shadows of the shape of Mr. Meyer scrambling across the room.

I drew in a deep breath and stepped into Percy's room.

"Quick!" Mr. Meyer exclaimed. "Grab some wet cloths!"

Pa's face went blank as he rushed past me, leaving me standing dumbly in the doorway.

"He's running a fever!" he said.

Mr. Meyer's voice was distant against the buzzing in my ears. My feet were grounded, my eyes fixed on what was before me. As much as I wanted to, I couldn't pull my eyes from Percy as his body heaved up and down in dramatic convulsions.

CHAPTER 28

The scent of kerosene hung heavy in the room and I thought I might be sick.

"Carrie!" Mr. Meyer jerked me into the present. "Carrie, hold his side!"

I lumbered to Percy's bedside and following Mr. Meyer's lead, attempted to restrain him, but was no match for his strength as he thrashed around in a sort of frenzy I'd never seen. I thrust all my weight onto him, pressing my upper body upon his flailing arm as he kicked the bedsheets loose. His skin was slick with sweat and the fume of kerosene profusely flooded my nose as the salve radiated off his chest.

"Carrie's here, Percy," Mr. Meyer said loudly, as if to mute out the frantic flopping of the body we were holding. "She's here to see you."

Pa rushed in beside me, placing cold wet rags against his forehead.

"Press this against his tongue." Pa's voice was steady and reassuring as he handed Mr. Meyer a tongue depressor.

I was taken back to the time when we had horses. I must've been about five or six years old. Millie, one of our leads on the farm, was pregnant. I didn't know the true nature of what was going on, other than I couldn't wait to see that foal. I'd already named it Buddy, pretty smart I thought, given I didn't know whether it was male or female.

What I remember most about that day is Millie's desperate whining and Pa's calm. I couldn't stop pacing, chewing my nails to the bone as if Millie's pain had consumed my own spirit.

Pa rested his hand on her cheek, whispering to her as he pressed her tongue down and the neighbor began to pull the foal from her body. Buddy was a special horse, but as much as I begged, we just couldn't afford to keep her during that time, having no idea our glory days of golden wheat were just around the corner.

Percy's body continued to lurch up and down, the sickness possessing his body, the same way the storm had caused the land to tremor as it reaped havoc on all it touched. I fixed my eyes on his chest, a better alternative to the vulnerability on his face.

What seemed like hours passed by in this way. And then, when I felt as if all my strength was gone, Percy let out a deep sigh and his body went limp.

"What's *wrong*?" I frantically screamed.

"He's still breathing," Pa said, placing his hand on Percy's chest as it rose and fell rhythmically. He pressed the back of his other hand on Percy's forehead. His cheeks were flushed, but his face was peaceful, his eyelids closed as if he were simply taking a nap.

Mr. Meyer left the room. From the silence of the hallway came a wailing, an unrecognizable sound like that of an animal, which I came to realize was Mr. Meyer's sobbing. Pa gave me a nod and went out to console the old man.

When I rejoined them downstairs leaving Percy to sleep peacefully, Mr. Meyer was composed and listening to Pa. "They got no empathy," he was saying. "The way they swing by here knowing what you're going through. They've got some nerve."

"Yes, we passed one on our way in driving his fancy truck," Pa scoffed. "Only a banker would wear such formal attire to a farmhouse."

Mr. Meyer seemed surprised until realization crossed his face. "Oh, that wasn't an agent," he said, giving a dismissive wave.

"Oh?" Pa raised his eyebrows, his cheeks flushing.

"Never seen the man," he said and shrugged. "Said he was a friend of Percy's."

He pulled a glass from the cupboard, rinsing out the dust before filling it with water.

I didn't realize Percy had any real friends 'round here other than me and of course, *Bethany.* I was ashamed to admit I was both jealous and intrigued.

Mr. Meyer took a long drink of water, gulping loudly before setting the glass in the sink.

"How many episodes has Percy had like this?" Pa asked, breaking the silence.

I'd wondered the same thing but didn't dare ask. Part of me didn't want to know.

"First one," he said, pulling a chair out from behind the table. He braced himself with the table as he sat and absentmindedly rubbed his lower back with his weathered hand. "He's had the fever sure, but first time his body acted up like this."

Pa was quiet. I could see he was working something out in his head as he bit the inside of his cheek. "I've seen this kind of thing before with animals. Something spooks them and gets their heart rate and blood pressure up." He fumbled with his hat. "With animals, it's usually danger, so that doesn't make much sense for this situation."

A nagging feeling gnawed at my insides as I tried to fall asleep that night. I tried to push it down, but then my ears were filled with irritating sounds. The scratching in the walls had become a constant like wind or rain (dare I remember the sound of rain); the chirping of crickets in the Minnesotan summers of my childhood.

Percy had survived.

I reminded myself of what was truly important. I'd give anything to have him healthy. Even if he had lied to me about Bethany, even if he didn't trust me enough to confide in me, I couldn't be selfish. Percy was still alive.

But still, that wasn't what bothered me. Not in this moment anyway.

The picture of Percy's parents surfaced. His mother's face clear in my mind. I tried to find some sort of resemblance between them, but there was none, which wasn't unusual. Heck, most people would never place me with my fair-skinned, blonde-haired mother had they not known we were family. I had my father's cheekbones and olive complexion.

Percy's mother appeared much more high maintenance in the picture from the truck than the teenager in the photo at Mr. Meyer's place. The city had clearly changed her. Gone was the girl of simple cotton dresses and plain features. His mother, at least the Chicago version of her, had played up her features with mascara and dark lipstick, her hair delicately curled by rollers I supposed, a display of fashionable trends and expensive taste.

I tried to imagine how I'd change if I were to move to a city filled with billboard lights, clubs and restaurants. Access to stores on every corner. How quickly would I trade in my roots for another lifestyle?

My mind shifted to Percy's father. The strong nose and thick, dark mustache had stood out in the photo at Mr. Meyer's, his broad shoulders dwarfing his wife as she sat beside him.

And then, all at once it hit me.

The man in the photo at Mr. Meyer's was not the man in the photo with Percy and his mother. My heart nearly stopped.

That was *it*. I was sure of it.

The more I rolled it around in my head, the more I realized they didn't even resemble each other. Even his mother.

Though women can be elusive in how they presented themselves, chameleons in the technique used when applying eye shadows, lipliner or how they even plucked their eyebrows. I still didn't see the common features between the photos of his mother.

My mind was racing. There was no way I'd be falling asleep anytime soon. I was sure of the fact that the man in Mr. Meyer's picture wasn't Percy's father and was now doubting the resemblance between the women in the photos from the house and the one with Percy in the truck.

Percy was alive. That's all that mattered. I blushed; my shoulders were heavy with shame. Percy was fighting for his life, and there I was doubting his entire story.

CHAPTER 29

"**I**'ve seen this kind of thing turn both ways, Carrie," Pa said the next morning, shaking his head.

A neighbor was watching Benny, relieving Ma to come along to Mr. Meyer's. Now, as she sat beside me, she reached over and placed her hand on mine, giving it a squeeze. "Dust pneumonia is nothing to joke about."

Obviously.

Pa cracked his knuckles, a habit he often did when filling the empty lulls in conversation. "It's the same with animals," he started again. "They inhale too much dust and—"

"Stop."

I didn't care about hearing stories comparing Percy to Pa's dead farm animals. He didn't need to spell out Percy's fate. I already felt it in my gut.

Percy looked peaceful. Thank God for that.

Ma set herself up for heating soup on the stove and within minutes, the house filled with the comfort smells of fresh biscuits baking in the oven. I began to wipe the shelving in the kitchen, but sensing my distraction, Ma gave me a sympathetic nod of permission to leave the room and stay with Percy instead.

Whispers of wind slipped through the windows, stirring the lace curtains. My stomach momentarily tightened and my palms grew sweaty, an immediate reaction to any indication of a storm.

I pulled up a chair Mr. Meyer had placed beside the bed and rested my hand on Percy's arm. Could he sense my presence? I hoped so.

I never realized until that moment just how difficult it was to talk to someone who couldn't talk back. Sure, I'd talked to Goldie, but this was different. I tried to think of the things Pa often talked about, but it always seemed to circle back to the weather and crops, which I couldn't bear to talk about now, let alone depress Percy with.

I missed his voice. Missed his constant teasing. I begged God to bring him back to us, frustrated at not knowing if anyone was actually listening to my pleas.

"Carrie," Mr. Meyer's voice interrupted my trance.

I glanced at the clock. I'd been in the room for an hour.

"No need to plant yourself beside him all day," he sighed. "Come eat lunch with us."

I had to admit I was hungry. I hadn't eaten a bite since the visit yesterday. Hadn't slept much, neither. The uneasy feeling of not knowing what was going to happen kept me up later than the moon and left me restless, tossing the blankets from my body just to pull them up again.

The table was filled with the aroma and efforts of Ma's cooking, which somehow relaxed me. Steam billowed from the biscuits in the basket as we passed them around the table, along with Ma's vegetable soup. I could almost taste the robust sweetness of the stewed tomatoes and the richness of the beef broth. We hadn't had it in ages. Not since long before this whole disaster started. Ma must've saved a few jars in the cellar, dusting over it, just waiting for some tragic situation to rear them out.

"What a treat," Mr. Meyer said, praising Ma's cooking. "With just the two of us here, most days we throw together whatever is quickest. This is a fine thing you've done."

Ma's face lit up.

I should complement her more.

"It's the least we could do, Algott," she said, her voice quivering. "Percy is such a nice young man."

"That he is." He sniffled as he smeared a pat of butter across a biscuit. "Talked to his folks yesterday. They're devastated, of course."

I waited for him to say more.

"I can imagine," Ma said. She must've been as curious as me because she remained quiet, leaving room for Mr. Meyer to go on.

"You know, they haven't had it the easiest. But as people find out, all the luxuries in the world can't buy you a good marriage. And when all the luxuries disappear, you're left with the bones of it all and then it's up to you to decide how to build upon it."

The next day, I was surprised to find a polished black Chrysler parked at the farm.

"Looks like Percy has visitors," Pa commented as he parked our own dusty vehicle closer to Mr. Meyer's barn. I thought of the young chap we had seen the other day and wondered if he'd come back and if so, who he was. There were many secrets to Percy.

"Let's wait here, Carrie," Pa said, pulling a chair out from the table once we were inside. He pulled his hat off and groomed his thinning hair across his head. A muffle of voices came from somewhere upstairs.

We waited in silence, the ticking of an old grandfather clock keeping track of the stretched moments of heartache as Percy lay dying. After what seemed like hours, the thud of descending footsteps echoed against the hollowed pine stairs.

I glanced up, expecting to see the chap from the other day. A distinguished man somewhere in his mid to late sixties eased his way down the stairs, balancing himself with the railing as he gingerly approached us. He tipped his hat to us and left the house.

"Doctor Morgensen," Pa said.

I wasn't sure how he knew who he was. We'd never visited the doctor's office, always relying on Ma's homemade concoctions to get us through whatever ailment came along.

"Hello there!" Mr. Meyer greeted us from the top of the stairs. "Great news! Percy's lungs are clearing! He prescribed a bottle of Sulfapyridine for good measure."

My heart swelled. He was going to live! Percy was going to live! My eyes burned as tears slipped from my eyes.

"Algott, that's great!" Pa's eyes gleamed. "How long before he's back to fighting shape?"

"Doctor figures a good couple of weeks at the least. More than likely, he won't remember much of the time he's been laid up, thank God."

My chest lightened, pushing out the heavy feeling that had consumed me over the past several days.

"There's only so far kerosene can go before a doctor is needed," Mr. Meyer added as we climbed the stairs to meet him. "How anyone can even afford medical insurance is beyond me. I would've given anything to fix this boy. My own lungs if I could."

Pa agreed, knowing all too well the struggle to be able to afford the luxury of health insurance or doctor visits.

"Had it not been for Bethany's family," Mr. Meyer said, "I don't know what would've happened."

My breath hitched in my throat.

Surely, I'd heard him wrong. What the hell did Bethany have to do with this? My shoulders tightened into burning knots.

Pa's eyebrows knitted together in confusion.

"Don't know why they felt so inclined to help us out," Mr. Meyer was saying, patting the sweat from his forehead with a red handkerchief. "Just plain good people, I guess."

I knew it was selfish, but a pang of jealousy stabbed me in the gut.

Bethany.

I pictured her begging her banker father to help Percy. Or maybe her parents had met him and already treated him like the son they never had, just as my parents adored him.

Get a grip, I told myself.

She was after all, the reason he would live. How could I ever compete with someone who had essentially saved his life? The idea swallowed my worth in one gulp.

"Carrie," Pa's voice was faint over the buzzing in my ears. "Are you okay?"

They were both studying me, worry lines across their faces. I forced a smile.

"Yes," I lied. "Just overwhelmingly happy to hear the news."

CHAPTER 30

Percy slept.

His chest rose and fell with the soft outward and inward pull of his breath. I would give anything to hear his voice right now. What were the last words he'd said to me? I tried to remember, but it was a blur. The day of the storm carried the highest elation and the deepest sorrow I'd ever known. It had never occurred to me how one day could be big enough to hold both.

Through the window, I saw Mr. Meyer and Pa as they crossed the yard, their bodies obscured by specks of dust that clung to the glass in Percy's room.

"Carrie."

The sound was so faint I thought I had imagined it, but when I looked at Percy, his eyelids flickered.

My heart jolted.

I awkwardly pulled my hand from his, unsure of where we stood with each other. I leaned in closer so he could hear me.

"Percy?" His eyelids fluttered at the mention of his name. "You awake?"

"Carrie, get inside," he pleaded softly.

Beads of sweat bubbled up on his forehead and he curled his hands into fists. He mumbled something I couldn't make out.

"Percy," I said, resting my hand on his arm. "It's okay. We're safe. We're all safe. You saved Benny. He's okay." Tears welled up in my eyes knowing I could never repay him for what he'd done for my family.

His fingers uncurled like the fern tendrils we had once had in our Minnesota garden.

He could hear me.

"Percy," I whispered again.

I waited. For something. *Anything.* When he remained still, I knew I could take a chance.

"I love you."

I squeezed his hand, and after several minutes, stood to leave the room. Ma would be expecting us home to help fix supper and do the evening chores. Not even visiting Percy could get me out of that.

Percy mumbled something again. Maybe a name? *My* name?

I stopped, straining to hear his voice over my own heartbeat.

"Percy?" I asked, urging him to go on.

Butterflies flew dizzily in my stomach.

His eyelids opened ever so slightly as if it took all the energy he had to do so. His body was coming back to life one nerve at a time. Painfully slow, the doctor had said, but excruciatingly necessary for a complete healing.

I held my breath, hoping to hear him say my name, but what I heard was both equally fulfilling and heart-wrenching.

"Love you."

So faint, it was barely a whisper. Within moments, his eyelids stilled and he was snoring softly once again.

Something pinged in my stomach, indiscernible between elation and anxiety. What was it that had me so uneasy and restless?

Who? Who did he love? My heart demanded.

His words were clear, but who were they meant for?

CHAPTER 31

For the next several days, Percy gained consciousness more often. I didn't see any of this as Mr. Meyer kept visitors away for a period of time to avoid any confusion or possibility of further infection. I filled my days with meaningless tasks, helping Pa wherever needed. I was fidgety and nearly ran to the truck when Percy finally regained his strength enough to get the clearance to come on over.

"I better not strike a match around you," I teased, grateful to have him back, even if he did smell strongly of kerosene.

"Grandpop's orders," he insisted, mocking offense. He'd lost a good ten pounds and his voice was raspy, but was the most beautiful sound in the world. "The old man's got me on a tight leash these days. Surprised he even let me leave the house."

"Well, it's better than smelling like onions. After the storm, Ma rubbed Benny down with an onion poultice. Poor kid smelled for days, not that he noticed. How are you feeling anyhow?"

He shrugged. "Pretty soon, I'll be hitting on all eight again and then Carrie Lexington, you better watch out." He raised an eyebrow and for a moment, locked eyes. I could feel goosebumps settle on my arms. "Doctor fixed up a salve of kerosene, lard, and serpentine for my chest and Grandpops made me some kind of cough syrup concoction involving sugar and a drop of kerosene. Made me sweat it out like some kinda exotic animal at a blind pig."

"Sounds lovely." I laughed, having no idea what a blind pig was.

I thought of mentioning Bethany, but decided better of it. The last thing he needed was to deal with my insecurities. I had to win him over. That was all there was to it.

"Well, this morning we swung by one of the Red Cross Emergency Stations. They're all over town. I brought you some things." He reached down into a box beside his feet and pulled out some black tubing of sorts.

"A new mask for you," he said and grinned, handing over what appeared to be a homemade contraption with goggles. "Keen, ain't it? I know how spiffy you like to be." He flashed me his same old dimples and a reassurance swept through me.

"Gee, thanks," I said, pulling it over my head. "How do I look?"

"Like a dish for sore eyes." He eyed me up and down. "You look swell."

"You'd be seen with me like this?" I raised my eyebrows.

"Only if I could keep you in the truck."

"You wouldn't!" I pulled the mask up and without warning, he leaned in and kissed me quick.

A steady heat rushed through my veins and my heart felt as if it was going to burst.

"Well," he challenged, "I guess you'll have to go to town with me to find out."

"Guess so," I mocked. "What else you got in there?"

His mouth stretched into a smile as he bent down and pulled a stack of folded linens from the box. "Grandpops saved these," he said nonchalantly, handing them to me, his cheeks flushing. "I thought you might like them."

It was a stack of sugar sacks, neatly ironed and folded, some displaying patterns of roses in blush pinks, others with pale yellow sweet pea blossoms or vibrant sunflowers.

"They're beautiful," I said, my cheeks growing warm. I ran my fingers over the fibrous material. Not many people, my folks included, could afford sugar, even if the packaging doubled for clothing. It was the most thoughtful gift I'd ever been given.

"This one's my favorite." I unfolded a bag.

"Peonies," he said, his voice gentle.

Fuchsia blooms popping among lush green leaves covered the canvas, their petals intricately jagged.

"I figured your ma could make you a dress or something."

Something flickered in his eyes, sending a flash of heat through my body, creating an intensity between us. I waited for him to grab me and pull me close, intertwining his fingers in my hair as he kissed me. His gaze met mine. He suddenly cleared his throat, then picked up the empty box, fumbling with the lid in an effort of breaking it down.

"You talk to your pa today?" he asked.

My shoulders dropped as my lungs released a gush of air I didn't realize I'd been holding. I wanted to shield my face from him. Run and hide.

"Not yet." I hugged the stack of linens tightly to my chest.

His eyebrows twitched, his lips turning up at the corners.

"Percy James," I scolded, putting a hand on my hip. "What are you hiding?"

He smirked, throwing his arms up in mock surrender. "Nothing."

"Your brows twitch when you lie."

"I do nothing of the sort," he said, his eyebrows twitching again.

Pa's car pulled into the drive. Percy's eyes locked with mine and he grinned, causing my heart to beat nearly out of my chest. I wished he'd think simple gestures through first and realize their consequences. The slightest smile or the way he looked at me could throw off my entire day, sending me into an analysis of what his intentions were.

Mr. Meyer's truck appeared in the drive and he parked alongside Pa, grasping the door handle as he eased himself out.

"I'd shake your hand, but I'm too afraid I might shock you," Pa said, greeting Mr. Meyer.

The electricity from the storms lasted for days. Coupled with the dryness of the plains, it was as if nature was trying to separate even neighbors.

"No need," Mr. Meyer said, tipping his hat. He looked as if he'd aged years since Percy's illness.

"Thank you for the sugar sacks," I said. "They're lovely."

"Well, I figured we've got no use for them. Percy wasn't too keen on using any of them himself," he chuckled, "and Lord knows, neither of us can sew anyway."

"Really?" I asked, casting Percy a glance. "I think you'd look quite lovely in the sweet pea print."

He clammed up, his face flushing.

Benny ran out of the house, the door slamming behind him. "Where's the surprise?" he yelled.

Surprise?

I cocked my head at Percy. His eyes sparkled. I knew he had been hiding something.

"Percy?"

He smiled broadly, throwing his arms up in the air. "Innocent."

Pa pulled a crate from the back of the truck, its contents hidden by a thin sheet.

"What is it?" Benny asked as he stood on his tiptoes, reaching up as Pa lowered the crate to the ground and swooped Benny up into his arms, despite his protesting.

"Carrie? Do you want to do the honors?" Pa looked at me with expectant eyes.

I hesitated, not trying to be ungrateful, but I didn't have it in me to love another puppy. Not yet. Maybe not ever. A surge of frustration seared through me. How could they not feel the same way? Goldie had even won Pa over, following him between the house and the barn, always at his heels. Her favorite place to be in the evenings was curled up on his feet while he sat on the couch and read. Something balled up in the middle of my throat.

"Go ahead," Pa urged.

Everyone watched me, gauging my reaction. I forced a smile for the sake of them all as I tugged the sheet off the crate. My heart stopped. Could it be?

"PUPPY!" Benny squealed.

"Not just any puppy," Pa said, setting him down.

"GOADIE!" Benny was now jumping and clapping.

My heart seized, and for a moment, all I could do was stare. Goldie peeked out, her eyes warm as melted chocolate, seemingly heavier than the rest of her body. *It was her.* Oh goodness, it *was* her.

"Careful, Benny," Ma said, approaching us from the house. "She's been through a lot."

I lifted the ball of dirty fluff from the crate and pulled her to my chest as I kissed her matted head and Benny's sticky fingers combed her rough fur. Her heart pattered against my own and I pressed my face into her side, inhaling her scent, a mixture of lye and cedar chips. She wriggled in my arms but I couldn't let her go.

"How?"

"Pa found her in the shed," Ma said, her eyes gleaming with tears. "Can you believe it?"

Goldie licked my face in a series of wet sandpaper kisses. My heart burst and tears instantly streaked my cheeks. I was dreaming. I had to be. To an outsider, she was a sad sight of skin and bones. Hardly the weight of a large cat. But to me, she was the most precious thing in the world. She was family.

"After you went to sleep that first night after the storm, I was determined to dig out that shed if it killed me," Pa said.

Mr. Meyer stood by Percy, his arm wrapped across his shoulder as they listened.

"I went inside and started carefully digging, preparing for the worst. With every shovel of dirt, I braced myself for the worst." He blinked hard. I'd never seen him cry and he wasn't about to start now. "As luck would have it, I heard a faint whimper. Could hardly believe my ears. Thought maybe I'd imagined it. But there it was again, over by the stacks of pallets." He shook his head in disbelief.

"I prayed it was true. Sure enough, there she was, shaking and whining. Dirty as ever, but alive," Pa explained.

All the times she'd chewed up his boot laces or the legs of the couch and Pa had just shook his head and sighed. Now I realized how much she meant to him after all. Like everyone else, she'd won him over and was just as much a part of the family as Benny or me.

"Smart pup," he said, patting Goldie's head. "She'd bunkered down under the old cloth I'd thrown over the tractor and got buried there. Not even a full-grown dog could've dug his way out of that sand."

I kissed her head again.

"She was pretty dehydrated, and it took a while to plump her up," Ma added, "but several weeks later, here she is, nearly the weight she was before the storm."

My heart ached. "Why didn't you tell us sooner?"

Ma frowned. "We just couldn't bear to break your heart again if she didn't pull through." She stroked the fur on Goldie's muzzle.

"Well, we oughta be heading out," Mr. Meyer said.

I was torn between hugging Percy good-bye and not wanting to put Goldie down as if either one could be ripped from my life at any minute.

Percy, as if unsure himself, glanced at me and nodded.

Mr. Meyer and Percy drove away, the brown world swallowing their truck as they disappeared into the horizon.

For a moment, everything in the world was perfect. The thought even crossed my mind that quite possibly God had returned to fulfill some prayers.

But how many miracles could one person be allowed?

CHAPTER 32

"I look absolutely ridiculous." I dreaded Percy seeing me like this and couldn't believe I had to wear such a thing, but Ma insisted on it.

Percy laughed. "Don't worry, I'll wear one, too." He adjusted the mask around his neck. "Hey, maybe people will think we're button men ready to bump off some criminals."

"Great," I groaned, but I couldn't help but laugh. He looked more like an alien than some kind of enforcer. I searched the bulging plastic protrusions where his eyes should be. "It's a good look for you."

"Thanks," he smirked. "I try."

We'd been spending more time together in the past few months as Percy regained his strength and neither of us were needed anywhere while Pa wandered about the farm, putzing with things or gazing at the sky.

With Ma's permission, I accompanied Percy to town in an effort of trading some of the few eggs from his last two chickens for food at the store. Mr. Henley, the grocery store owner made a point of knowing people's names and was as much a part of the town as the gravel roads or the buildings themselves, and seemingly just as old.

"I'm worried about Benny," I told Percy during the drive in.

I didn't plan on saying what had been tumbling around in my head, but there it was, the words floating in the air between us.

Percy frowned. "How so?"

I glanced out the window, diverting my eyes.

I cleared my throat. "Not eating. Doesn't matter what Ma makes, he won't touch it." I thought of the Texas gravy made of flour and water, which was hard for even me to choke down. But unlike Benny, I knew the consequence of not eating.

"What does he like?" he asked, his voice calm and steady.

"Bacon," I scoffed, shaking my head, tears stinging my eyes. "And green beans."

I was keenly aware of my own emptiness that had crept into my stomach as my mind drifted to meals of mashed potatoes and freshly baked bread with ham. My mouth began to water.

Percy's lips were pursed, his jaw set tight enough to bulge the muscles in the corners of his mouth as if quietly deciding something. I kicked myself for spilling my personal thoughts, but I thought my head might explode if I held them in any longer.

When we got to the store, we stood in line behind a woman in rags who was pleading with Mr. Henley. His eyes were drawn together in concern, his clothes hanging on the bony frame of his shoulders, tucked in place by the ties of an apron that was worn down to the threads. Now he was putting a hand on the woman's shoulder as a little boy tugged on her dress, his face caked with dirt, holes in jeans that were much too short for his growing body.

"Please Mr. Henley," the woman begged. "I have nothin'. You know I'm good for the barter once things turn 'round. Between the critters and this God-awful heat, my garden is dead. Our calves long died. We got nothing."

Mr. Henley sighed, his shoulders dropping as if carrying the weight of the world upon them.

"Ma'am," Percy said and stepped forward until both the woman and Mr. Henley regarded him. "I've got an extra egg. Sorry it's not much, but it's all I got. It's yours for trade."

The woman hesitated, glancing at her son as if the decision rested with him. "Thank you," she said and nodded to Percy, her eyes filled with tears. "Thank you."

After the woman had left with some milk and cheese, Mr. Henley shook his head. "Wish I could do more. This ain't right. All this suffering. And the farmers even."

"You rate good," Percy said, reassuring the old man. "This town is lucky to have you. The economy's been hard on everyone."

"I'd give all this food away if I could, but I can hardly feed myself and my wife." He slid his hands in his pockets. "Anyhow, what can I get you son?"

"Whatever three more eggs can get us," Percy said.

I shifted uneasily. Nearly five more people had lined up behind us.

"Give me just a minute," he said, accepting the eggs from Percy.

Percy drew in a deep breath and let it out, his face red. "Think I'd rather go back to working in the fields than go on begging like some kind of bindle stiff hobo."

"Least you got something to trade," I said. "Most folks round here don't. Heck, even our grain is nearly gone. What hasn't rotted is overcome with mice."

A tightness gripped my throat.

Percy grabbed my hand and gave it a squeeze as I blinked away the tears. People behind us began to grumble. At 110 degrees, the heat was almost unbearable, squeezing the sanity out of everyone.

Mr. Henley returned with a box in his hands. "I appreciate your kindness," he said, handing it to Percy. A few tomatoes, among other vegetables were in there.

"I've known your grandfather for years," he went on. "He's a good man. Helped me more times than I can count in the early years. Give him my regards."

Outside, the sky was white and hot, aiming on killing us all. The street nearly empty, most likely the result of people trying to stay cool in their cellars. Mr. Williams stumbled from an alley, his white shirt wet with sweat or whatever was in the jar he was drinking from.

I glanced at Percy, who shrugged. It was nearly noon on a weekday and school had been canceled for the remainder of the week due to the heat.

"Bank's closin' up for good!" he yelled to us, liquid spilling out of his jar and forming a puddle of mud in the dirt. What did that mean? What would this do for her family? How would we ever get new equipment or money for the new crop season?

"What are you saying, Mr. Williams?" Percy asked, his eyebrows knitting. His face was pulled together in concern, and I thought of Bethany and her fancy clothes. Thought of how her family had saved Percy's life and I couldn't help but feel sorry for Mr. Williams.

"I'm sayin'," he slurred, "*what I already told you.* Bank's closin'." He took another drink, streams dribbling out each side of his mouth and down his chin. "*Closed.* Closed for good." He stumbled away, leaving a trail of spilled liquid in the street.

"You think he's drunk?" I asked, a slow burn settling into my shoulder blades.

"Sure is, he's drinking corn whiskey, but…" He frowned and I could tell Percy was somewhere else entirely. "Let's get this in the truck before the sun spoils it all."

We made our way to the truck where he opened the box, his eyes glistening. "Take this," he said, handing me over a small package of burger, along with a few potatoes and onions. I didn't know what to say.

"I couldn't."

Truth is, I wanted to. I wanted it for Benny, who was getting skinnier by the day and for Ma who worried constantly.

Percy set the package in my hands, his skin brushing against mine, sending goosebumps up my arms. His eyes met mine, kind and gentle. "Please. Grandpops would want you to have it."

My heart melted and I couldn't help myself. I slid over, and before he could say anything, pressed my lips to his in a slow kiss.

When I pulled away, a surprised look crossed his face as he regarded me for a moment, his eyes locked on mine.

And then, as if deciding something, he pulled me toward him and kissed me urgently, his hands in my hair, chills running through my body.

When Pa came in for supper later that day, he slumped down heavily in the chair at the table.

"Is it true?" Ma asked, incredulously. "The bank's gone insolvent?"

Pa swallowed hard, shaking his head. Ma got up from the table and walked to the counter, her back to us and head hung low as her body shook with silent cries.

"Cawie!" Benny sang from his chair. "Cawie, Cawie."

"Quiet, Benny!" I snapped.

He froze, as if my words had slapped him across the face.

"I'm sorry, Benny, it's just…"

Too late. He'd already started crying.

I thought I might blow up into a million pieces. I felt horrible.

Goldie rolled her eyes up at me before laying her head back down. She didn't even beg anymore. There was nothing to beg for. How ironic that we'd switched places and I was the one begging now. I'd resorted to feeding her ground-up thistle, but could hardly stand to see the way her bones protruded from under her fur. I'd let her down.

"We'd be further ahead if we'd spent the past year sleeping," Pa said.

"Can we move back?" Ma's voice was tentative. *Move back?* In all the years we'd lived in Kansas, they'd never once talked about moving back.

"No use," he said. "Nothin' back there. Besides, times are as tough there as they are here."

I forked the fried-up onions and few pieces of rabbit on my plate that had been rationed out. I wanted to cry but felt too weak, as if my emotions were starving along with the rest of me.

Pa rubbed his temples, his hand calloused from years of work, covering his face as he tried to rid the stress from his head.

"We've got a few coins under the mattress," Ma offered. She wearily approached the table, composed, but her eyes were red and glassy.

"Best off holding tight to the little we have," Pa said. "Harder times are coming."

Despite how hungry I was, I no longer had an appetite and slipped bits of hamburger under the table, dropping them to the floor.

Harder times are coming. Harder times are coming.

It was a mantra I couldn't get out of my head. Words I could stomach no more than the food. I already thought we were in the thickest of hard times and couldn't imagine how it could get any worse.

CHAPTER 33

"Heraldson believes he can make it rain," Pa read from the paper he'd brought home from town. His voice was bleak, but a hint of optimism played in his eyes.

Ma tugged a sheet from the window, blinding the room with streaks of bright dust, giving the room a more cheerful appearance. Every morning she'd replace the dirty sheets with clean damp ones.

Pa then began to chuckle. Quietly at first, and then into an outright roaring laugh. I glanced to ma who shrugged and joined him.

I let my shoulders relax as I closed my eyes in the warmth of the sun.

"Says here, we should all bring raincoats and umbrellas." Pa skimmed the rest of the article quietly, mumbling the words to himself.

"Dear God," Ma started. "Do you think it's true?" She reached up to the corners of the window, abruptly cutting off my light source as she slipped a new sheet over the nails.

I opened my eyes.

"Worth a try," Pa said, folding up the paper. "Prayers ain't helping none."

The event was held a few blocks up from Main Street. Percy and Mr. Meyer were there by the time we arrived, waving us over to where they stood amongst several other families.

"Quite a turnout, ain't it?" Mr. Meyer said. "Folks crawlin' right outta the woodwork for this fella." He pulled a red handkerchief from his pocket and wiped the sheen off his forehead, soaking the cloth with dark wet spots. "Mighty hot one today."

"That it is," Pa said.

Percy grabbed my hand and pulled me away from them into the gathering crowd.

A rush swept through my body, and I briefly shifted my gaze to Ma to see if she'd noticed, grateful she was too busy spreading out the blanket she'd brought.

"You bring your umbrella, Mr. Meyer?" I raised my eyebrow.

Percy flashed me a mischievous smile and with a glance over my shoulder, pulled me in close to him, his lips landing on mine. With his arms wrapped protectively around my waist, he kissed me deeply before pulling away and regarding me with a cocky grin.

"You don't know how long I've been waiting to do that," he smirked. "And about the umbrella. We don't need one."

"You sure 'bout that?" I asked. "You seem overly confident. You got some weather credentials or something?"

"Nah," he said, shaking his head. "Just common sense. The man's a hype selling the buzz to whatever pushovers will buy it. I believe it about as much as the truth with dry farming to begin with. The ol' cattlemen are the ones they should be asking. Not these so-called weather experts. Doesn't take long for people to forget. Two generations and it's a distant memory."

I thought of the cattlemen from the late 1800s who'd lost most of their large herds to lack of grass to eat. Most of the locals knew about it, especially the old farmers. The problem was that most of the farms were now run by transplants who had followed the promise of easy money and new farming innovation techniques.

"Well, hopefully President Hoover can help us out," I offered.

"Hmph," he replied.

The murmur of voices was escalating, creating a buzz of energy. Several bystanders had filled the space between us and Ma, and now we were nearly shoulder to shoulder, making the heat that much more unbearable.

"You better watch it," I teased, pointing a finger at his chest. "You might just be cut out for politics."

"I'm offended," he scoffed. "Nothing but highbinder crooks who consider themselves the big cheese. They're in denial on who really runs their cities. Not the life for me."

"LADIES AND GENTLEMEN," boomed a voice. "PLEASE TAKE YOUR SEATS."

We made our way over to a fencepost to watch the spectacle unfold around us. I figured over a hundred people of all ages were there. All to witness the miracle of rain. The murmuring lowered to a few whispers as people settled onto their blankets, their umbrellas readily available in their laps.

I glanced to the sky. Not a cloud in sight.

"JUST AS THE EARLY TRAINS BROUGHT RAIN INTO THE GREAT PLAINS WITH THEIR DISRUPTION OF THE AIR WITH THEIR STEAM." The man in the black suit stretched his arms dramatically to the sky.

I nudged Percy, resisting the urge to give in to a giggling fit, but his eyes didn't waver from the speaker's face.

"I WILL ATTEMPT TO DISRUPT THE NATURAL STATE OF THE AIR AND PULL THE SUSPENDED WATER RIGHT OUT."

Murmurs grew louder and gave way to an eruption of clapping and hollering. I found Pa in the crowd, his face pulled together in both a mixture of curiosity and scrutiny of this man whom the papers had proclaimed as our last hope.

Heraldson's mustache was dark and groomed as if he'd just come from some kind of fancy barber shop in the city. Every so often he removed his hat to wipe the sweat from his forehead, his waxy hair gleaming under the sun. He dug his hand into a jar of jelly of some sort and smeared it onto the balloons that were tied to the post in front of him.

"NITROGLYCERINE JELLY!" he noted in exasperation.

A few of the younger men in the crowd nodded, while some of the other older men shook their heads as if they couldn't believe what they were seeing.

Percy leaned forward.

Within minutes, he released the balloons; a hundred or more pairs of eyes fixed on the seemingly ordinary spheres as they floated upward into a cloudless sky.

"NOW, FINE FOLK OF KANSAS, THIS IS THE MOMENT WE'VE ALL BEEN WAITING FOR." He pointed to a woman in the crowd. "I hope you didn't fuss too much with your hair today." He winked at her.

Percy rolled his eyes. "This chap's a proper ass."

All of a sudden, an explosion pierced the sky, followed by a high pitch shrill ringing in my ears. Instinctively, I clutched Percy's shoulder as the fence post I was leaning upon shook, sending vibrations up my arms and a booming in my chest. It was as if a heavy magnet had been suspended above us, rolling all of our eyes to the sky at once as we covered our ears.

"Dynamite!" Percy yelled, his voice distant beside me.

I wanted to believe in the method. I really did. With everything in me, I wanted to believe it would work.

But instead, the ground began to lift; clouds of dust rolling over the land and into the sky. I could hardly see my own hand in front of my face. People were coughing, choking on the thick cloud of particles that only moments ago we'd been walking on.

My throat went dry and scratchy as if being scoured with sheets of sandpaper. I gasped for air, drawing more dust into my already burning lungs. Percy jerked me away, his arm shielded over his mouth.

My heart lurched. We had to get out of here. Had to get Percy out of here.

People were frantically shoving their way through the crowd while pulling masks and wet cloths up over their mouths. Some were opening umbrellas against the shower of dirt that sprayed from the sky.

Another stick of dynamite boomed, and my heart felt as if it might burst.

Percy threw his arm protectively around me as particles peppered our hair. "LET'S GO!"

I hung onto him for dear life, his hands capable and steady, guiding me as I stumbled dumbly to where Ma and Pa were scrambling to gather their things. Dust enveloped us, browning the sky with unsettled dirt.

Ma hardly glanced up, her arms full of blankets and umbrellas while Pa carried Benny. "Can't create rain, but sure can create a dust storm awfully fast!"

Once we were safely in the truck, I turned to Percy. His dark eyebrows were light with dust, his cheeks streaked with dirt. "You okay?"

His shoulders dropped, his hands on the steering wheel as his eyes met mine. He was more handsome than ever. Dirt and all. His lips curved up into a smile and then, he was gut laughing. Honest to God, gut laughing.

"What a show!" he said.

We laughed for several minutes, and it felt good. Felt good to laugh away the worries and pressure of it all, our laughter rolling up into the air as easily as the ground had in this forsaken place.

Tears rolled down my cheeks. If bystanders had the chance to see us, I'm sure they'd have thought we were all out crazy. Maybe we were.

I brushed the dirt from my arms, my skin gritty and raw as I shook from the adrenaline surge. I glanced over at Percy, and my heart nearly stopped. His face had grown serious, as if he couldn't believe what he was seeing.

I scanned the area ahead of me. Nothing alarming. Just people scrambling to their vehicles.

"Percy?" I raised my voice, but his face was frozen, his mouth open as if he needed to say something but couldn't speak. "Percy!"

He jerked out of his trance and searched my face, his eyebrows furrowed. "Nothing," he said. "It's nothing." He slid the key into the ignition and roared the engine to life. "Just thought I'd seen a ghost. That's all."

It didn't look like nothing.

His face had froze, and I'd seen that look before when the storm came. My stomach churned. What had upset him so much? *Who* had upset him so much? The Percy I knew wasn't afraid of ghosts.

When Mr. Meyer jumped into the truck, he chattered the entire way home, but I was hardly listening. My mind was on Percy.

His face had paled as he gripped the steering wheel with white knuckles, glancing often in the rearview mirror. He dropped me off with a slight nod of his head and a measly, "Later, Carrie."

The celebratory dance that was scheduled for the onslaught of rain was permanently canceled and not a word spoken of it again. The only reminder of the event being our scratchy eyes and burning throats.

But I didn't care about any of these things.

The fear frozen on Percy's face had overshadowed any threat nature could've thrown at us.

CHAPTER 34

Percy and I became inseparable over that summer, spending most of our days together, exploring sand dunes, training Goldie or sometimes just sitting and talking.

In that season, as the life in the prairies died around us, something took root within the deepest hollows of my heart in a place I never knew was empty. He planted *meaning*, securely rooting me in this world and like an attentive gardener, he nurtured it with each smile and every kiss until its vines permeated throughout my body, choking out weeds of worry.

Our conversations were casual. I never questioned his past, even when I told stories of my own upbringing in Minnesota as he listened carefully and nodded, fully understanding the seasons that came with Midwest living.

I would often run errands with him around town, grateful to escape the void of life in the country. At least in town, there were people moving about and it was easier to pretend things were as they had always been.

"Where we off to today?" I asked as remnants of farmhouses began popping up in the fields, signaling our approach to town. I tried to imagine the brilliance of their existence when they were first built in contrast to the shambles they had since become.

"Henley's store." His eyes momentarily flicked to mine and then quickly back to the road.

"Why?" I asked.

A fleeting expression crossed his face. "Drop off milk."

That was Percy. It frustrated me to no end, but knew it wasn't worth nagging about, either. If he didn't want to talk about something, he wouldn't—unless it was on his terms.

Already the sun was descending, its last attempt of lighting the world blocked by buildings that cast long shadows and encroached upon us like spilled oil.

"It says it's closed," I said, reading the sign on the door as we approached.

He hesitated. "We're meeting him out back."

"Really?" Pa never met him out back. But then again, Pa usually didn't stop by and Ma only did when needing groceries, which never happened at eight at night.

Mr. Henley was heaving a bulky bag I presumed to be garbage into the metal can behind the store, placing the lid on it as he waved us over. Percy backed the truck up to the door.

"You can wait in here," he said to me, shoving the truck in park and turning off the key. "I'll only be a few minutes."

He abruptly jumped out of the truck, shutting the door behind him with a loud thud. Their conversation was muffled between the scraping of the crates as they slid the splintered boxes of milk from the bed of the truck and into the door which had been propped open with a rock. When all the crates were unloaded, Percy disappeared inside where I imagined him to be helping the older man put the milk into refrigeration.

As promised, minutes later he returned with a smile. "That was painless," he smirked. His mood had lightened.

"I want to show you something." He locked eyes with me, an intensity within them that set prickles on my skin.

"*Really*," I taunted. "And what's that?" I glanced away, the weight of his stare sending a jolt of electricity through my veins.

"You'll have to trust me," he said, fixing his eyes back on the road.

He drove until town became nothing more than small boxes on the horizon behind us, pressed between the vast emptiness of an inky black sky and the gray fullness of the ground and all that lay beneath it.

We drove in a comfortable silence, and when he slid his hand over and grasped mine, our eyes momentarily met and the world swirled around us.

Several miles later, we pulled into an area I'd never been. In the dark, mounded hills rolled into the shadows of the ground in gentle waves. My stomach tightened at the possibilities of what lay before me.

He turned the truck off and faced me in the darkness. "Ready?"

"Always."

Outside, the wind had died into a slight breeze. I imagined the sound to be like the ocean on still days, even though I'd never seen the shore. A blanket of stars shone upon us and when my eyes adjusted, I could easily make out Percy's shape from behind the bed of the truck.

He fumbled around with something and within moments, a soft glow illuminated from a lantern he held, its beam of light swaying back and forth, a rolled blanket tucked under his arm.

"Where are you taking me, Percy James?" I teased.

His eyes flashed in the light as he raised an eyebrow. "You'll see."

I followed him, grateful for the light as we climbed the height of a hill toward the stars. I clung to the back of his shirt, my legs struggling to gain footing. It was several minutes before we reached the top. I tried to catch my breath as he handed me the lantern and shook the blanket out onto the ground.

"This is the most beautiful thing I've ever seen," I said as I laid beside him on the blanket. In the solitude of the hills, it seemed wrong to raise my voice above anything other than a whisper.

"It's a sacred place." Percy's silhouette was turned to the veil of stars that had covered the sky in points of light. "A burial ground where the

Osage would send their loved ones to the next world by burying them in the sky."

I couldn't find words for many minutes as we lay there, small in the expanse of an endless sky. He slid his hand over and intertwined his fingers with mine. An intensity burned, a magnetic pull that clutched my stomach.

He pulled me close, his hands radiating heat as it sent electric pulses through my body. Our faces were inches apart as he regarded me for a moment, as if gauging whether to kiss me. My pulse raced even while I expected him to pull away.

He hesitantly brought my hand to his lips as if contemplating a decision. And then, before I could process what was happening, he pulled me into his arms, his solid chest pressing against mine as he slid me on top of him, the scent of his aftershave filling my senses and raising my body temperature.

Suddenly his lips were touching mine, soft and tender at first, and then more urgent. All at once, I released every worry and inhibition. I kissed his soft lips hungrily as his hands grasped my hips and then he wrapped his arms around me, the intensity almost too much to control.

I slid my hands under his shirt, sending goosebumps to his skin. The welts from the dust storm had resided, only slightly raised under my fingertips.

"Carrie," his husky voice slipped out between heavy breaths, sending a chill through my body.

I brushed his neck with my mouth, his body going rigid against my own.

"Carrie," he said breathlessly.

"Hmm?" I moved to the swell of his neck and his pulse quickened beneath my lips. His breath hitched as I fumbled with a button on his shirt.

"We can't," he muttered, but then his lips found mine again and his hands were buried in my hair.

I leaned into him, but he quickly kissed me one more time before sitting up.

What was wrong? What did I do?

Suddenly self-conscious, I ran my fingers through my hair as I tried to slow my breathing when he stood.

"It's getting late," he said, pulling me up to standing. "I need to get you home."

"Where were you, Carrie?" Pa asked. He was watching me, making me suddenly aware of how late it was. My mind raced.

"Running errands." I pulled my shoes off, placing them by the door, avoiding eye contact at all costs.

"With Percy?" he prodded.

"Yes," I said, retrieving a glass from the cupboard.

I rinsed off the dusty film before filling it halfway with water and gulping it down, the cool water an oasis for my parched throat and a shield from Pa's scrutiny. I didn't want to think about what had just happened. What started off so right, ended so wrong. When I turned to face him, Pa's face didn't express disappointment but a slight smile.

"I remember that age," he said. He shook his head, lost in some distant memory. "Just be responsible, and Carrie, remember how one choice can impact the rest of your life." He rubbed his temples in an effort of easing the tension from them, the creases in his forehead stretching and bunching.

"I will, Pa. I always do."

"Where'd you go?" he asked.

"Nowhere special, really," I said, choosing my words carefully. My heart raced at the thought of what our *errands* consisted of. "Percy needed to get something for Mr. Meyer at the hardware store. Something for the tractor."

Really, Carrie? Something for the tractor? I didn't even believe it.

"Oh, and Henley's," I quickly added. "To drop off milk."

"Hmph." Pa's eyebrows furrowed.

I sighed. My eyelids were heavy, and sleep was sneaking up on me. Tomorrow would be an early morning of helping Ma mend worn clothes. I just wanted my bed.

Pa stood and stretched. "I didn't realize Algott still had cows. Far as I knew, he'd sold them for the little bit of meat they had on em, which wasn't much. Couldn't even produce milk anymore."

My shoulders dropped with relief, thankful it was Pa who'd been drafted to wait up on my account and not Ma. I shrugged and walked to my room, leaving him to turn down the lights and lock the door.

All I could think about was climbing into bed and rehashing the last hour with Percy.

Percy.

The thought of him sent chills up my arms, even if he *was* confusing as hell. I hardly even noticed the tapping from within the walls as spiders and God knew what scuttled about.

I replayed the evening in my mind, but something hitched in my brain.

Percy liked me, didn't he?

Or at the least was attracted to me. But why did he pull away? My shoulders bunched into burning knots. Was it the guilt of Bethany?

I pushed the thought aside, refusing to let her screw up the memory, but the uneasy feeling lingered in my gut. I sifted through the details of the evening and my mind rested on Pa's words. Algott no longer had cows, which meant Percy didn't have milk to deliver to Mr. Henley. My stomach sank.

Percy had lied to me.

CHAPTER 35

Ididn't see Percy for the remainder of the week. I thought about asking Pa for a ride to his house to check up, but Pa was distant, always watching the skies or mumbling to himself. I didn't want to weigh him down with anything more than he was already carrying.

That Saturday morning, I awoke to Benny's footsteps thudding throughout the room.

"Benny," I moaned, covering my head with a pillow. "What time is it?"

"Lunchtime," he giggled. Benny was shaking me. "Wake up, Cawie!"

"I'm up, I'm up." I stretched as my eyes adjusted to the streams of light pouring through the window. Benny watched me, noisily crunching down on something.

A carrot?

"Where'd you get that?" I exclaimed, jumping out of bed. He ran away laughing.

Ma was whistling in the kitchen, pulling vegetables from a box on the table. Seeing the look on my face, she laughed. "Tomatoes!" she said, stating the obvious. "Can you believe this!"

She shook her head in disbelief, a smile plastered across her face. "Ladies' Aide dropped off a box of food. Pa won't be happy, but…"

I peered into the box, taking in a rainbow of fruits and vegetables.

"That's not all," she said, crossing to the countertop. "There's some meat, too."

Breakfast consisted of fresh eggs and greasy bacon (bacon!) with toast. Ma even gave a bit to Goldie who hardly tasted it as she gulped it down greedily. I couldn't wait to tell Percy when he came by later that afternoon.

"Hey stranger," I said to Percy when he got out of his truck.

He frowned, his expression holding something between agitation and insult until his eyes held mine and softened. "Sorry," he said, diverting eye contact. "Been busy."

I brushed it off, unable to stay frustrated long. Not when we hardly ever had time together.

"No matter. I have a surprise for you!" I took his hand and led him to the kitchen where I pulled an apple from the basket and tossed it to him.

"Ladies' Aide." I smiled.

He bit into it, closing his eyes as it sprayed juice into the air.

"Did they swing by your place?" I asked.

He hesitated. "Sure did." He searched my face instead. "Look Carrie, I need to talk to you about something, but I'd rather do it when I have more time."

My stomach tightened. *More time. More time.* There was never enough time in Percy's world. Least not for me.

Something had changed. The slightest shift, like a breeze in August, with just enough hint of fall that you could sense cold weather coming. I felt it, but didn't have the courage to face it. Not yet anyway.

He pecked a quick kiss on my forehead and turned to go. I wanted to grab him, to stop him from leaving, but couldn't bring my pride to do so.

Not yet.

As the months went by, more neighbors left town. Left it all. The house, the furniture, all of it. Most didn't even bother to lock the doors. Just packed up whatever they could fit in their jalopies and hauled off to California, with not much more than hope. Hope to find food, find work, find another shot at life. If it weren't for Percy being here, I'd be tempted to do the same.

According to the papers, nearly 28,000 businesses had already failed, along with over 2,200 banks, our own little local one included. It didn't seem possible that our branch bank could even be connected to those big ones you see in the papers, but I guess it's so. Seemed the entire nation was bleeding money. Papers ran cartoons with pictures of snakes labeled as the "Banking System" wrapped around farmer's necks.

I went out to the shed one day to look for Pa. The door slid heavily across the metal track as I pulled with most my weight. When the sunlight spilled into the building, I couldn't believe my eyes. For the first time since I remember, the place was empty. Not a thing in it outside of the tins of oil and cloths.

That evening, I'd never seen Pa so dismal at supper. I hated to even ask.

"The shed…"

"Sold it all, Carrie," he replied, without so much as looking up from his plate of food.

I shook my head in disbelief. Ma reached her arm across the table and placed her hand on his. He abruptly got up and went outside, leaving his food untouched.

I couldn't decide whether to like the system, which had loaned us the money for all the equipment in the golden years or despise it for taking it all back and selling it for much less. In the end, I guess it was never ours to begin with.

The land was moody, spitting dust at us in hot breaths that made wearing our masks a necessity. A vast emptiness filled the fields. Dust storms would roll in, howling and causing all kinds of noise, but after the howling of the wind stopped came the worst kind of silence. The deafening, thick kind that spilled into every crevice.

Please God, I pleaded, looking to the sky. *I know I haven't been the best Christian, but please save us.* I was desperate enough to give prayer a shot. For the sake of my Pa. Too many farmers had hanged themselves and I couldn't take it if mine became one of 'em.

Nonetheless, the skies were a bleak gray, not with the promise of rain, but with sand that could choke the life right out of you at any minute.

I searched the vast expanse of land that had once been a lush field against blue skies. It was land that would sustain us, even as the stock market was crashing. The land, when treated right, was reliable or so I was told. More reliable than placing borrowed money you never touched into places in the market you never saw or knew existed.

But Pa was wrong. They all were. Either that, or they disregarded the probability that the land would rebel when not treated right.

And that's just what it did.

Most things I could deal with. A few spiders. Garden snakes. A bat every once in a while. The bugs, I couldn't.

Bugs I'd never laid eyes on in all my years of living here, joined the many spiders that had built residences within our walls, slipping through the cracks and skittering across our floors and walls. It was as if they had been waiting beneath the ground.

It was during the nights when I was lying in bed, drifting off to thoughts of Percy and what our future might hold together.

It was faint at first, just above my head. I thought it was my imagination playing tricks on me. But as I lay there, the scratching got louder.

I squeezed my blanket and held my breath, straining to hear. It came again, a collective scratching from within my bedroom wall as if a wild animal was desperately trying to get out. Only it wasn't the typical mouse sounds, but hundreds, maybe even thousands of tiny things.

I jerked the covers off and lit the kerosene lamp, pulling it to my bed as I inspected the wall.

Nothing.

But all night long, there was the sliding and tapping of legs crawling and slithering between the thin wood planks of wood. I couldn't see them, but I could feel their bodies tickling my arms. Thousands of pointy legs dragging their writhing bodies across the surface of my skin. I rubbed my arms and legs until my flesh was raw, but nothing was there. They're all within the walls, invading my mind through my ears.

I refused to sleep with my head near the wall, only inches away from the centipedes, spiders or anything else contained by the thin sheet of wood that separated my body from theirs.

Benny, on the other hand, embraced the creatures like newly found friends. One morning, I caught sight of him playing with something on the floor.

"What you got there?" I peered over and stopped dead in my tracks, my heart thudding as a chill radiated up my legs.

Percy's legs were spread out in a makeshift fence for a black army of centipedes. Every direction they squirmed, their multitudes of legs frantically pulling their bodies across the dusty floor.

From then on, they were everywhere, as if invited.

In the walls, on the floors, up the walls.

Ma said we should be thankful we didn't have Black Widows like those in town. She told me of kids who had to routinely check their beds for them. And to think, it couldn't be worse.

I have to get out.

I have become claustrophobic in this life. I didn't want the farm. Didn't want to live in this place. I wanted to run away and never look back. I thought I might go crazy within the confines of these four walls in this empty place of dirt.

Percy was my only hope and I wasn't even sure if he loved me enough to provide an escape.

CHAPTER 36

"Carrie!" Ma called from the back room. "Get the door!"

I pulled my hands from the little bit of water we had for soaking dry beans and dried them on a towel. The thought of beans and wheat porridge for another lunch was nearly unbearable, but I reminded myself how fortunate we were to have food at all.

Someone tapped again from the front door.

Not many people came by this way. Too much gas to get out here and not many could afford it. Heck, even school had been canceled several months prior. Teachers could only get by on so many I-owe-yous before needing some other means.

Percy. My heart raced and I pinched my cheeks.

I pulled the door open and my shoulders dropped. The wrinkled faces of two women peered back at us, goggles around their necks.

"We're with Ladies' Aid," the woman with silver, curly hair announced.

"We're here to offer help," said the other woman gingerly.

Ma eyed me and I shrugged.

Pa, who had been out back, came way to the front door. "Can I help you?" he asked.

It was the first time we'd been home when they dropped off the food boxes. The women repeated themselves, diverting their attention to Pa.

I held my breath.

His face registered aggravation. "We appreciate you coming out all this way," he said, "but we don't need any help."

The silver haired lady threw the other one a hesitant glance. "We understand, sir," she said.

Ma's body went rigid as she stood beside me. We wanted help. We needed food. I could hardly feed Goldie anything besides ground up tumbleweed.

"We're going to all the areas. This drought got people all around lacking in—"

"Ain't no drought," Pa said, pulling his straw hat from the hook by the door and slipping it on his head. "Just a dry spell. Give it time, it'll turn around."

For the longest minute of my life, no one spoke as Pa slipped past them to the shed. Ma shifted uncomfortably.

"Thank you for comin' on out here," she said. "It's very thoughtful." She pulled the door closed with a deep sigh, the house going dark and cool, her hand lingering on the door handle.

An engine mumbled to life outside.

They couldn't go! We'd starve!

My heart pumped loudly in my chest, flooding my veins with a bursting pressure. *Food.* All I could think about was food.

Whether it was survival instincts or just plain desperation, I threw the door open and scanned the yard, squinting my eyes against the blinding sun. The women were gone.

I ran to the end of the drive, my cotton dress scooping the pillows of air that tried to hold me back. The car of food must've been forty, no, fifty yards ahead of me, rolling slowly down the sand-blown road.

Dear God, please don't let Pa see me.

I doubled down. My legs burning from the energy I used.

I had to catch that car.

Through the brown cloud of dust, there was a faint flicker of red lights and the screech of sliding gravel. The dust settled, making the car visible as it stopped in its tracks.

The silver haired woman was driving. She cautiously peered out the window and met my gaze. My face must've held some kind of desperation. Enough to get that woman out of the car and send her walking toward me through the dust. Dust that was clinging to my slick skin, caking the perspiration to the pores.

"Excuse me," I called out. What should I say? I'm scared of starving? We were losing everything? The fields weren't producing?

"It's okay, dear," the woman said, somehow reading my mind. "We're here to help. No use being ashamed. The depression has hit nearly everyone in some way. This drought hasn't helped."

I cringed at the word *drought,* as if it were some kind of curse word and glanced over my shoulder to be sure Pa hadn't caught sight of me.

"We have a few things," she said, reaching into the trunk of the car and pulling out a box. "Not much, but enough to go around."

She placed a heavy box in my arms, the glorious weight of canned peaches and corn, a bag of flour and sugar. *Sugar!*

Aware of the half-cocked smile on my face, the woman let out a small laugh.

"Bootleggers," she affirmed. "Sheriff kept all the sugar he confiscated and gave it to Ladies' Aid Society and the American Legion for distribution."

"Thank you," I said, my voice a sigh of relief.

The words weren't enough; didn't equal the weight of the food. I could hardly keep the tears from starting.

"You've all done so much. Last time, we ate nearly everything within a couple of days," I added sheepishly.

A look of confusion momentarily crossed the woman's face.

"There must be some misunderstanding, dear," she said, her face smoothing into a smile again. "We began delivering this week."

I thought about her words as I advanced to the house, balancing the weight of the produce in my arms as I cast glances toward the shed.

Ma didn't say a word, but hugged me and took the box. She swiftly unpacked everything, concealing the items within the bottom cupboard where Pa wouldn't see.

That night, I lay in bed, full enough to not dream of food. Ma had made toast with Kansas gravy made of paste with flour, water, salt and pepper. She was discreet in mixing up the overlooked ingredients and if Pa noticed, he didn't say so.

With my stomach fuller than it had been in weeks, my thoughts drifted past food and settled on Percy once again. His smile, his dimples, his unruly golden hair. His image warmed my insides like an inviting campfire.

Pa was too prideful to talk about the boxes of food when they mysteriously showed up each of the three times in the past two months. His livelihood had been stripped away and it hurt him to not be able to provide for his family. He had always told me, 'you take away a person's livelihood and pride, there's not much left to his soul.'

I really hoped President Roosevelt would follow through on the Public Works Program everyone was talking about. Something needed to happen soon or we'd all starve to death like the animals had long ago.

Percy stretched the width between his visits.

He'd hardly kissed me in weeks. Everything seemed to be vanishing, like grains of sand through an hourglass, so slightly that I didn't notice but could feel my life slipping slowly through my fingertips.

I'd see a glance of worry over his shoulder while walking through town—as if someone might see us together. A hesitation in his voice when asking about future plans. Or a sort of sadness in his eyes when looking at me.

And in the depths of my soul, I knew something was dying as fall leaves did just when they were most brilliant. Unexpected. A leaf here and there until before you knew it, the entire tree was bare and vulnerable as the harsh cold took over.

I knew in my heart it had to be Bethany.

"They're still holding the dance this spring," I said one day, while sitting in his truck. I held my breath, waiting for his excuse to come, testing his commitment, but not wanting to accept the confirmation of it.

He gripped the steering wheel with white knuckles and his face held the weight of the world.

"Percy, what's going on?" I asked gently.

"Nothing," he said, his eyes fixated on the road. He sighed and glanced over, forcing a weak smile.

"Then tell me what I did wrong."

My voice came out pleading and whiny. I pushed on. I needed to know. "Why are you pushing me off? Avoiding me?"

An unsettled look crossed his face. "What do you mean? I ain't got no beef with you."

"You're evasive. You aren't around." I took a deep breath, studying his face. "Is there someone else?"

I exhaled. I'd gifted him with an opening. A chance to tell me the truth.

"You savvy? Carrie, I…" His eyes flicked to mine, a burning intensity in them. *Tortured.*

I regretted my words immediately but waited for him to pull over and grab me as he'd done before.

"I can't do this right now," he said evenly. His face was unreadable and cold.

My heart sank and nausea seeped into my stomach. *How dare he?* I wanted to scream at him and demand the truth, but my breath hitched in my throat and threatened to choke me if I tried to utter a word. Pride.

Instead, we drove in silence until he dropped me off with a slight wave and a "see you tomorrow."

My heart had become a million-pound anchor and was sinking, making it devastatingly clear.

He was about to break it.

CHAPTER 37

Of all the changes happening around me, I'd be foolish to say they didn't pierce my heart the way Percy could, my internal world as fragile as that around me and its consequences just as devastating.

When Percy came by, I knew something was wrong. He was nearly impossible to read—as if there were two sides to him. The charismatic, spontaneously impulsive side that would grab me in his arms and make me feel as if I was the most important woman in the world to him.

But then, there was his other side.

The one he brought today. *Distant. Secretive.* Making me feel like a fool for ever believing he could like me, knowing he was sweet on another girl and probably playing me. Something was building and I was scared to discover what it was.

"Got your costume?" I smirked, attempting to lift the mood between us. I already had my goggles around my neck and a couple of wet rags for our mouths.

A smile slipped through his pursed lips.

I shifted uncomfortably.

"I brought a bag for tumbleweed, too." I stretched my neck. "For Goldie."

"Let's breeze then." He alleviated me from the weight of the bag before walking ahead of me.

The air was hot, sucking any moisture it could from the cracked earth. Already, my forehead burned from the sun.

"Think we'll find any arrowheads?" I asked, trying to make casual conversation. It wasn't uncommon to find all kinds of treasures in the dunes. Last time, we found an old wagon wheel Percy had turned into a tire swing for Benny. But our biggest goal was to discover blown over arrowheads from the time when the Comanche had run wild over a field of plains, through fields of blue buffalo grass in pursuit of the bison that ate heartily on the deeply-rooted plants. We hadn't found any yet, but there were stories of others stumbling across them while mending fences.

Today wasn't about the arrowheads, though, but spending time with Percy.

"Hard to say," he replied. "There's a few dunes I've been wanting to check over by where the Cimarron used to flow."

Unease settled in my stomach. I don't know why, but something was nagging at me. We walked a few strides in silence, the air thick between us.

"Pa says there's a new federal program brewing." When he didn't reply, I went on. "They're paying for any healthy farm animal to be slaughtered and canned for families who need food. Including horses."

He snorted. "Well, a little late. A government agent stopped by not long back," he said. "Deemed the two cows we had as unfit and paid a buck a head. Couldn't produce milk anymore and were skin and bones. Hell, they cut them wide open and guess what they found in their stomach cavities?"

He blinked hard, his eyes brimming with defeat. *"Sand."*

The thought sunk in. God knew how much sand they'd all inhaled, despite the masks and precautions. I swept the thought away, the root of too much anxiety already.

"Grandpops bargained with 'em and they paid a little. Sure, cattle-kills take care of the overstock, but the rising prices don't help anybody when people can't afford to buy the meat to begin with, canned or not."

His face was unreadable, his jaw set. My heart knew this conversation, his hostility wasn't about the economy.

"Percy, look." I rubbed my temples in effort of alleviating the headache that was brewing. "I know it's me. I've felt it a while now. If you don't want to be with me, just tell me."

He abruptly stopped, searching my face. His expression softened. "Is that what you think?"

I diverted my gaze, unable to choke out the words in fear of breaking down.

"Carrie." His eyes narrowed in concern. "I don't want to hurt you. I just…" His shoulders dropped. "Can't be with you."

I let out a breath I didn't know I'd been holding. Holding for quite some time. My shoulders burned. It sliced into my stomach, my heart, anything and everything within me, hurting worse than losing everything. The tractors, the new shiny car, things bought on credit during the good times. Nothing could cut like Percy's words.

"I don't want to hurt you," he repeated, a tortured look in his eyes.

Heat flushed my cheeks. My head throbbed. "I can see that."

My words came out sarcastic, but I didn't care anymore. I was tired of this game. His eyes fixated on me. I wanted to run away. He was a great actor. So good in fact, I almost believed he wasn't like all those city boys I'd been warned about.

"Is it Bethany?" I demanded.

The muscle in his jaw bulged, but he didn't answer.

"Why?" The question came out as a near scream. It had been building for some time now. Tension thick as pudding.

He rubbed his temples. "I can't, Carrie. It's not fair to you *or her*, and I don't want to hurt either of you."

My heart stopped. I knew it.

"I'm going home." I turned away before he could see the tears welling up in my eyes.

"Carrie, wait," he said, reaching out to stop me.

"*Without* you." I jerked away, stomping off toward the house. "Good luck finding those arrowheads!" I called over my shoulder as he watched on in bewilderment. "I'm sure *Bethany* will *love* them!"

Tears streamed down my cheeks and I dared not turn around. How dare he? Didn't I at least deserve to know why?

Trying to figure him out was like trying to put together one of those jigsaw puzzles, but without a larger picture to go by. Every now and then, I'd take a piece and examine it closely, holding it up to the light and comparing it to the rest.

One minute he was a constant in my life, helping out on the farm, going treasure hunting, leaning in for quick kisses behind the dunes. The next minute, he was distant and cold, avoiding me for days at a time.

His relationship with his parents was strained. That I had gathered.

"You've got a good family, you know," he'd told me one day. It was just like Percy to throw out some wise comment, as if he were much older than he was. I laughed.

"It's true. Your pop's one of the good ones. Honorable. Patient. *Loyal.*" A hint of sadness had been in his voice. He had stuck a blade of grass in his mouth, gazing at some point in the horizon as if lost in a memory.

I had thought of my pa in comparison with his own family, though I didn't know much about them. Surely my father had never spoiled my mother with the riches of finer things as his father had. In the one photo I'd seen of them, his mother wore a dark flapper dress, stockings and a stylish hat, a feather boa wrapped casually around her neck as if an afterthought. His father wore a suit and top hat, a cigar in his mouth.

Clearly, they once had money. Times had to be good then, didn't they?

I tried to imagine living a life like that, so far from the dusty sweat of farming, and sewing our clothes from whatever material Ma could salvage. I imagined his father gifting his wife with jewelry they had seen through the clean windows of a shop on the streets of Chicago, the bright lights reflecting off the glass.

What would my life had been like had I been born there? Or, even if we'd stayed in Minnesota?

Ma didn't own any jewelry. Not much anyway. Just a simple wedding band that was once my grandmother's and a locket that had been passed through the generations from a great, great grandmother who came here by boat, nine children in tow, from Norway. He'd never given her much for luxury outside of our stove and refrigerator during the agricultural boom. Even those were bought used from the downtown appliance store.

"Your father has a good work ethic," I reminded him, from that first conversation at our table over a year ago.

"So I thought, from all the hours he was gone from home," he said, his voice turning cold. "Turns out, he just had a floozie on the side."

It took me by surprise. Not that his father was a cheat, but that Percy had actually opened the door to his past life, if even just a sliver.

"My relationship with my father growing up seems similar to yours," I had said. "Didn't you go see some ball games with your dad?" I thought of all the times Pa and I had played checkers or ran errands together, just the two of us.

Percy and I had been laying on our backs, watching the clouds slide across the blue sky like sheaths of billowy smoke. He had turned to face me, propping his chin onto his hand.

"Some, yes."

"Did you talk to him?" It came out sounding ridiculous. Of course he talked to his dad. "I mean, did he *listen* to you when you talked to him? Ever give you advice?"

He thought about this for a minute before carefully answering. "I suppose we bumped gums a little during the game."

"You know, a man can be a lousy husband but a good father. Seems inconsiderate to judge him any other way."

For a few minutes, we had said nothing, both lost in our own thoughts as he seemed to take in what I was saying—as if considering it for the first time.

"Tell me about the Chicago nightlife," I had finally said, trying to change the topic to something lighter.

Percy had laughed. "Carrie, I've told you. It's a lot like Minnesota. Cold in the winters, hot in the summers besides the breeze coming off from Lake Michigan."

"No, I mean the city itself."

He let out a sigh. "Well, to be honest, it's dirty. It's industrial. There's new factories and stores going up all the time." He had sensed my disappointment. "But, there's another side of it too, I guess. A side with speakeasies where stages rise from the floor while some canary played piano on it and sang to a brass jazz band.

"Many of the people there try to be hotsy-totsy like the starlets on the silver screens—Rita Hayworth, Joan Crawford, Greta Garbo— wearing their glad rags to clubs and hitting on all eight.

"Little New York is what they call it. But the people, Carrie," he had said, gazing into my eyes, "they're nothing like you."

A shot of pain had stung my heart as I thought of my old wardrobe. Absentmindedly, I ran a hand over my worn dress.

"That's a compliment," Percy said, grabbing my hand and pulling it to his lips. "Why can't you see how beautiful you are?"

My cheeks grew hot as his lips brushed my skin.

"So many pushovers trying so hard to be someone they're not. They got ice and oyster fruit around their necks and fingers and it's still not enough. It's never enough. The lights, the buzz, the constant purchasing," he shook his head in disgust. "Carrie, living here in this place this past year has been the best part of my life." He paused. "*You've* been the best part of my life."

Without warning, he had leaned in and kissed me deeply, without any care or concern that someone may have been watching. The world around me melted away as he pulled me in closer, heat radiating from his chest. He was all I needed in that moment. In all my moments.

Yes, I had the edges of the puzzle put together, a border of a mysterious picture I couldn't see. Edges that had been softened and smoothed with wear were easy to piece together. But there were too many middle pieces missing for me to even possibly make sense of the larger picture I was gathering about Percy James.

"I'm going to town," Pa announced after a late lunch. "Have to pick up some oil."

"I'll go," I said, slipping on my shoes. The walls of the house were closing in on me, squeezing the air out of the space between them, with Percy's lies growing bigger than the love he had for me. I wanted to scream. I wanted to sob. I was too numb to do either.

We took the usual route to town so Pa could assess the fields, something he'd done since before I could remember. His face was strained and every so often he'd sigh or shake his head. We drove in silence, each lost in our own thoughts.

Percy didn't love me anymore. Maybe he never had. It was a gut punch to my being and I regretted ever knowing him. I couldn't stomach conversation and the mundane of daily life. Chores and tasks of the simplest nature had become insurmountable mountains.

Bethany's house came into view.

Don't look. Don't look.

The ground fell out from under me; a hurricane of emotions thrashing every bit of anxiety and desperation harbored in my heart, leaving wreckage in its wake. My gut told me not to look, but I couldn't resist.

I'd passed it a million times in my life and knew it by heart. The gray siding, the blue shutters, now peeling and flaking into the dirt like everyone else's. The white lamp post by the door, always painted a bright white as if they had an endless supply of paint. The entire house was fading into the horizon, but there stood the beacon of hope and prosperity in the damned white lamp post.

A figure emerged from the backyard. An invisible force squeezed my stomach.

A shadow in the dusk. Maybe my eyes were playing tricks on me, but my heart knew even before my mind did. Bethany was sneaking in another boy. It wasn't the first time. She knew how to get their attention and had stakes on most chaps in town.

Only this time, I knew who it was. His hat was unmistakable.

I couldn't pull my eyes away.

All at once, every suspicion living within me slit the veins of any hope for a future.

How long?

How long had he been toying with me? Tears stung as my heart shattered into a million jagged pieces, shards of glass cutting my insides and setting my skin on fire.

"Carrie?" Pa was watching me. "You okay?" His voice echoed from somewhere outside my head. "What is it?"

I couldn't answer. Couldn't breathe.

He glanced in his mirror in an effort of catching what had made me so distraught.

But Percy was already gone.

CHAPTER 38

Someone was knocking at the front door the next morning. I checked my face in the mirror. My eyes were swollen and red, my skin blotchy. I pulled the hair off my shoulders and yanked it into a ponytail just to rip it out again. I decidedly threw my hair up when the knocking rattled out again, this time more urgently.

My gut twisted. I sucked in a deep breath and pulled the door open.

Mr. Meyer stood there with his hat in his hands, his eyes droopy and rimmed with wrinkles; his broad shoulders slumped over as if his hat weighed more than he could manage to hold.

"Mr. Meyer." My voice was weak, but all I could muster.

"Good day, Carrie," he said, his eyes falling to the ground. He fumbled with his hat, an uncomfortable silence coming between us. My stomach lurched. I was going to be sick. He was apologizing for Percy. I glanced over his shoulder, but Percy wasn't even man enough to show up and own his decision. I grit my teeth, my jaw aching, waiting.

"He's gone," he said slowly, the lines creasing between his eyes.

What did he mean *gone?* My breath hitched in my throat.

"Percy? Gone where?"

My head throbbed and I didn't care anymore. I just wanted to crawl back to my hole.

"I'm afraid I have no idea, Carrie," he sighed. "Can I come in?"

I stepped aside.

"Everything okay?" Ma asked, coming in from the back room and pulling out a chair for him. Benny yelled out from the bedroom as I imagined him slamming his toy car into the wall in a mock collision.

"I'm afraid not," the old man said, placing his straw hat on the table, exposing thin wisps of what was left of his hair.

I couldn't breathe and could hardly hear him over the beating of my heart.

"Percy left," he said.

"Left?" Ma asked, raising her eyebrows. "To where? Home?"

"Not sure," he said. "Just left a note that he was leaving. Didn't say where. Said not to worry." He shook his head, rubbing the stubble on his face. "Said he'd write when he could."

"Have you spoken with his folks?" Ma asked.

"They haven't heard from him. Of course, they're sick with worry. We were hoping Carrie might know something."

They shifted their eyes to me, but my lips quivered and all I could do was shrug. I ran my fingers through my hair to keep them from trembling.

Pa came in and Mr. Meyer rehashed what he'd told us.

"Maybe he got sick of the suffering and headed south," he suggested. And then their conversation turned to mumbling just beneath the buzzing in my ears.

The idea hurt. *It was me.* I'd pushed him too far. I wasn't enough for him to stay in this desolate place. Did he leave with Bethany? Were they running away together to avoid watching me suffer, along with so many other things in this place?

"Who would they be from?" Ma's voice was distant and my ears pricked as I strived to rejoin the conversation. "Where on earth would they get them? Who could afford them?"

Ma turned to me. "Carrie? Do you know?"

"Know what?" I asked, not quite grasping what she was asking me.

"Who would send Percy such an expensive floral arrangement?"

CHAPTER 39

*W**hy?*

I couldn't wrap my head around it. He'd been pulling away, a broken dam dislodged and scattered as it swept down the river, just out of reach. Was it me? In the depths of my heart, I knew the answer.

He'd left intentionally with his grandpop's old truck. No good-bye. Just gone. How could someone so protective of my feelings suddenly vanish without any regard for how it would devastate me?

I knew three days in he wouldn't be back.

People who'd left this hellhole never returned and I wasn't enough to make him stay. Not in this place anyway. Maybe in California or who knows where, even back home in Minnesota where dirt didn't constantly fill the sky. But not here in this place.

"Sorry, Carrie," Pa said, resting his hand on my shoulder. He'd just come back from Mr. Meyer's place.

I blinked hard, squeezing back the tears.

"It's not you," Pa said. "No one's heard from him. Not even his parents. Times are tough. You can't blame him for leaving without much to inherit here."

"Not much to inherit?" I jerked away from him. "What? Like two hundred acres of barren dirt?"

It was as if I'd slapped him across the face.

"Carrie!" Ma scolded, her eyes murderous. "You do NOT talk to your father like that!"

I'd crossed a line, but now that the words had violently escaped, there was no taking them back as they lingered in the air between us.

"Pa, I…"

He held his hand up to silence me, his shoulders humped over as he trudged his way outside.

"Ma," I pleaded, my eyes brimming with tears, blurring her body into a puddle of blue as she turned her back on me.

"Do you even know how hard this has been on your father?" Her voice wavered. "He doesn't even have the little luxury of complaining. He just tries and tries and tries. For *what,* Carrie?" she sniffled. "For YOU! For this family."

Tears spilled down my face. Not only had I hurt Pa, but I'd hurt her, too.

"We might not be wealthy and you might be embarrassed by us, but you have a father who loves you. *You* are his wealth. This family…" She sighed. "If that's not enough, then shame on you."

Despite my hunger, I couldn't eat for several days. An oppressive darkness occupied the house, pressing heavy on our shoulders.

My heart ached.

I missed the way we were before the skies started eroding our pride. I tried to ease into neutral territory with Pa through small talk, but he dismissed himself early from the table nearly every time.

The overabundance of cruel words I'd said to him outweighed the lack of words I'd said to Percy. I never told Percy the things I meant to say. How he was everything good in this world. Minnesota snow on Christmas morning. The smell of pine after rain in the woods up north.

He had detoured my life to a scenic road of still waters and a sun that slipped from the sky and melted into the horizon in an explosion of colors. His presence had become the starting point and destination to any relevance in my life.

And for the weight of his existence, his absence was an empty depth on starless nights.

He was gone.

He'd abandoned us while Pa stayed and fought.

But as furious as I was with Percy's betrayal, I'd give anything to have him back. My cruel words had been used on the wrong person. I knew that now.

PART III

1932

CHAPTER 40

Percy

Ileft in the middle of the night.

Driving Grandpop's old truck, I resisted the temptation to check the rearview mirror. Glance, but don't stare is what people say. I'd done too much looking over my shoulder the last few months and it was time to leave the past in the dust and keep my eyes fixed south.

I turned out of Bethany's driveway, guilt rushing my body. As the truck belched up Kansas dirt, thoughts of Carrie crept into my mind. Not necessarily memories, but glimpses of her. I imagined the look of disappointment on her face when she'd found out I'd left. Knowing I had caused that pain stabbed me in the heart.

Lies.

It was the only way to protect her. To spare her the pain of knowing my involvement with Bethany.

I should've told her in the beginning to save her the heartache of betrayal later. Bethany had known the terms of our relationship from the start, but the timing never seemed right to discuss it with Carrie. I never planned on getting close enough to care.

Had she known my background, she would've been more careful. Would've expected it even. But the way she looked at me and hung on every word as if she was truly interested in whatever stupid thing I was about to say... She believed in me like no one had before. Enough to make me believe I could be a better person...to make me *want* to be a better person. Selfishly, I sucked it in like a fish in water until my heart betrayed me.

The glow of my headlights softly lit the road in small stretches, a dim cone of light cutting through the engulfing shadows of the dark prairie. It was a road I knew by heart and without animals to intersect the vehicle, there weren't any threats to divert my attention from the sickening feeling that bubbled in the pit of my stomach.

Guilt that had been lying dormant at the bottom of my gut, now erupted, searing into every tendon and muscle in my body. I rubbed my shoulder in an attempt at easing some of the burning tension.

There I was, not much better than my father. Keeping Carrie in the dark to avoid hurting her the way my father's lies hurt my mother. The thought of disappointing her were razor blades to my flesh.

And my feelings for her? I hadn't planned on that. It scared the shit out of me. My parents claimed to have loved each other at some point. But had they? Before the charade of their marriage?

Either way, no matter how I molded or twisted the situation in my mind, it always came down to the simple truth that there was no other way than to lie. It was a double-edged sword that kept them safe. And I'd rather have the blade to my neck at the expense of my reputation than have the blade to theirs in knowing.

My first stop was the grocery store. As always, Mr. Harrison was punctual, beckoning me through the store to a private room in the back where dusty crates were stacked half-hazardly in the corner, his desk overrun by piles of papers and envelopes. He didn't say much. Never did. Just pulled a key from the chain he wore around his neck and unlocked one of the desk drawers, sliding it open with a screech of the scrape of wood.

He nodded as he quietly handed me the envelope and thanked me for my help. I didn't count the cash until I got to the truck and after thumbing through the dollar bills, made my way to the gas station.

I saw her in every stretch of mile on the way to Santa Ana, marked by nameless faces of children, fathers and mothers who held up signs reading *Will work for food.*

Leaving was pruning a tree you had planted and watched grow as you tenderly watered and fertilized it, standing in awe of its massive beauty. I'd severed those closest to me. Grandpops. Carrie. Her parents. Bethany.

Well, there's nothing quite like the sweet sickening smell of death to jerk you to your senses.

Gardenias.

He'd found me.

I had come home, anticipating seeing Grandpops in his tattered twill chair, a newspaper tucked beside him as he snored. I didn't even make it through the door. I smelled them before I saw them.

If Big Al didn't take me out, a goddamned heart attack sure would.

Gardenias.

My past had finally caught up with me. I now knew how Lefty had felt the day I'd placed the bouquet in his office. The bouquet I had ordered. The reason it was ordered in the first place. I was so young and eager to prove myself. Just a foolish kid.

I had promised myself to never chase fast, easy money again. But that was before I'd met Carrie. Nothing can ever prepare a person for the agony of watching someone you love die a slow death. I couldn't do it. I goddamned couldn't do it. So, a seed of a thought turned into a simple decision I still don't regret.

Willy wasn't hard to find; hell, he'd probably never leave Chicago. He connected me with Dudley and the southern bootlegging circle who'd been running strong since I'd left on good terms with Big Al. As much faith as these farmers put in the fields and the skies, I put on liquor. People's demand for it was always reliable and much more predictable than the dusty fields of Kansas or the skies that pressed down upon them.

No, I wouldn't watch them starve or die on account of me and my mistakes. I'd rather have Carrie hate me and live, than love me and die.

And so it began.

I summoned my dead past and once again, became a runner for Big Al's Enterprise. Smuggling and running whiskey by night allowed me to make enough money to slip boxes of food onto Carrie's doorstep by morning. Grandpops', too.

But, as economics went, the cost of fruit and vegetables was high with demand and in order to feed them all consistently, it required a little skimming off the top. I knew I'd be sniffed out for squeezing it. I knew it wouldn't take long. I knew the risk.

And with pruning a tree, yes, the limbs suffered, but in the end, it is for the strength of the tree.

CHAPTER 41

As I drove south on Route 66, the air became too thick to breathe, settling on my skin in a thin veil of stickiness. I stopped checking my mirror for Big Al's droppers, looking to blip me off into the big deep sleep, after driving over a day without any sign of them. The muscles in my shoulders began to relax and I started noticing things around me instead of looking back. I'd been to the slummiest dives in Chicago and still, they didn't compare to this.

Shantytowns and squatter camps were scattered on either side of the road, their cloth sides flapping in the wind while kids chased each other around in the dirt, their parents perched wearily on barrels or crates, their bodies humped over like sacks of flour.

The tents were temporary, provided by the California Relief Administration, and locals were not as welcoming to the millions of bindle punks who'd settled there. *Okies & Negroes Not Allowed* was a common sign that decorated many of the businesses I passed, even as local sharecroppers promised wages for sixteen hours a day of work, seven days a week, picking grapes, plums, peaches, potatoes, lettuce, or whatever crop they had.

I settled on a government camp just outside of Santa Ana, set up by the Farm Security Administration for migrant workers. It was a dollar a week to stay, but it offered hot showers, toilets, and a place to lay my head. Hell, they even had their own school and ball diamond. Breakfast was a penny a day.

Breakfast.

Something so simple and yet held so much. Had I not lost everything that mattered to me in my life, I might've been overjoyed. Or optimistic to say the least. But all I could do was think about how Carrie and Grandpops must be feeling.

With everything in me, I wished things could have turned out differently. But as life often goes, fate disagreed with my plans, as well-laid out as they were, putting me behind the eight ball. So there I was, nearly homeless, but grateful for whatever a penny a day could get me for grub.

CHAPTER 42

Carrie

I stood in front of the house I'd driven past a thousand times, without having ever stopped. It had been weighing on my mind and I knew what I had to do, even if my heart yelled to turn back and let things go. I had to find out what I could about Percy.

Sucking in a deep breath, I rapped my knuckles against the splintered wood.

Silence.

This was a horrible idea. I suddenly didn't know what I was doing here in the first place. What would this solve?

I turned to go, but someone stirred within the house. My stomach lurched as stomping noises grew louder. A moment later, Bethany's face appeared in the doorway. I opened my mouth to speak and closed it again, words escaping me. She wore the same flour sack patterned dress I had in my closet.

"Carrie?" She glanced over my shoulder before stepping outside, closing the door behind her. "What are you doing here?"

"Percy's gone."

She nodded her head in agreement, her face sullen. A glint of sunlight reflecting from her wrist caught my eye. *His watch.*

"What's going on?" I whispered, sounding pathetic and desperate. She gave a sideways glance to the street.

"They found him," she whispered.

I couldn't hide my confusion. His parents? "*Who? Who* found him?"

Her eyes were wide and vacant, a colorless blue. I couldn't tell what she was thinking.

"The mob."

For a moment, neither of us said anything. And then all at once, I laughed, my stomach releasing the tension I'd been holding onto. I couldn't help it. What a line! They'd thought of everything, and now I realized just how naïve they thought I was.

Her eyes widened, but I couldn't stop.

"Mob? Really, Bethany? The mob got him?" I shook my head in disbelief, having no idea why I was laughing, but it felt good to release all the pent-up emotion I'd been harboring for so long.

She scrunched her eyebrows in concern, but I knew she didn't care. Not about me anyway. They'd had a thing for at least two months.

"Look, my dad would kill me if he caught me outside. I can't talk. My family's packed up…we're leaving as soon as dark settles."

I stifled a chuckle, but her face had gone blank. Was she serious?

"My father," she said, her eyes welling with tears. "He's one of them. He's in the ring."

I waited for her to laugh. For Percy to pop out from the back room and realize the joke was on me. But now, tears streamed down her cheeks.

"You're serious?" I asked incredulously. My heart stopped as the realization sunk in and questions filled my head.

"Look, Carrie, I'm sorry. I urged Percy to tell you the truth, but he insisted on keeping it quiet to protect you. He couldn't bear the thought of putting you at risk."

Percy? Mob? How?

Gauging my expression, she sighed. "You really didn't know, did you?"

I shook my head no.

"Percy was one of the connecting runners," she said dismally. She glanced at her watch. "Gave this to my father for enough money to get outta here."

I shook my head again, as if I could shake loose the thread of thoughts.

"So how long were you two…" I swallowed hard, trying to wrap my head around it all. *"Involved?"*

Her eyebrows pulled together in confusion. "Involved? Like in the mob?"

"No." My cheeks flushed. "Romantically."

"Hmph." She stifled a laugh. "Percy is like a brother to me."

A wave of guilt washed over me, drowning out her words as she slipped off his watch and handed it to me. I hated her only ten minutes ago and now a tornado of emotion swirled within my chest.

"My father'll never notice." She wrapped my hand around the last thing Percy had of his family. "He'd want you to have it. I believe it was all he owned." She glanced to the street. "My folks should be home any minute. I have to go." She slipped back into the house.

Percy. Mob. Chicago.

I walked away, my mind reeling, when she called out, "He really does love you, you know."

Pausing, I turned and thanked her, knowing there was so much more to say, but having no idea what it was. The door clicked shut.

My hands were trembling. I thought back to the many stories I'd read in the paper about the Chicago Mob. It all made sense now. His evasiveness. His paranoia.

Terror clutched my heart, gripping it with sharp blades and sending a tremble through my hands. Images of washed-up bodies floated in my mind. Bodies missing limbs. I knew what the mob did to people. Everyone did. Even down here.

That was the last time I'd see Bethany.

CHAPTER 43

Percy

My new home was a shamble of a place, but a place to sleep nonetheless. The tent was situated on a wooden platform, with cloth sides that flapped gently against the wooden frame anytime the winds decided to remind me of their presence. I hadn't grabbed much from Grandpop's when I left and now I realized how much I'd overlooked. Like soap. And towels.

I let out a deep sigh as I unrolled the thin quilt I had brought along. I knew there was an order of importance to what I had to accomplish here and hoped to do so in a timely manner. Right now, though, all I could think of was the grime on my skin from days of traveling in the dust-filled air and the humidity of California pressing that dirt deeper into the pores of my skin. I thought of Carrie's reaction if she were to see me with my matted hair, insisting I wear my "fancy hat" as she called my mob hat.

Walking through camp, the place was quiet considering the number of tents that held evidence of occupancy…remnants of campfires, tattered clothing drying on clotheslines, a few scraggly dogs as worn down as the old ropes that held them loosely to the spikes of tents. As dismal as it was, it offered me a good sign of possible work.

When I reached the main office building, the dame at the front desk regarded me with weary eyes that suggested she was as underpaid as everyone else near these parts.

"Ma'am," I said, giving her a nod. "I'm looking for work. *And soap.* I also need soap almost as much as work." I smiled, waiting for her to warm up.

"Aren't you all," she said flatly, clearly unimpressed by my dimples.

I wanted to tell her I wasn't like the other bindle punks here, but kept my mouth shut at the realization that maybe I was more like 'em than I was ready to admit. I regretted not wearing my hat. How much I woulda loved to come across her in my swanky days when I could saunter in with all the confidence of a fella backed by the Chicago Mob and throw down some Cs. But instead, I just smiled.

"Yes, I suppose we all are."

"Postings are on Sundays." She said, peering over her glasses, her bony fingers spread across the desk. "Today is Friday."

I couldn't help myself. "Oh, so the time works the same here as it did in Kansas?"

She pursed her lips.

"Look ma'am, I'm just trying to make it like everyone else. I have a family back home I'm trying to provide for. If I had any control over the stock market or the weather or hell, even the farmers, I'd change things. I'd make you wealthy over those scummy highbinders who forced hardworking people like you and my folks to the streets. But, as luck would have it, I don't." I considered something for a moment. "But there is one thing I *do* have—if it helps any in putting my name maybe a little higher on a list…" I leaned in closer.

The woman tilted her head ever so slightly, listening.

If there was one thing I'd learned in the mob, it was how to read people. I had her attention.

I glanced around to be sure no one was nearby and reached into my bag to pull out one of the important things I *hadn't* forgotten at home.

I pulled the weighty bottle out and put it onto the desk, its gold liquid contents sloshing around gently.

Her eyes grew wide, her gaze shifting to the door before wrapping her fingers carefully over the bottle and sliding it closer to peer at its contents. "This real?" she asked, her voice containing as much excitement as I'm sure this woman could muster in that thin body of hers.

"Real as rain," I said, chuckling at the irony of it, though she didn't seem to notice.

"Where did you…" she eyed me carefully. "I've seen this before. This is…"

"Tiger milk. The good stuff. Not the hooch you find in some dive. Templeton Rye," I finished for her. "Al Capone's whiskey of choice."

Her eyes shifted from the peeling yellowed label to me and back again, as if trying to decide how I rated.

"How did you come across it?"

I wanted to tell her. How I'd met Big Al and worked with him, touching expensive whiskey before hardly anyone else. How there were rooms full of whiskey crates (full!) where we'd play rats and mice for stacks of cabbage like it was nothing at all, but also everything. About the walls of moonshining families' homes that were insulated with straw and bottles of bathtub gin. In the end, I lied.

"Won it." I shrugged, leaning in closer and lowering my voice to a whisper. "Playing dice against some high binder who looked important."

Her eyebrows raised as she turned the bottle over in her hands, tracing the label on the back. My ambition got the best of me. "Rumor has it," I said, lowering my voice. "It was a front man of Machine Gun Kelly's."

She drew in her breath, her eyes growing wide.

"Machine Gun Kelly?"

I nodded.

"You know of him?" I asked, knowing the effect the famous button man had on women. Whether it was the legend of him or his looks, I hadn't a clue. "Anyhow, I have a couple of these and I'd love to offer them to someone who would really appreciate their value."

She nodded furiously.

"My husband," she started, her voice barely audible as she cautiously glanced around to be sure no one else was listening. "He was a cotton farmer. Did some business in Tennessee. Told me all about Machine Gun Kelly. Even saw where he grew up. Can you believe it?"

Her gaze shifted to the bottle again.

"Do you think he's touched this?" She swirled the whiskey around, mesmerized by the amber waves.

"Of course," I lied. "Rumor has it he inspects most of the bottles for quality and such."

"Well, my husband would appreciate this more than anyone I know." She smiled slyly as if this was the most exciting thing that's happened to her in quite a while, slipped the bottle into her purse and straightened up, all business again. "I might be able to see what I can do with the list."

"Thank you, ma'am." I nodded, turning to go. "You struck me as the high pillow 'round this joint."

"Wait!" She called out, standing from her chair.

I turned back.

"Soap!" She tossed a green bar to me. "Consider it an agreement piece."

"Thank you, ma'am. You are truly the kindest dame I've come across so far in California."

Little did she know, she was the only one I'd come across in California so the bar wasn't set high. But two days and several showers later, I fought my way through a crowd of men, most of whom were shaking their heads in disgust as they walked away from the papers which had been posted at the main building.

"Good luck, kid," an older man told me. "I've been here nearly three months and still get the crap jobs."

I crossed my fingers and slid through the men to the list.

My heart nearly stopped.

Turning away, I shook my head and sighed.

"Sorry, kid," another man said, patting me on the shoulder. "But at least there's *some kind* of work."

Once through the huddled group and well on my way back to the tent, I smiled. Whiskey, again, had proven to be much more reliable than the weather and definitely more real than rain.

And then, I said a silent thank you to Machine Gun Kelly and his notorious reputation with women.

CHAPTER 44

Carrie

From somewhere outside, a car door slammed shut. We followed Pa outside to find a sheriff climbing out from an unmarked vehicle.

My stomach cinched.

I'd seen him around town, but never at my house. Never at anyone's house, save for the time when someone's wife in town was found dead. Shot cold in her living room. Her husband didn't get far, either.

Pa stiffened. "What can I help you with, Officer?"

The sheriff's lips pursed as he pulled a folded paper from his back pocket and handed it to Pa. "You seen either of these men?"

Pa's eyebrows scrunched together. His eyes flicked to me and then back to the paper. "Nah," he said.

"Heard that one of 'em used to work on the farm here." He spat a wad of brown juice to the ground, his eyes steady on Pa. "Small town. I thought maybe you'd know where to find him."

Pa shook his head, his cheeks flushing. "Haven't seen him in quite some time. Just up and left."

The man rubbed his chin in thought.

"He's a very dangerous man," he finally said. "Wanted for bootleggin' and possibly murder."

Pa swallowed hard, the bulge in his throat prevalent.

"Anyhow, we'll find him. We always do." He turned to go and added, "Keep the photo in case you forget what he looks like."

We stood frozen.

Percy? How could it be Percy?

Later, Pa went to visit Mr. Meyer and refused to have me with. My stomach was in knots. Several times I went to the bathroom and kneeled on the floor, thinking I might be sick, but all that would come up was bile.

Ma went about the house, picking up and setting down objects at random, to dust beneath them. Her hands trembled. She glanced out the door often.

When Pa returned, he sat us down, setting his hat on the table as he combed his fingers through his thinning hair. His face had aged several years within the past one and I regretted this place for that.

"Turns out," he started, squeezing his eyes shut momentarily, "Percy is a felon."

My throat constricted.

"There must be some mistake," Ma choked. "Percy? I don't believe it."

"Quite the background. Crime. Bootlegging. Murder schemes." He sighed.

I jerked my head up.

Ma's eyes grew wide. "What?"

He shook his head. "Algott thought he'd help. You know, get him out of the Chicago crime scene. Then, the thug just up and left. People like that don't change."

I slammed my fist on the table. "He's no thug and you know it! He might have a past, but you know he's good."

"Carrie, that's enough!" Ma said, gripping the edge of the table. "Turns out, we don't know anything about him."

Pa let out a deep breath and stood. "Carrie, he's trash. I shoulda seen it and that's on me. I brought him into this family and will be the first to correct things. If he resurfaces, I want to hear about it immediately."

"But—"

He cut me off, leveling me with his stare. "IMMEDIATELY."

I choked down sobs. My soul shrunk within my body to some small corner to die.

He turned to face us, his eyes locked with mine. "You play in the mud with pigs and you're bound to get dirty."

CHAPTER 45

Most days, I couldn't stop my mind from racing. I tried flushing out thoughts of Percy with tedious jobs around the house, but the physical nature of it couldn't reach the voids in my heart or spinning in my brain.

He'd run away, I kept reminding myself. He'd said as much in his note to Mr. Meyer. He was clever. If anyone could escape the mob, it was Percy.

But still, my heart ached as endless hours stretched into days.

It was my last year of school and to help the family, I signed up with the National Youth Administration to stay after classes to work. Many of the boys my age, along with older men in the area, had been contracted by the Civilian Conservation Corps, getting paid to build bridges, drill wells, and work on other projects for a government paycheck. The once wealthy stood in the same lines as the rest of us for whatever government handouts were accessible.

Pride cast a small shadow on starvation.

It was nearly a hundred degrees when I finally finished scrubbing desks and sweeping floors in the school. The grit of the air irritated my skin as I made my way home, a forty-five minute walk on a good day. Percy's face popped into my mind as it often did during empty moments like this. I imagined him smiling, a strand of wheat sticking out of a goofy grin.

Was he in Oklahoma? Had he gone north to Chicago?

The unknown nagged at my heart, stinging it over and over again. I wanted to scream at him for abandoning me, for not trusting me with his whereabouts, while a small part of me ached, knowing why he hadn't.

In the distance, the figure of a man began to take shape. I squinted. *Pa?*

With his back to me and so much distance between us, it was hard to tell. I'd never seen him on my walks home. I jaunted into a light jog and as I got closer, the form began to morph into recognizable broad shoulders and faded overalls.

"Pa!" I called out breathlessly.

Startled, he whirled around, his face set in confusion.

"Pa," I panted, stopping to rest my hands on my knees while trying to catch my breath. "Where you comin' from?"

"Work," he said, a glint in his eyes.

I was struck by the familiar kindness in his smile.

"Work?" I was taken aback. The fields were dead, and he'd never worked outside of 'em. "Where?"

"Works Progress Administration." He shrugged. "Who would've ever thought the government would turn out to be the nation's largest employer. We're rebuilding some roads nearby as one of FDR's New Deal projects."

My heart swelled with pride. "You like it?"

We had started walking again, my feet keeping pace with his.

"Well," he considered, "it's not like farming."

To me that was a good thing, although I knew how heavy the words were for him to carry.

"But, yes I do. It's good to feel productive again and to see the immediate results of what you're investing time in."

I nodded, feeling the weight of my conscience float to the surface of my ribcage. "Look, Pa…"

"No need, Carrie." He raised his hand up to stop me and gave me a sideways glance. "You were right."

My breath hitched in my throat. He wasn't the kind to admit defeat *or* failure.

"You can't eat dirt. That farm ain't worth nothing to anybody but us." He shook his head. "And it wasn't the farm. It was never about that. It was what it represented. I've never wanted anything more than to create a legacy for our family. Something to pass down."

His eyes, kind and willing to do whatever it took to care for our family, welled with tears and he looked away.

"You *have*, Pa. Your work ethic. Your determination. *That's* the legacy you've passed down to me and Benny."

His eyes fixed on some point in the distance as we quietly made our way home. Soon, our yellowed house became visible, its wraparound porch, though decrepit with uneven boards that creaked when walked upon, welcomed us. It was a home held together not by the timber in the walls or the cement of the foundation, but by the spirit of love, determination, and optimism. Things more important to pass down than any amount of land.

CHAPTER 46

Percy

Droplets of rain soaked through the roof of the tent, clinging heavily to the cloth above me as I lay down. My heart pounded rapidly, my face drenched, whether from sweat or rain I couldn't tell. My breathing slowed at the realization that the spray of machine gun bullets were pellets of rain tapping the tent.

Rain.

I nearly began to cry, trying to remember the last time I'd actually *heard* rain. I rubbed the sleep from my eyes, relief giving way to anticipation. Moments later, under the tent awning, I cupped it into my hands and splashed it onto my face like some kind of crazy person.

The papers won't sell themselves.

Pop's words echoed in my head. Something pinged in my stomach. Sadness? Regret? I drew in a big breath and pulled myself away from the memory.

That morning, I was certainly the youngest in the bed of the truck. Mud, following the occasional bump, sprayed from the tires as we followed county roads for at least half an hour on the stretch to Mr. Jenkins's fields. Already, the sun was fighting to break through the clouds as fog gave way to pops of color as fruit fields began to appear.

Groves of oranges stretched as far as I could see, brilliant bursts of color speckled against the horizon as the sun began to burn off the mist of morning. For a moment, I closed my eyes and inhaled the sweet smell.

"Nice, ain't it?" a man's voice said, causing me to open my eyes. "Could be worse. Could be working for one of them cheap farmers who don't pay squat. Full of empty promises. They're a dime a dozen 'round these parts."

I nodded with a smile and a twinge of guilt. How long had he waited to make this list?

The driver pulled the truck over, signaling us to climb out. Not long after, a heap of canvas sacks were passed around. I kicked my boot against the tire of the truck, dislodging chunks of mud that plopped into the wet grass.

"Remember, fellas," one of the older men said, "unless you like to drink sour orange juice, make sure the ones you pick are smooth and heavy, no soft spots. Be careful when you put them in your bag so you don't go and bruise 'em. Lunch break is at twelve. Half hour, then back to work."

We all scattered, spreading amongst the endless rows of orange trees. I was directed to the far end of the grove, requiring a walk through a patchwork of both cool shadows and sunny spots with wet grass clinging to the sides of my boots.

I drew in a deep breath and relaxed my shoulders.

Birds sang melodies of optimism and cheer, unaware of the devastation that was happening outside of their little community; a utopia in the midst of a dirt hell.

Carrie would've loved it.

More than anything, I wished I could pick this grove right up and land it in the middle of their field. I imagined her running through the trees, laughing as Goldie chased her. And then her lips were kissing mine. A rush flooded my body and I pulled myself from my thoughts.

My job was simple.

I was to carefully reach up into the trees and pluck the brightest, firmest and heaviest oranges, placing them into my bag until someone came around to swap them out. It wasn't long before I was whistling along with the birds and nearly missed the sound of the lunch whistle when it distantly shrilled out signifying lunch.

When I approached the group of men, they had gathered around a beat-up pickup and were pulling boxes from the bed, claiming tree trunks to lean against as they unwrapped sandwiches and bumped gums about politics, the weather and other topics.

"How much?" I asked, eyeing the ham and turkey delicacies. I didn't have any money with me, but if I could set a little aside I could treat myself once a week. Maybe Fridays.

"A good morning's worth of work," an older man commented as he handed me a box and pulled a crate of oranges forward.

I misunderstood.

"Honestly," I said, passing the box to a man who had lined up behind me. "I'll bring money next time."

The older man chuckled. "Are you confessing you didn't work hard this morning?" His eyes gleamed as he regarded me.

"Not at all," I started. "It's just—"

"I'm teasing, son." He handed me another box. "Take the lunch. It's free."

When I was settled under the shade of a tree, I unwrapped my sandwich. Nothing had tasted better. I closed my eyes and let my body relax. The job might have been simple, but that didn't mean it wasn't hard work. I rolled my shoulders and absentmindedly rubbed the upper part of my picking arm in attempt to relieve the burning sensation. It felt as if it weighed about three times more than the other.

"I don't recognize you."

I popped my eyes open. It was the old man from the truck. He turned over an empty crate and eased himself gingerly upon it, leaning his arms across his legs as he sat and regarded me.

"I'm new," I said, slicing the peel of the orange with my thumbnail. It sprayed a fine mist across my hand. "Just got here Friday."

The man nodded. "You like it so far?"

"Depends. You referencing California or these fields?"

He chuckled. "Both, I suppose."

I thought about it.

"Crazy as it seems, I miss Kansas. It's dirty and desolate, but it's home, you know?" He nodded his head in agreement.

"And the job?" He regarded me with inquisitive eyes.

"I can't complain." How could I? I'd never really traveled, but this was one of the most beautiful places I'd ever seen and would confidently rank it against any distant place. "The job keeps me on my toes, literally speaking. I have time to think. As silly as it sounds, I have space to reflect, you know, on my past and things like that."

He nodded again and for a few minutes, we ate our sandwiches, lost in our own thoughts.

The man took a sip of water and cleared his throat. "Citrus, you know, is just behind oil in California."

"That so?" I asked, grateful I'd landed amongst the Citrus Belt.

"Sure is. You can thank the Spanish missionaries for that." He crumpled his sandwich paper into a ball and clasped his hands together, leaning forward as if letting me in on a secret. "But the mother of all citrus can be traced to one tree in Washington. *One* tree." He shook his head as if he couldn't even quite believe it. Either this man had been working the fields a while or knew the finer workings of a bullshit story. I smirked to myself, but if he noticed, he didn't lead on.

"*The Washington Orange,*" he said, rubbing his lower back.

I no longer owned a watch, but knew the break was nearly over.

"That one tree produced the wealth that created cities such as Pasadena, which was founded by the San Gabriel Orange Grove Association." The man smiled. "Always remember this. Despite contrary belief, money *can* sometimes grow on trees."

The whistle blew.

I jumped up and offered my hand, helping the old man to his feet. "How long you been working here?"

He smiled, grabbed the crate and turned to go. "Longer than you've been alive I reckon."

After the shift ended, my body ached and many of the men rested their eyes, soaking in the sun as we traveled the dirt road back to camp. I marveled at their stamina. Then I wondered how long the old man had worked the fields before finally getting the job of delivering lunches.

"Mr. Jenkins is a class act," someone said.

My ears perked up.

"Does he ever come around?" I asked, hoping to join the conversation and eager to learn about someone who was so wealthy, but not from running in a crime circle.

The men looked from me to each other before erupting in laughter.

"What?" I asked, suddenly feeling like a chump, but appreciative to be part of the talk unlike the button men I knew from Al's circle who were always too important to mingle with their subordinates. My cheeks burned and I felt as if I were the new kid in a classroom with long-established friendship circles.

"You must be new, son," an older cat I reckon to be in his fifties said. "You did after all, just spend your entire lunch break with the fella."

I raised my eyebrows and seeing the confusion upon my face, the men laughed louder. It couldn't be. The older man I sat with wasn't dressed in a fine suit, nor smelled of wealthy cologne. Hell, he didn't even have any ice on his fingers. He passed out lunches for God's sake, even knowing how I rated, which was currently zero. A bindle punk.

A nagging twitch took over the back of my brain, deep within my conscience. The kind a person got when realizing their view of the entire world had somehow shifted. Like when viewing the photos of my father with his mistress…the realization that his and my mother's marriage wasn't what I thought it was.

I shifted in my seat and rubbed the back of my neck, thinking of Mr. Jenkins, but kept coming to the same conclusion: he either wasn't as wealthy as everyone believed or I'd been fooled most my life on what wealth really looked like.

The man I sat with drove a beat-up pickup and wore work overalls.

CHAPTER 47

Carrie

The space that stretched between the fullness of Percy's presence and the vacancy of his void was the heartbeat between breaths of life and the stillness of death; a heavy endurance to carry.

More and more suits began to appear in town.

Always with new instruments to measure and calculate, predict and prevent. Soil scientists urged farmers to practice new methods of using terraces and plowing along the land's contour to minimize runoff. Some farmers still clung to enough hope to entertain these specialists, but most just shook their heads and scoffed at the ideas or even possibility of recovering the fertility of the soil.

"There's talk among the men today," Pa commented one evening at supper. "Government is paying seventy-five cents an acre if you're willing to try wind erosion strategies to knock down the dunes." He sighed. "Can you believe it? They want us to use the ol' lister plow before planting the crops, rotating crops each year. Says it'll keep the soil and nutrients in place." He took a bite of carrots. "They're even willing to pay us for it. All the newly invented machinery and they want us to use that ol' lister."

"You think you'll give it a try?" Ma asked, attempting to sound hopeful.

I slathered a dollop of butter on Ma's freshly baked roll, watching the streaks of gold trickle down and drip on the plate. I closed my eyes, savoring the richness that melted within my mouth. Memories of prosperous farm days and running through the kitchen while the women baked for the men in the fields came to mind.

"Carrie?"

I drew my eyes up to meet his gaze.

"What do you think?"

I was taken aback. I knew nothing about farming, nor was in any position to add to the conversation. "About what?"

"What do *you* want for your future?" he asked.

Ma smiled, waiting for my answer.

Pa had never asked such a thing. Honestly, I didn't know what my future held at this point. Just a few months ago, I couldn't see myself anywhere without Percy and now, he was completely severed from my life. I released a breath I hadn't realized I'd been holding.

"I want dogs," Benny commented, giving Goldie a pat on the head. Goldie thumped her tail against the floorboards as if in response.

"The farm," Pa said, gesturing with his silverware, "or what's left of it, is in your hands. Is it worth trying to revive?" He gauged my reaction and as if sensing my hesitation, went on. "I'm willing to try all the fancy tricks these soil scientists and government workers have up their sleeves, but in the end, it's *your* legacy. If it's not in your heart, I'll let it go."

Ma and Pa's eyes were on me. I could feel my cheeks burn.

I didn't want it. Any of it.

I'd known that for a while, but knew what the land meant to him and what it represented. All the hours and days and years of sweat poured into hopes of reaping a legacy productive enough to last through the generations.

"Carrie?" Ma prodded, placing her hand on my arm.

I sucked in a deep breath and steadied my gaze on Pa. "I appreciate all of your work. I don't know a harder worker than you and I know you did it all for us. For the family."

Pa nodded.

"But I also saw the struggle and desperation that came from it." I thought of the land's retaliation against us caregivers, who were responsible for violating its trust. "I want to build something upon the foundation of work ethic you instilled in us." Feeling a surge of inspiration, I couldn't keep the words from spilling out.

"I want to fall in love with something the way you fell in love with the fields. Love it enough for it to pull me out of bed as the crops do for you, if nothing other than to watch their stalks glow under the rising sun, their draw bringing you back again in the evening for quiet walks after a hard day's work."

If the words hurt Pa, he didn't let on, his face neutral and even as he listened. I swallowed down a lump that had formed in my throat.

"I want that relationship with something, but I'm not sure it's here in this place," I clarified.

For a moment no one spoke. I felt my throat constrict and took a sip of water, diverting any eye contact. Were they disappointed in me? Angry? I hoped not. The last thing I wanted to do was to hurt them and now, I questioned saying anything at all.

Pa rested his silverware on his plate and slid it out in front of him.

"That's fair," he said.

My heart stopped, another lump forming in my throat.

Rising from my seat, I made my way over and wrapped my arms around his broad shoulders, pressing my face against the roughness of his whiskered cheek.

"Thank you," I said, my voice barely a whisper. "Thank you."

He hesitated for a moment and then hugged me back.

When I finally pulled away, I caught a gleam in his eye. A look I'd seen several times during the best days of harvesting.

"But if you change your mind," he said, "many of the guys are taking their government checks to buy new combines."

I laughed along with him, releasing the tension that had built up over some time, knowing that there wasn't anything in the world that could take the spirit of farming from his body.

CHAPTER 48

Percy

Every day near lunch, Mr. Jenkins would drive that old truck to our worksite and drop off boxes of food, sometimes with so many oranges, we'd each grab a few and take them back to camp. He'd inherited the land and started with a small operation, growing from there. He and his wife could never have kids and she had passed nearly ten years back, leaving him to run the orchard alone.

He was a withered man, his small frame hunched in a sort of way that only happens with time and labor. The creases of his face suggested much experience in his lifetime, World War I being one of them. Despite his physical stature, his hands were large and calloused from years of manual labor.

He took a liking to me and I found we had much in common, including a love for whiskey. Every day at lunch he would plop beside me, bringing extra food and stories from his life. One day, he brought me the most delicious strawberry shortcake I'd ever tasted. Turned out, not only did he harvest oranges, but also walnuts and flowers.

"One hundred fifty trees," he commented one day, his eyes reminiscent while he sipped on a glass of lemonade. "We got our first tree some years ago as a wedding gift."

His comment brought back a Bible story I'd heard as a kid in Sunday School. The one about a tiny mustard seed growing into the kingdom of heaven.

"We had humble beginnings," he said, fixing his eyes on me with a smile. "In the beginning, it was just my wife and me."

"So how'd you do it?" I asked. "How did you grow it into what it is today?"

He chuckled. "You might not like the answer, son."

I waited for him to go on and tell me about the many connections he'd had, being in the right place at the right time with some high binders or buying out smaller family operations to add into his large one. But he mentioned none of these things.

"That's the secret," he said, his eyes gleaming. "Hard work, the *slow way.*"

I thought of the methods of picking that seemed to be outdated. "Why not use more spiffy machinery and modernization? You could grow it bigger, faster."

He regarded me with inquisitive eyes. "Now, why would I do that?"

"I don't know, efficiency I suppose."

"The land has always been good to me," he said, looking around at the thriving trees. "Why would I ever compromise that relationship?"

I pondered this and how different it was from what I'd grown up around. Chicago, a city of mass production, speed, and efficiency at the cost of the blueness of the sky. This mass production of industrialization stretched south, trading in family farms for factories but at the cost of the greenness of the land.

"What are your interests?" he asked, changing the subject.

"Flowers." I shrugged.

My answer surprised even me. I didn't have any hobbies. Especially not anymore since I wasn't with Carrie exploring. I'd never told anyone of my past and even now, my stomach started bunching into knots. Something about the ease of conversation between us and his gentle nature made me feel as if I could tell him anything.

"Oh?" He raised his eyebrows. "I have to admit. They were my wife's passion, but I don't know a perennial from a weed in her old flower beds. How'd you come to learn about flowers?"

I debated how much to tell him, opting for the safe side of things. "I had a job that involved ordering large bouquets while living up in Chicago. I caught on, I guess."

"Sounds interesting," he said. "My first job was on a farm, milking cows and cleaning horse stalls. I think you got the good end of the stick."

I chuckled. If he only knew.

"Well, I could stay back after work is done and take a shot at naming your flowers," I suggested. Part of it was avoiding the loneliness of camp and the other part of it was straight out curiosity at seeing the rest of his property.

His eyes sparkled. "I think that can be arranged."

He met me by his pickup nearly four hours later. Instead of taking a left at the end of the gravel drive, we took a right and drove the road a few miles down, past the neat rows of planted trees to where the driveway wound beneath an arched sign that read Citrus Valley View in bold letters.

The farmhouse itself was modest, built of limestone with dark wooden doors and matching shutters on each four-paned window. A chimney popped out the top, more of a nostalgic factor than for warmth, the house itself framed with hydrangeas and ornamental grasses. Surrounding it all were lush gardens with gravel pathways that wound between them.

"Home sweet home," he said, pulling his truck up to a shed that matched the house.

"It's more than anything I could've imagined."

I'd once biked past Big Al's brick manor in Chicago, marveling at the three stories, dreaming of what life must be like for someone of that stature and envisioning myself inside, but it didn't compare to Mr. Jenkins' home.

This was an estate.

Mr. Jenkins rested his hands on the steering wheel, assessing the grounds. "At one time, this house held large groups of church gatherings and whatever social events Lucille liked to host." He smiled, turning to face me. "She made the sweetest chocolate ganache cake you've ever tasted."

My mouth watered at the thought, remembering the corner bakery in Chicago that touted cream puffs with raspberry filling and petit fours in a rainbow of colors. Another place I'd love to take Carrie sometime. My heart ached.

"It must be hard, missing someone so much." I couldn't imagine losing someone after a lifetime together. I'd been crushing on Carrie a couple of years now and if she were gone…

"Yes," he sighed. "It is. Do you have anyone back home?"

I hesitated.

"Did." I squeezed my eyes shut. "I couldn't tell her I was leaving. Call me a coward, but I knew if I saw her face, I'd had selfishly stayed and never let her go."

I didn't have to say more. I could see it in his eyes he understood.

From then on, every Friday we walked his gardens after work. I'd point out different flowers and a little of their history, but the conversations mostly turned to stories of our lives. Our families and our pasts.

Months went by, and on one Friday, when we sat out on his porch sipping iced tea, I opened up for the first time since my youth and told him of my time in the mob.

He listened intently, without showing any emotion of surprise nor appall. When I was finished, he took a moment before speaking.

"Are you still on the run?" he asked gently, concern in his eyes.

I nodded.

"I don't think they'd take the time to bother looking in shantyvilles and camps, but I don't think I can safely ever go back to my family."

He nodded. "I see."

"Have you ever done something you regret?" I asked. "I mean *really* regret?"

Lefty's face flashed in my mind and a surge of nausea rolled into my stomach. It was revenge. Selfish revenge and the stupidity of youth. Skimming to keep Carrie and our families fed was entirely different in my mind. Justified, even if it broke my moral conscience as I vowed to never steal again after Lefty's demise.

"Sure have," Mr. Jenkins said, rocking in his chair. "We all have. And if people don't admit it, they're lying to themselves. That's life." He shrugged. "Life can be brutally hard. I used to think of it in terms of black and white but learned over the years it's a lot more muddled than that. What counts is if you learn from it. That you keep getting better and make things right with God and with yourself." He looked out to the orchards. "The latter being the toughest. Good luck, son. It won't be easy."

CHAPTER 49

Carrie

Slowly, my heart had healed, scarred as it was, over the lashes Percy had carelessly made.

I hated how he'd changed me. How he somehow had the ability to bring out both my best and my worst self. How I had to force my smiles and push myself to get out of bed, the air itself too much pressure as it weighted down my body and added thousands of pounds to my legs, the thought of facing the day an overwhelming task of endurance.

He'd stolen the mistaken belief in life itself. The assurance that things would always somehow turn out how they were meant to be.

My stomach churned. I desperately wanted him back home. I needed him to be alive, but was he? My heart was shattered, my mind was fragmented, jumping from one incoherent thought to another.

He was out there somewhere, wasn't he?

Now and then, my mind wandered to the strong possibility he no longer existed. The possibility shook through my body like a tremor to the earth, sucking all the air from the room. No, I had to believe he was still alive, even if it meant he didn't trust me enough to know the truth. It squeezed my heart 'til it hurt but was a better alternative to the other.

I threw myself into mindless work, scrubbing away sneaky thoughts of what life with Percy could've been like and instead, focused inward.

What did *I* want for my future?

I turned the question over in my mind day after day, wanting to live up to something Ma and Pa could be proud of. Someone I could be proud to become. More and more, I was beginning to feel it wasn't where I was currently. But then where?

Dust storms continued to blow in as if imagined by the memory of the crops themselves. Gusts of winds blasted our house with granules of sand that chipped away the paint, leaving our home in a state of shambles constantly. Heartache was the only thing that grew from the dirt.

Every other week, the Red Cross brought crates of food that we couldn't afford with our wages. Not if we wanted to keep the house anyway. I would never grow tired of the excitement of the rapping of knuckles against the door, signifying the next week's meals. Would there be more of the crisp apples and snap peas? Last time, there must've been at least three varieties of tomatoes in vibrant colors of yellow and orange.

Today, as always, the dark-haired man smiled as I opened the door to greet him. "Thank you," I said, shifting the weight of the crate into my arms.

"Just doing my job." He smiled, his teeth white against his sun-kissed skin. I'm sure he had many ladies after him with the enthusiasm his eyes carried and his spark of energy. I knew I had to move on, but even at Ma's urging, I wasn't ready.

I had to try.

"You've been running our route for months," I said, forcing the corners of my mouth up into a smile. "I should at least know your name so I can formally thank you. The Red Cross has done so much to help us."

A look momentarily flashed across his face, an inward pull of his eyebrows quickly replaced by a full set of dimples. He wasn't Percy, but he was handsome, I had to give him that.

Percy's gone, I reminded myself.

The man tipped his hat and did a little curtsey, and for the first time in forever, I giggled.

"Dudley. My name is Dudley."

CHAPTER 50

Percy

Pineapples. They were everywhere in Mr. Jenkins's house. Intricately carved into the dark oak trim that cased every doorway, topping each pillar that separated rooms, crosshatched into carvings of pineapples, their leaves flowing out as if melting from the wood.

The floor creaked behind me as Mr. Jenkins approached with a smile.

"My wife had most of the say when it came to decorating," he said, handing me a glass of what smelled like raspberry tea. The ice cubes clinked gently against the sides of the weighty crystal as I brought it to my lips, savoring the sweetness of the drink.

It wasn't lost upon me how much the turn of events could change. To think that just a few months ago I had to turn all my cups upside down and rinse them to clear them of the dust. Scrounging for food, desperate to be useful. Now, here I was, drinking lemonade of all things, from a swanky crystal glass with the owner of a large orchard in a place where plants weren't only surviving, but thriving.

"So," I began, as we headed out the back door and toward the gardens. "Tell me about the pineapples."

For a moment, his eyebrows pulled together in thought.

"I noticed they're throughout your house."

"Ah yes," he said, upon realization. "A symbol of prosperity. A sign of worthiness."

I tried to imagine such a humble man of giving nature ever being the type to have to prove himself to others. Although, I had once been that same person and knew people could change. As if reading my thoughts, he laughed.

"It wasn't to reflect our worthiness, but the worth of our guests to us. We wanted more than anything to have a full house. One in which people felt welcomed and valued. After the devastation of not being able to have children of our own faded, we decided to fill the house often and always with friends."

I imagined living a life with the amount of wealth as to deciding what types of symbols you wanted to decorate your home with. Ma would love to see a place like this. My heart swelled a bit and I quickly swallowed.

"Where did it come from?" I asked. "The pineapple idea?"

He squinted his eyes against the sun. Bees were buzzing about the patches of color which sprung up in waves along the gravel pathway that rounded through the garden.

"Christopher Columbus," he said.

He took a sip from his glass. "Before he found what he had hoped was Asia, he'd visited several islands and brought pineapples here. They weren't grown here so they were seen as a delicacy. A symbol of prominence and value, often given to guests."

He reminded me so much of Grandpops in the simplicity of their lifestyles and how they viewed wealth in general, as if money were just an afterthought to the richness in the life you chose to live.

My heart ached. It wasn't safe to go back yet, I was sure of that. But I could write. I'd write him a thank you for taking me in and for guiding me in a time when my family life seemed splintered to the point of having to leave to avoid stepping on the broken shards. My parents might've chosen to walk barefoot on the glass, but that didn't mean I had to.

CHAPTER 51

"You're on special assignment today, Percy." Mr. Jenkins pulled me aside as the men unloaded, going about their separate ways after offering him a hello.

It was the first time I'd seen him wear anything other than his straw hat, as he adjusted his black fedora, matched with gray slacks and a freshly pressed white shirt. I glanced down at the same worn jeans and shirt I'd wore every day since moving to California. They looked like something I'd gotten out of a hock shop.

"Where we dusting off to?" I asked, trying to conceal my anticipation and suddenly feeling inadequately dressed as I climbed into his truck. He didn't strike me as the kind who would hit up some ritzy juice joint, but he was sure dressed spiffy enough.

"Farmer's Market in Santa Ana." He shifted the truck into gear and put it into drive. "You ever been to Santa Ana?"

"Can't say I have."

"Well then, this might just change your mind on California all together." He smiled.

It was about a three-hour drive as I took in scenery of boulevards lined with palm trees and deciduous plants that reminded me of the fake ones from our apartment back in Chicago. We talked about many things, but mostly about his late wife. He told me how they'd met at a dinner party hosted by their church and as Mr. Jenkins said, "She was the most beautiful person he'd ever laid eyes on."

When the conversation turned to Carrie, the old man's eyes sparkled as he glanced from the road to me. I told him of our adventures. Of the waves of sand walls that swept over houses and ate farms. He listened quietly, shaking his head as if in awe of this world he had never experienced but only heard about.

We unloaded crates of oranges and walnuts and set up a stand just behind the truck next to another man who was busily doing the same, while trying to keep two young boys in tow.

"I've been coming to this same place for over twenty years," Mr. Jenkins said, tipping his hat to fellow farmers as they shuffled about their stands. "Once a month. It's become a part of me like Sunday service."

I thought of how special that was. Here was this fella who had contracts with large citrus companies and he hadn't lost value in what truly made him happy. The little things.

"Anyhow, I want you to meet my long-time market neighbor. He's one of the most gracious and humble men you will ever know." I followed him to a man who was neatly arranging baskets of snap peas and green beans.

"Mr. Noguchi," he greeted the man. "This is my friend, Mr. Percy."

The man extended his hand to me and smiled warmly.

"Nice to meet you," he said, tipping his hat. He was small in stature but had large sparkling eyes that seemed to dance when he smiled.

"Robbie!" he called out after one of the boys, about ten or eleven years old. The boy raced over, ball glove in hand. "This is my Robbie," he said proudly, resting his hand on the boy's shoulder.

"You like ball?" I asked.

"Is there any other sport?" the boy grinned. A little cocky for his age, he reminded me a lot of myself in my youth. I liked him immediately.

Mr. Jenkins tossed him an orange, which he readily caught before running off to join his friend, Jimmy.

"Look around a little." Mr. Jenkins encouraged me with a nod. "We don't officially open for another fifteen minutes."

I wandered the road as all around me, people set up stations like a well-organized fair. Tropical fruits I'd never seen were neatly arranged into enticing piles while scarves hung from wood sticks, their silks flapping in the breeze. A few tables in, something caught my eye.

"Real as rain," the man said, donning a neatly trimmed mustache and red bowtie. "I grew up on a ranch and anytime we'd till the gardens, we'd find these and throw them in a jar."

I picked up an arrowhead, carefully examining it before setting it back beside the others. I did this a few times before settling on one the color of amber.

"Good choice." The man neatly wrapped it in paper, folding it a few times before handing it back to me. I passed him the money, a few days' worth of breakfast costs.

Already, the air was sticky and a thin sheen of sweat had settled upon my skin. Mr. Jenkins dabbed his forehead with his handkerchief and poured two glasses of cool lemonade from a thermos. It was a busy day of greeting customers, most of whom knew Mr. Jenkins by name. We didn't pack up until the sun had tucked into the horizon.

"I have one more thing to show you before you make any judgements on California," Mr. Jenkins said while packing empty crates into the back of the truck.

Not long after, we were driving again, turning the opposite direction from which we'd come.

We drove about ten minutes before the road opened up. My breath caught in my throat. A rushing feeling of tranquility passed through my body, and I imagined this to be the place where the Holy Spirit could've lived.

Mr. Jenkins killed the engine and gazed out into the horizon. As beautiful as the setting sun could be over fields of copper and even the city skyline, it was nothing in comparison to this. Cresting waves of aqua and teal crashed into foamy bubbles against the beach, the wet sand reflecting the captured reds, oranges, and violets of the sunset before nightfall.

Silently, I got out of the truck, slipped off my shoes and squished the sand that had wedged between my toes. The world and all of its troubles were momentarily lost. I'd never felt as grounded and full of purpose, yet small and insignificant, as standing there facing the ocean.

Mr. Jenkins stood beside me, placing his hand upon my back. "You haven't seen California until you've seen the majesty of the sun setting upon her ocean."

We drove home in silence, the sky lit with the glow of a billion stars, Carrie on my mind. I wondered what she was doing, five months feeling more like five years since I'd last seen her. My heart ached.

When we pulled into camp, Mr. Jenkins turned toward me. "I've been meaning to tell you, Percy…" He hesitated, as if carefully choosing his words. "Your problem. It's solved."

My problem? The mob?

Seeing the confusion on my face, he nodded.

"*How?*" I thought of Big Al's hatchet men and how easily they could go off the tracks, and shuddered.

"Did I ever mention all of the swanky parties my wife and I hosted?" His eyes twinkled. "Well, let's just say we didn't drink orange juice at them. And we held large parties frequently."

Questions swirled my mind as I registered what he was telling me. And then a horrifying thought crossed my mind.

"You didn't…"

"Take anyone out?" He cut me off with a dismissive wave and a laugh. "I have some friends who have friends who know who to pay."

"But," I stammered. "It was a significant amount of money. I can never repay it."

"And I don't expect you to. I told you I was never able to have any kids of my own. I have no one to spend my money on. This brings me joy. The economy has done enough to split up families. You don't have to be one of them."

"Thank you," I said, choking back tears and shaking my head in disbelief. "For everything."

Not only had he taken away my debt, but my running. No worry of someone putting the screws on me. So much fear. And now, it had been lifted from me. I rested my hand on the old man's shoulders, wishing more than anything there was something I could do to thank him, but knowing nothing could ever be enough. "I hope someday I can be half the man you are, Mr. Jenkins."

"You know, Percy," he said, his voice quiet, "I didn't have much of a father growing up. He wasn't usually around and left us when I was a kid."

I thought of my own father and a bubble of regret ballooned in my stomach at how we had parted ways.

"I helped my mother in raising a younger sister, who has already been gone for fifteen years now. I did whatever I could, working odd jobs here and there. Always working. There were many times I wanted to throw it all in and give up and I could've really used the approval of someone telling me they were proud of me. That they saw my efforts and my heart and would reassure me I was going in the right direction. Seemed the only thing I was sure of was my work ethic."

Though his silhouette was black against the window, I could tell he had turned to face me. "Hard work and looking for the good in people is what's turned me into a person I can be proud of. Anyway," he cleared his throat, "I wanted to tell you that I'm proud of what you're doing for your family."

It was as if every burden I'd ever carried had been taken off my shoulders. All the stories my father had told of his work when he was my age and his rise to the columnist position, and I realized in that instant that all I've ever wanted was for him to say these words to me. Mr. Jenkins reached over and placed his hand on mine, his callouses a testament to the life he'd lived—and it was enough.

"But," he said, "none of this should matter to you. In the end, the only approval you need of yourself is your own."

I could hear in his voice that he was smiling, even if I couldn't see his face.

"Now," he said, clearing his throat again. "Go home to your family."

CHAPTER 52

Carrie

It was a Tuesday afternoon, four o'clock p.m.

Already I was growing hungry, the gurgling in my stomach reminding me that I hadn't eaten since eleven. I pulled the wastebasket out from under Mrs. Hallard's desk, dumping the contents of crumpled papers and the occasional gum wrapper into the bigger metal basket. On Friday I would get paid again. Not much, but enough to save.

I slid the empty wastebasket back under the desk before grabbing the full one. I squinted against the sunlight as I made my way to the garbage can outside.

"Carrie Lexington."

I froze.

My legs locked up, rooting me to the ground. Chills swept over my skin and up my neck. The loud thumping of my heartbeat overpowered everything around me.

Percy. Was I imagining him now?

I spun around.

"Carrie." His voice was hesitant as if he couldn't quite believe it was me.

"Per-cy?" The words came out stammered from my mouth, barely audible. My breath hitched.

His eyes welled with tears, his face unreadable. He looked the same and yet older somehow. Relief flooded my body, followed by a rage I'd never experienced. My mind buzzed in a flurry of emotion.

"Where?" My mind spun. "Why?" I stammered a little louder.

His face was pained, deep lines creasing his forehead. "Carrie, I—" He took a step forward.

"Don't!" I yelled, throwing my hand up to stop him. I couldn't hear it.

Months.

MONTHS. I didn't know whether he was dead or alive. Why he'd left. And now, he thought he could just make the rules and waltz back into my life without any warning? I was finally coming to terms with life without him. Adapting. Adjusting. Altering.

"Carrie, I'll explain everything."

I turned my back to him and shook the garbage basket with forceful motions, the contents tumbling out into a disarrayed pile of rubbish in the garbage can.

"Carrie," Percy pleaded. "Please…"

Don't turn around.

"Leave," I said, looking beyond him. I drew back the weight of my anger and disappointment, the despair and isolation, aiming before letting it go. "It's what you do best."

The words hit their mark.

His eyes looked tortured. He opened his mouth to say something, but I cut him off, slamming the door behind me.

I wanted to stop him. To run to him! To tell him how even still, I couldn't live without the thought of loving him. But he needed to hurt. Hurt like I did for all that time. It wasn't possible for him to ever know the depth of that feeling, but I had to at least sting him.

Because truth be told, I didn't think I had it in me to survive again without him.

I hated myself for it.

CHAPTER 53

Percy

I flipped the eggs in the skillet, their edges sizzling and crackling in the heat of the oil when a knock on the door nearly caused me to jump out of my skin before I remembered Mr. Jenkins's words. No more running. No more fear.

Carrie?

Warmth flooded my body as I lowered the heat on the gas stove and made my way to the entrance. When I opened the door, it wasn't Carrie, but a large man, seemingly lost somewhere in his fifties, who stood a good foot taller than me with broad shoulders. He wore a pair of black slacks and a neatly pressed white shirt with a blue tie that screamed banker. Or mobster. Sometimes, it was hard to tell the difference. My stomach twisted.

"May I help you, Sir?" I asked.

"That depends. Do you know a Percy James?"

"In person," I said. "Nice to meet you."

He hesitantly shook my hand, his eyebrows twitching as if unsure of whether to believe me. He steadied his pale blue eyes on mine, the bags underneath suggesting several sleepless nights. He pulled off his hat and held it at his side. "Then yes, you can help me."

He wasn't with the mob, I reasoned. He'd have busted in the door or come during the night, and I knew Mr. Jenkins was a man of his word.

I motioned him inside.

The man cleared his throat as he pulled the chair from the table, its legs scraping loudly against the pine flooring. He set his hat on the table and bent down to pull a manila folder from the brown leather bag he'd set on the floor beside him. It dawned on me that he might be a head doctor or something.

He turned to face me as he steadied his gaze on my own, his bushy gray eyebrows raising as he assessed me with a solemn face.

"How old are you, son?" he asked.

"Twenty-one," I replied. What was he here for? My thoughts shifted to my folks and I let out an involuntary sigh, suddenly wishing Grandpops would make it back from the store.

The man shook his head and chuckled to himself as he slid a business card across the table.

Mr. Donalds, Family Attorney

"I'm sorry, Mr. Donalds?" I searched his face for confirmation. "I'm not sure what this is in regards to. Am I in some sort of trouble?"

"Not at all, son, but it appears we have a mutual friend in Mr. Richard Jenkins," he explained.

I dropped my shoulders in relief, wondering what he was doing here. "Yes, wonderful fella."

He frowned. "I'm sorry to be the one to tell you, but I'm afraid Mr. Jenkins has passed."

My heart stopped.

"Pardon?" My voice came out in more of a whisper than a question.

Mr. Donalds swallowed, his Adam's apple disappearing under the collar of his shirt. "Mr. Jenkins passed peacefully in his sleep Friday night. A housekeeper found him Saturday morning."

I tried to wrap my head around it. It felt like just yesterday we'd planted the bush of magnolias in his garden. He was so resilient. Now thinking of it, I wasn't even sure how old he was. He had a spark about him that made him appear so much younger. The type of person you'd trust to live well into their nineties if not one hundred.

The clock above the table ticked rhythmically.

"Turns out," the man went on, his words quickening. "He left nearly everything to you and St. Michael's Women's Group, at the request of his late wife of course."

My ears buzzed. Somewhere outside a dog barked.

"I… I'm not sure I understand."

"The orchard and the home are yours to do what you see fit with it. It's all in here," he said and slid over the envelope that for the first time I noticed was addressed to me.

I blinked my blurred vision into focus, enough to read my name.

"You can always sell it," the man suggested. "I mean, an orchard can't run itself and requires endless days and a lot of dedication. It'd be an easy sale as Mr. Jenkins had been approached a few different times by larger corporations."

I didn't know what to say. His words swam around me in a current of confusion.

He stood and offered his hand. "I've known Richard Jenkins for years," he said, his mouth turning into a smile. "He always wanted kids, but it wasn't in the cards. He spoke of you often, Mr. James. When I questioned his decision to leave the estate to you, he assured me you'd be capable of running things as you saw fit."

We both stood as I followed him in a daze to the doorway.

"I nearly forgot," he chuckled, bending over to pull something from the bag he carried. "He wanted to be sure I gave you this."

He pulled out a ripe, yellow pineapple and shrugged. "He could be an odd one at times."

I watched him walk to his black Chrysler as I stood in disbelief, the pineapple a rough and weighty confirmation of the reality of the situation. Tears sprung from my eyes and trailed down my face.

And then, I chuckled, thinking of Mr. Jenkins's toothy grin. It was the first pineapple I'd ever received.

CHAPTER 54

A burning sensation twisted into my shoulders like knotted snakes, spewing their venom within me. It was too late. Carrie had moved on. How stupid of me. Of course, she would have found someone else by now. It had been nearly a year since I left Kansas. It was selfish of me to think she'd spend her days aching for me the way I did for her.

She'd changed.

Maybe I was mistaken and she wasn't crushing on me the way I had on her, mesmerized by some teenage romance that never really existed. Exploring the sand dunes seemed like a fabricated memory. Another time altogether.

"Tell her," Grandpops urged me, lifting his fork in emphasis as we ate baked chicken. "She'd understand."

He was the least of people who I'd normally take relationship advice from, but the only one I had at the moment.

"Tell her what?" I scoffed. "That I was a bootlegging grifter who lied to her for over three years but now I'm reformed and ready to settle down?"

She *had* trusted me.

So many times I had come close to telling her and I had let my ego and fears get in the way of the truth. And now it was too late.

"Yes," he said. "The truth. Women always like that."

He was right. But where to start? How could she ever forgive me?

"Lucky for you, son," he said, chewing his food thoughtfully, "I've arranged a visit with her family. It'll be the perfect opportunity to come clean."

CHAPTER 55

Carrie

"It's my fault," Mr. Meyer stammered. He pulled his hat into his hands as we stood outside of our house.

I stole a glance at Percy and for a moment our eyes locked, sending sparks through my body as my heartbeat accelerated—just like it used to whenever I was close to him. He'd gotten ready for dinner and he looked good. His hair was slicked neatly to the side of his head, his arms tan from wherever he had been for the past several months. He wore slacks and a button-down cotton shirt, with boots. I forced myself to look away, trying to slow my heartrate.

"No, it's not," Percy said, shaking his head. "I'll tell them."

"Tell us what, Percy?" Pa demanded. He gave Percy a deadly stare and I was afraid he'd throw a punch at him.

"Maybe we should all sit down." Ma beckoned us into the house and sat beside Pa at the table. I could feel Percy's eyes on me as I chose a chair on the other side of Ma, leaving him to sit beside Mr. Meyer on the other side of the table next to Benny.

Goldie sat beside Percy, smiling like a dog who couldn't choose alliances as he reached down and stroked her golden fur.

Somehow, I felt betrayed.

Percy sucked in a deep breath before he told us about his days with the Chicago mob. Pa listened intently, his mouth opening as if to question him and then closing it again, unsure of where to start. I was sure he was skimming over some of the details, but nonetheless it was incredible and had it not been for Bethany, I would have thought it to be unbelievable. His elusive behavior, always looking over his shoulder. It was all beginning to make sense.

"It was time to leave," Percy ended his story. He rubbed his shoulder, the tendons in his arm taut. "I couldn't handle the stress of any of it anymore. It didn't matter how much money I brought in or what kind of clothes I wore, nothing could earn my father's approval or buy them a happy marriage. I wanted out. I wanted to leave all of it. It wasn't worth it anymore."

He glanced at Pa, who nodded, urging him to continue.

"So, when my friend, Willy, offered to have me stay with his grandfather in Kansas, it was my shot to get out…to make a clean sneak. Mr. Meyer graciously took me in, which I'll forever be thankful for."

No one spoke as Percy shifted uneasily in his seat. Mr. Meyer clasped his hands together, resting them on the table in front of him. Ma glanced to Pa. He'd calmed down some, and just kept shaking his head in disbelief.

Slowly, things began to click within my brain. Why he had been gone for so long had nothing to do with me, but for his safety and the family's safety. The family photos on Mr. Meyer's walls weren't of Percy, but of another family all together.

"When are we going to eat?" Benny whined, breaking the tension.

Ignoring Benny, I turned to Mr. Meyer. "You're not really his grandpa?"

Percy watched me, gauging my reaction, his face unreadable.

"No, Carrie," Mr. Meyer said, "I'm afraid not. It was vital for his protection and yours for us to lie. I'm sorry for that."

"The sheriff who swung by…?" Pa asked.

"One of the mob's men," Percy broke in. "One of Big Al's tricks. Have one of his men pose as a sheriff or some kind of official to try to snuff out whoever did him wrong."

Pa shook his head, still incapable of believing this crazy story. He rubbed his chin, his eyebrows scrunched as he pieced the puzzle together.

"But you're safe now?" Ma whispered, leaning in. "*We're* safe?"

"Yes," Percy said, nodding. "I would've never returned if it brought any danger to you. I'm sorry," he added, wincing. "To all of you for bringing you into this mess."

"Now wait a minute," Mr. Meyer said, resting his hand on Percy's arm. "If it weren't for you, we would've all starved long ago. Dudley has been a Godsend in delivering food every week."

Dudley?

I thought of the handsome chap who always brought crates of produce to our house. Realization sank in. "That was you?"

Percy flexed the muscle in his jaw but kept quiet.

"But how?" I asked.

He shrugged, settling his gaze on me. "Remember my friend Willy from Chicago?"

I nodded yes, my heart sending a rush of blood to my cheeks.

"Dudley's his cousin—"

"Other side of the family, of course," Mr. Meyer added as if bringing clarity to an obscure situation.

Percy went on. "He's been down here on business for quite some time."

"But how?" I repeated, afraid to ask what kind of business. "How did you get the food? I thought it was from the Red Cross."

"The only way I knew how. Dudley had connections to bootleggers and runners for the ring down in these parts. Mr. Williams being one of the leaders."

"Mr. Williams?" Pa asked in disbelief. "The banker?"

Bethany. I still couldn't believe it. How in the world did her family get wrapped up in bootlegging?

"And a few other locals who are safer if I don't name them." Percy's late-night runs to the grocery store. It wasn't milk in those bottles after all. "Skimming money was the only way to get enough to purchase food every week."

He stood from the table, glancing toward me. "I should go."

I couldn't stand it any longer.

I jumped up and despite everyone's stares, wrapped my arms around him, burying my face in his neck as tears spilled onto his shirt in a wet mess.

I loved him.

He had lied to *protect* me. To save me. To save us all from starvation. He'd risked his life, not only for Benny during the storm, but for all of us.

For a moment he hesitated, and then wrapped his arms tightly around my waist, his shoulders dropping in relief. "I love you, Carrie," he whispered. "I can't ever lose you again."

"Ewe," Benny's voice called out. "Are you going to kiss?"

I choked back sobs, barely aware that Pa and Mr. Meyer slipped back outside the house. I pulled away ever so slightly, long enough to wink at Benny, who was watching us with a scrunched-up nose.

Percy's eyes gleamed just before he pulled me into a tender kiss. I never wanted to let go.

Percy was home.

EPILOGUE

Percy

They were all here.

My folks had come in the day prior. Separately, but still there to support us just the same. I did the thing I never thought I would.

I proposed, and she said yes.

It was a simple proposal, perfect in every way, just like Carrie herself. We were out on one of our treasure hunts behind her place. I could hardly contain myself, patting my pocket nearly every minute to be sure the ring was still there. I'd been in some of the slummiest mob dives and seen dust offs and shoot outs, and none of it caused my hands to tremble the way they were now as I followed her, watching the slow swishing of her skirt with each stride she took, my heart nearly jumping out of my ribcage.

She suddenly stopped, causing me to stumble into her.

"Percy James," she exclaimed, turning to face me with a wide grin. She wrapped her arms around me and kissed my cheek. "Haven't you been busy?"

"I try." I shrugged, taking in the scent of her hair. Truth was, I had a lot to make up to her.

I led her to the plaid blanket I had laid out upon the dirt earlier in the day while she finished her chores, the setting sun casting long shadows upon us as I lit the kerosene lamp and pulled her close. I'd packed a few slices of pineapple and some pound cake, but my nerves had gotten the best of me. Food was the last thing on my mind.

"Cat got your tongue?" She giggled, poking me in the ribs.

I drew in a deep breath and wiped my palms on my pants. I couldn't wait any longer.

"Carrie," I began, nearly losing myself in her inquisitive eyes as they searched mine. "I've seen the brightest lights of the city and been in the swankiest places where ladies and gents drank from the finest crystal glasses under chandeliers of diamonds, but none of it compares to the sparkle of your eyes."

She chuckled and shook her head. "Percy, I—"

I placed my finger on her lips. I'd rehearsed this too many times in my head to get fumbled up now. "I've been fortunate enough to acquire anything a chap could ever ask for, but I've learned what true wealth *really* is and know that none of it is worth anything without you beside me."

She smiled, sliding her hand in mine, and I took pleasure in the crimson blush creeping up her cheeks. I swallowed down the lump in my throat, hoping she didn't think I was some kind of flat tire chump.

"It would be my honor to have you as my wife," I said, then hesitated. "If you could ever bring yourself to wed a fool like me."

For a minute, she didn't say anything. Not quite the reaction I was going for. I raised my eyebrows.

"Yes," she finally sniffled. "A million times yes!"

Tears trickled down her cheeks as I slid the single diamond upon her finger, and she smothered me with kisses.

I had known it from the moment I'd laid eyes on her that first day on the farm and now felt like the luckiest chap alive to have always been enough for her, regardless of my position in life.

Soon Carrie would no longer be my moll, but my wife.

The thought of it gave me more thrill than anything in this world. I was dizzy with the dame, plain and simple, and this week, we were tying the knot.

"I'm proud of you, son," Pops said, looking at all of this place that was ours.

I shook his hand and thanked him. I finally understood it had nothing to do with the size of the estate, but everything to do with the honest work that had been put in.

"Maybe you should consider moving here," I encouraged Ma later that evening over roasted chicken and steamed carrots. "You know there's quite a few movie stars in California."

Her eyebrows raised slightly as she smoothed the plaited fabric of her spiffy rose-colored skirt, her thin porcelain arms peeking from beneath the puff sleeves of a cream blouse.

Carrie watched her steadily as if viewing a tropical flower amidst a Midwest prairie of more practical beauty.

"Oh Percy," Ma sighed, waving dismissively as she poured herself another glass of scotch, "you know I could never leave Chicago."

I opened my mouth in protest and then closed it again. She'd always been a dreamer. That's what magnetized people to her. Who was I to take that away from her?

"If you change your mind," Carrie offered, "there's plenty of room."

"Thank you, dear," Ma said. "I'll get along just fine."

And somehow, for the first time, I believed her. She had after all, gained the independence she had always longed for, leaving Pops and working in a downtown clothing shop.

Pops seemed to be happy, too. I wasn't sure if he was still dating his mistress as he and Ma seemed fine here together. He was working at the factory, but had a supervisor position now.

The next day promised to be hot and already the sun was nestling in between the clouds, blanketing the ground in a thick haze of gray.

I inhaled deeply, letting the sweet smell of citrus overwhelm my senses.

"This will always be the most beautiful place I've ever seen," Carrie said softly, slipping her hand in mine as we stood on the porch and scanned the expanse of the orchard. Goldie stretched her legs before flopping down beside our feet, sulking at the boredom of our conversation. "I still can't believe it's ours."

I nodded in agreement.

No matter how many times I reread the will or pictured myself here in this moment, it still seemed surreal. Never had I imagined myself to be running a business. A legitimate one at least. Especially not in a place like this.

"It's too bad your ma wouldn't stay," Carrie said.

"Yes, but maybe it's supposed to be this way."

She gave me a quizzical look.

"Doing things on our own terms," I said. "Making our own way in the world."

"Maybe…" She smiled, her eyes reflecting light as she pulled me close and placed her lips on mine.

"We have a big day tomorrow," I teased, wrapping my arms around her waist. The Santa Ana farmer's market had already become a Friday ritual we anticipated each week. In a way, it kept Mr. Jenkins's legacy alive. It was how he built his business. His friendships. His life. No amount of machinery or mass production could replace it.

I raised an eyebrow. "Maybe we should get to bed early."

She smelled like roses and powder, her scent intoxicating. I placed a kiss on her neck, an electric shock running through my body. She was everything I could have ever asked for, and more. This dame had my entire heart and any future I had, I wanted her in it.

"Percy James," she scolded, playfully swatting at my arm. "You're scandalous, but I love you anyway."

Not long after, we retreated inside. Through the hallway where our wedding picture hung next to Mr. and Mrs. Jenkins, our similarities evident in the matching optimistic smiles, the future unknown, but ours for the taking. The apple tree in their picture replaced by the pear tree I had gifted Carrie with for the beginning of our new life together. Carrie had also framed two photos of our families and they hung there on the wall as well.

Later that night, when all was still, I reveled at Carrie's beauty as she lay sleeping, her body softly glowing in the moonlight that seeped through the ceiling to floor length windows of our bedroom. Her chest rising and falling in a soft rhythm of peaceful sleep under her shear nightgown, her shoulders smooth and delicate with her hands tucked under her chin.

This was my life. Sometimes, I still had to pinch myself.

It had been a long road full of gentle bends and sharp twists with unexpected detours. But in the end, it was the detours that had led to this place. To where I was in this moment.

I thought about the day I'd met Mr. Jenkins. That wet, sloppy day in the orchard when many had chosen to skip work. My father's words from when I was just a boy had rung loudly in my head. *The papers won't sell themselves.*

I couldn't help but grin at the possibilities. I finally understood Carrie's father's love for his fields and how difficult it must have been to see that dream die. But I smiled knowing that I almost had him on board with the idea of moving out here with Carrie's ma and Benny to run the distillery we were about to open.

This was my life. Throughout all the messes and adventures, in the end, it had all come down to a couple opportune decisions.

Again, my life was about to sharply turn directions.

Simply because I'd chosen to work in the rain.

AUTHOR'S NOTE

There are many contributing factors that led to what became known as the Great Dust Bowl. Despite the repeated cycle of grasses being stripped throughout history, whether in the late 1800s when buffalo were slaughtered and the "beef bonanza" began leading to fierce winds that killed herds, farmers were enticed to the Great Plains during the stretch from 1912-1915 in which they could homestead land for three years to grant ownership.

The 1910s brought a wet period and settlement was high. Realtors capitalized on this great migration and thousands of settlers migrated to Colorado, Wyoming, Texas, Oklahoma, and Kansas, coming in on excursion trains under the premise of towns possessing artesian wells, with broad streets lined in Elms and Maples and abundant crops.

Coupled with World War I in which German blockades cut off access to Russian wheat, thus creating a demand here (the 1917 Wartime Food Control Act guaranteed wheat prices of $2/bushel), famers prided themselves on saving the war. Modern machinery, such as gas tractors and the one-way plow replaced steam and horse-drawn plows and could tear through sod at a quicker and cheaper rate than ever before, and the combine harvester allowed for producing massive amounts of wheat fast. *More wheat grown, more plowed, more possessions* became the mantra for the Great Plow Up.

Between 1925 to 1930, enough land had been plowed to equal the state of New Jersey; about thirty-three million acres were stripped. Things had never been better. What could go wrong?

Modernization. Drought. The Great Depression. Overabundance.

The spring and summer of 1930 brought little rain and the winds began to kick up.

The 1930s blew away most of the farm fields. Without any native grasses to hold the fine dust in place, the entire top layer blew away. A severe drought proceeded, making it impossible to grow anything and leading to the deprivation and death of many farm animals. The demand for wheat had drastically dropped due to overabundance and most of it rotted away in grain elevators.

Storms rolled in. Black Blizzards, they were called, some rising as high as 7,000-8,000 feet and often accompanied by thunder and lightning rolled through the Great Plains, devouring animals and houses, leaving electricity and devastation behind them.

On May 9, 1934 dirt from Montana and Wyoming blew to the Dakotas, picking up speed as it went. By dusk, twelve million tons of dust fell like snow over Chicago, enough for four pounds per person in the city.

By May 10th, the skies of Buffalo, New York darkened and the storm was moving as fast as 100 mph. May 11th brought dust over Boston, New York, and Washington, D.C., and was reported raining down on fishermen in the Atlantic.

In the end, over 850 million tons of topsoil blew away in a single year and at times, there were over fourteen million grasshoppers per square mile. It was estimated to cost about half of that of World War I.

President Hoover's Federal Farm Board Agents urged growers to reduce their acreage, and in 1934 the Agriculture Adjustment Program paid wheat farmers to not plant crops at all. Many attempts were made to remedy the situation and in 1934, President Hoover asked Congress for $525 million in drought relief, including $275 million for emergency feed loans for cattlemen. They purchased starving stock to slaughter and can for the poor.

The Red Cross and Ladies' Aide stepped in, offering goggles and masks along with food. The Agriculture Adjustment Act offered payments to farmers who reduced their production of wheat. In 1936, the Works Progress Administration sent investigators to the Great Plains to assess the most deprived areas and allotted money for each of the persons still in those areas.

Migrant workers who became known as "Okies" or "Exodusters" moved to California, temporarily settling their families into shantyvilles or jungles as they searched for field work. Eventually, Government Migrant camps were created.

The government became the largest employer during the Dust Bowl, creating nearly eight million jobs between 1935 and 1943. F.D.R.'s New Deal included programs such as the Works Progress Administration (W.P.A./fondly known as "We're Probably Asleep" by some of those who were employed there), hiring displaced workers to drill wells, pave road, and build bridges throughout the country for 25 cents/hour. Many of these projects can be seen today, proudly stamped with the W.P.A. symbol.

The Civilian Conservation Corps (C.C.C.) employed young men to work in national parks, state parks, and national forests and the National Youth Administration (N.Y.A.) hired young boys and girls to make extra money at their schools.

The Soil Conservation Act proclaiming "soil erosion is a menace to national welfare" was initiated by F.D.R. in 1935, and he ordered state governments to study and prevent soil erosion, suggesting to give crops "breaks" every few years so the soil could replenish its nutrients and grasslands could be preserved. The Soil Conservation Service demonstrated projects and alternative processes to help hold soil and nutrients in place. Farmers would be paid $0.75 cents an acre if they carried out wind erosion techniques, such as plow contouring with the old-fashioned Lister plow so as not to pulverize the soil, plowing in circles versus straight lines and alternating crops.

The Dust Bowl inspired many of the modern techniques in farming. Many bizarre solutions were offered. New ideas came in through engineers from China, England, and several other places. There were attempts to "blow up" the sky in hopes of causing it to rain. Even suggestions to lay down wire netting or asphalt and mulch throughout the Great Plains. Eventually progress was made, and many of the methods used for topsoil and nutrient solutions are still used today.

BOOK CLUB CONVERSATION STARTERS

1. Percy references the billboards and advertising of big companies, along with the idea that many of them were capitalizing off from the Prohibition and largely influencing society. How has advertising and social media shaped current mainstream culture? How does this compare to the influence Baby Boomers had over products and brand positioning as they aged?

2. There are differing reasons for the Prohibition, ranging from a push from conservative religious groups to backing the war effort by cutting out ingredients used to make beer and using them for bread. What are your thoughts on the Prohibition?

3. The 19th Amendment gave women the right to vote. How do you see Percy's mother? How does she struggle with being progressive, while also adhering to the cultural norms of women during the 1920s? What are some clues that indicate she strives for independence?

4. Percy sees the mob as a way to make fast money but learns there are consequences to this. Where are other parts of the book where the idea of taking shortcuts and doing things the quick and easy way is present? Do you feel this is a character trait or social influence/ financial pressure?

5. How do Carrie and Percy's upbringings and surroundings contribute to their differences in viewpoints?

6. Modernization, along with the advancement in technology and "farm factories" contributed to the Dust Bowl, wreaking havoc on the land and the environment. Where do you see this today?

7. When Percy re-enters the mob while in Kansas, he does it for moral obligations. Do you feel his actions are justified?

ACKNOWLEDGEMENTS

It takes a team to publish a book, from the time the seed is planted as an idea to the time it finally blooms. I'd like to thank Ron Neuhaus, who provided the writing prompt and direction for *Becoming American* and for helping me cultivate writing skills that had been deeply buried since my youth.

I'd also like to thank Thekla Madsen, whom is an excellent author, for her guidance, encouragement, and willingness to read early drafts: you've been such an inspiration in the writing process!

Thank you to my parents, Dave & Pat Anderson, along with my brother, Aaron, for reading early drafts and being my largest marketers!

Thank you to Dave & Ruth Wood for your continuous support in my writing journey!

A large dose of gratitude to our local libraries and schools (most notably, River Falls) for supporting speaking programs and keeping history and literature alive within our community!

Lastly, a huge thank you to everyone involved in the creation of *Under the Dirt Sky*, including Brittiany Koren for her meticulous attention to both detail and the larger scope of character development and plotlines in her editing, Ed Vincent for the enticing cover design, Amit Dey for the beautiful layout, and Melinda Peterson and Melissa Krueger for their helpful assistance.

Thank you all for nurturing the growth of this book! Without you, it would still be a buried seed.

ABOUT THE AUTHOR

Callie J. Trautmiller resides in Wisconsin with her husband, their three teenagers and their dog, Penny. She has also written *Becoming American*, which went on to become a finalist in the Indie Book Awards, the Eric Hoffer Awards and was the runner-up for the Wisconsin Writers Award. *Under the Dirt Sky* is her second novel. You can find Callie on social media at: Facebook: CallieJTrautmiller, Instagram: CallieTrautmiller, or more info at her website: CallieTrautmiller.com.